Also by Marilyn Ludwig

Searching for Juliette

Haste Ye Back

The Secret of Kendall Mountain

It's Perfectly Safe . . . The Rulison Matter

Trust the Magic

The Geese that Won the War

The Ghost of a Tree Remembered

The Borrowed Days

Waiting Games

No Small Parts

Just a Stage

Code Pink

STAGE DIRECTIONS

MARILYN LUDWIG

ISBN: 9798989919611
LCCN: 2024914734

ZAFA PUBLISHING
Downers Grove, Illinois

*Sometimes the smallest step in the right direction
ends up being the biggest step of your life.
Tiptoe if you must, but take the step.*
— Unknown

Some stage directions you just simply have to throw away.
— Judd Hirsch

ACT ONE - We Put on Masks

No one reveals himself as he is; we all wear a mask and play a role.
— Arthur Schopenhauer

Hannah's Personal Essay - 200 words exactly

MY SUMMER VACATION
BY HANNAH RENDINA

I spent all summer in Germany with my mother. Because of my parents' divorce, we hadn't seen each other for a long time. At first it was a little awkward, but finally we remembered what we like about each other. My mother loves adventures. We rented a suite in a sixty-five-room mansion in Munich. My private bathroom was larger than my bedroom at home. The bathtub was enormous!

We walked all over Munich so many times that soon I knew it better than Chicago. I even went shopping by myself. I learned to speak a little basic German. I was surprised by how much it was like English. Mother and I took long bus rides around the country. My favorite was seeing Neuschwanstein Castle. It was supposedly the inspiration for the castle in Disneyworld. I also read thirty books.

Mother and I will now have happy memories and things to talk about. She plans to spend the fall in France and wanted me to stay with her, but I said it was time for me to return home to my dad, uncle, friends, and my dog Betsy. I'm excited about being in eighth grade at Castle Bluff Middle School.

Hannah sighed. It wasn't very good, but it might do. Fortunately, the new English teacher, Dr. Drake, insisted the essay had to be two hundred words exactly, so she didn't have to write much. She hated when teachers wanted something personal. Why would she want to tell some teacher she didn't know anything personal, especially since it would be graded? Maybe mentioning the divorce and things being awkward would be personal enough to suit him.

But, oh, what she could have written! Not that she had said anything that wasn't true; it was just such a small part of the truth. What Hannah hadn't said was she was alone much of the time and that was why she'd read thirty books. She'd found an English section in a used bookstore on Sendlinger Street, where the books were cheap. And she had learned so much German that she was thinking about taking it in high school next year.

Mother had a new boyfriend, Gavin, whom Hannah thought was creepy because of the way he looked at her. Toward the end of summer, Mother must have decided he was creepy, too, or maybe because she met someone else, who talked her into going with him to France. This turned out to be a good thing because the new man did not want Hannah around, so she was able to return home with Mother's blessings, after all.

At least she and her mother were talking again. This year might be less of a strain. Hannah had changed a lot inside, and she thought Danny and Porter had, too. At least Betsy was the same. Her barks of joy were still ringing in Hannah's ears.

Porter Walters
English, period 3, eighth grade

A GROWING-UP SUMMER
BY PORTER WALTERS

This was an unexpected summer that has caused me to change in many ways. I had planned to participate in the park district and high school's combined theater production, along with my sister, Beth, who had a paid position. Then my grandfather in Manitou Springs, Colorado had a heart attack. It turned out to be a mild one, and he has almost completely recovered, but my grandmother was a mess and needed family. Dad couldn't take time off work, and Mom needed to take care of my younger sisters. I was the logical choice. At first I was resentful, but it turned out to be the right thing to do. (One of the weird things about my family is that all four of my grandparents have the same last name. My parents met in college when they were lined up together in alphabetical order.)

I never really knew my grandmother because there were always so many people around us. This summer, though, we became very close. I helped her with chores, and she told me fascinating stories about her childhood and my dad when he was a little boy. We took taxis to visit Gramps in the hospital.

Manitou Springs is a busy, exciting town and was crammed full of tourists. I became involved in a community theater production of *Our Town*, in which I played Wally Webb, one of the children. It was a small part, but as the saying goes, "There are no small parts—only small actors." I learned so much from the adult actors in the cast and, especially, from the director. He emphasized character development. I'm looking forward to putting his ideas into action in CBMS's shows this year.

Most importantly, being away from home gave me some thinking time. Last spring, my school counselor advised me to skip seventh grade and go directly into eighth. This was a huge decision my parents said needed to be mine. Grams and I had many discussions on the advisability of doing this. She pointed out that schoolwork had always come too easily for me and that a challenge might be a good thing. I was worried, at first, about the social aspects. Finally, I came to realize that my strong friendships have little to do with school and that I would keep them and make new ones. I want to be an actor someday. Skipping a grade might make this happen a little sooner.

Gramps is home with Grams now, and one of my aunts is staying with them for a while. So here I am, back home in Castle Bluff, embracing this new school year.

Why do you always sound so pompous, Porter? He laughed at himself. Pompous Porter! He was hardly that. The way he wrote covered up so many of his feelings. He was plenty uncertain about skipping a grade, not so much for this year but later in high school. Beth had told him nicely that he'd never really fit in anywhere, so things wouldn't be that different. Of course she didn't use those words. "You'll always be unique, Porter, and do things your own way," was what she actually said.

In truth, he got along with everyone but had only two friends. Danny Kennedy, his best and oldest friend, had shrugged. "It won't make much difference," Danny had said. "We hardly saw each other in school last year anyway" — because of Danny's accident that had kept him homebound for most of the year — "and before that we went to different schools. You'll be busy with Drama Club, and I'll be back into sports." He grinned. "And everyone knows you're probably the smartest kid in the state."

Porter knew he and Danny would be fine. They were practically brothers and referred to each other's parents as aunt and uncle.

But Porter was worried about his other friend, Hannah. She was over the moon with delight that he was in eighth grade, too, and that they would go to high school together. They had become close friends, and they shared feelings that Porter normally avoided talking about. "The problem is—" Porter stopped himself. He was not ready to put into words what bothered him. "I'm not sure who I am anymore," he whispered.

Danny Kennedy
English, Section 7-2

ANOTHER SUMMER GONE
BY DAN KENNEDY

It was a great summer! One of the best! Most of last year was pretty miserable because I had a stupid accident and had to learn to walk again. At least this summer I was able to both walk and help a new friend, who had an awful fall and almost lost her arm. I helped her see that life can get better. She helped me, too, because most of my friends were away. They're back now, but everything seems different. It's hard to explain.

Most of my favorite things have to do with sports. Even though a lot has changed, that's still the same. I'll probably have to postpone Cross Country running and playing hockey for another year, but I'm becoming a really good swimmer. I joined a park district swim team and will try out for the new one at CBMS. My legs aren't as strong as they were before the accident, but my arms are amazing. Dad calls me Popeye. You should see my muscles!

We stayed home most of the summer because of my parents' work and because my sister, Kylie, was one of the directors for a theater program for little kids. We did spend a week in a cabin in Wisconsin with our old neighbors, who live up there now. While we were gone, my neighbors took care of my dog Bingo and cat Boots, who are great friends with their dog Betsy.

I'm glad to be back in school. This time I will make it for the whole year! I am determined to be a good student. It's hard for me sometimes, but I try.

And he was off to a good start, Danny thought. Kylie had proofread his essay and pronounced it just fine. "Should I mention Drama Club and the other things I'm doing this year?"

"No, the essay is about your summer. Your teacher is trying to know you a little and see how you write. It's not just about you. She's figuring out the best way to teach."

Kylie was growing up, Danny thought, not certain he liked the idea. She was a sophomore now and still going with her boyfriend, Brad. Then she asked him about Drama Club. "You're still going to join, right? Even though you don't have to?"

Danny nodded. "Whenever I don't have swimming, I'll be there. Maybe I won't act; I'll just help with the plays. I hope we have enough boys this year, but if they need me . . ." Drama Club members were there for him last year—when his sport team deserted him. Staying loyal to Drama Club was the right thing to do.

Laurel Mullen
English, Section 7-2

My Summer
By Laurel Mullen

I stayed in Castle Bluff all summer because I broke my arm right when school ended. My parents were supposed to go on vacation, but they stayed home because of me. My sister went to camp alone, and she was mad at me because she didn't like the camp. It wasn't my fault I broke my arm, although I'm not sure my parents believed that. The doctor did, though. He said it was a nasty break, and I needed to be very careful or I could lose my arm. I also had a concussion. He told my parents that no one should touch me and that my sister should go away to camp.

I made several friends when we did the play, *The Secret Garden,* last year. One was Danny, who learned to walk again, just like Colin in the play. He came over this summer to play games and talk outside. He couldn't bring his dog because my mother thought Bingo would be too rough around me. My friend Beth also stayed in Castle Bluff. She worked on the play in town. She said she could find a small singing part for me, but my parents didn't think it was a good idea. The doctor agreed. They were probably right. My arm is much better now.

I guess it wasn't a very nice summer. I'm glad to be a seventh grader and back in school. I'm joining Drama Club and Chorus. I hope I'll be in a show again.

It wasn't a happy essay, Laurel thought, and it certainly was short, but that was all she was willing to write. She'd have to go back and check every word that had a red squiggly line under it, and figure out if all the green squiggles meant something else was wrong. According to the computer, which she was seldom allowed to use, she had many grammatical and spelling mistakes. Because of her singing and acting, people were always surprised that she wasn't a good student. She just managed to keep her grades high enough so she'd be allowed to participate in what mattered to her. Being in *The Secret Garden* was the best thing to happen in her entire life. She thought she was good at writing poetry, too, but teachers never asked for that.

Her sister Avery was back from camp, as sour and angry as ever. Avery would never admit to deliberately pushing Laurel out of Hannah's tree fort. Instead, she insisted that Laurel had been clumsy, but that she had been blameless. Laurel knew the truth, but Avery was an awfully good liar. At least her parents understood that Avery often lost control of her emotions and had listened to the doctor when he recommended a camp for young teens with "anger issues."

Issues is right, Laurel thought, wondering if the doctor might have made threats, like contacting authorities. Issues and arm tissues. She used a real tissue to hold back tears. Her arm hurt today and was making it harder to proofread the pathetic essay. She wasn't sure her arm would ever be one hundred percent again, but she was absolutely certain she and Avery would never be friends. "I wonder if Mom and Dad know they shouldn't adopt me," she whispered.

"**Y**OU'RE LOOKING MIGHTY FINE for an ordinary school day," Uncle Martin observed at breakfast. "Or maybe it's not so ordinary?"

Hannah kissed a spot on his head that was starting to bald. "Yes and no," she said. "Drama Club starts today, and we're going to meet, officially, the new director. I already know him because he's my English teacher, but this is different." She wanted to make a good impression because he hadn't been that complimentary about her essay—B minus. She had redeemed herself somewhat with all the book reports.

"It's a shame Miss Armstrong couldn't stay," Dad said, joining in the conversation. "You'll miss her."

Hannah shrugged. "We knew it was only temporary until she could figure out what she was doing next. Her sister is in Canada getting a new treatment for her eyes." Hannah knew that Robbie wished people would stop fussing over her. She'd accepted her blindness and thought that others should, too. Hannah didn't think Miss Armstrong ever would.

"How are you getting home?" Dad asked. "Need me to pick you up?"

"No, thanks. Danny and I will walk. It's still a novelty to him." A novelty that would wear off soon enough, she thought. Odd that he wasn't going to attempt Cross Country. Maybe he thought he wouldn't be as good as before or maybe because he'd become really interested in swimming and planned to try out for the school's new swim team.

An impatient honk put an end to breakfast. "Oops! There's Mrs. Kennedy! See ya later!" Danny's mom, a busy real estate agent, had a house showing near the middle school and would drop them off.

"Laurel, over here!" It was Danny, sitting with his friends, Hannah and Porter. All three were waving for her to join them for the first Drama Club meeting of the year. No longer cramped into a small classroom, their venue was a large room that even had a small stage with a curtain.

"Hi," she said, joining them, determined to be upbeat, even though most of the day had been difficult, starting with both parents and Avery being cranky at breakfast.

"This room is great!"

"It is," Hannah agreed, "but we're hoping we can still go to the castle on Saturdays."

"I guess it will depend on the new director and Leland," Danny said. "I wish Miss Armstrong were still here. She was terrific! You've got the new guy for English, Hannah. What's he like?"

"Strict and old."

Laurel thought the old part didn't matter, but she was a little worried about strict. It was likely she wouldn't get any decent roles if he were to examine her grades too closely. Danny had agreed to help whenever she was in trouble.

The room was filling quickly. More boys this year, Laurel noticed, and they weren't just new sixth graders. She wondered if the success of *The Secret Garden* last year had inspired them to come. The new director walked onto the stage. Yes, he was old—maybe in his sixties or seventies—but he looked nice. It was time for her to forget about her impossible family and painful arm. It was time for her escape, Drama Club!

Old is right, Danny thought. It seemed like they were letting just about anyone teach these days. Some of the substitutes looked about Kylie's age. Lots of them didn't even have college degrees. Well, you'd never catch him teaching, although he enjoyed helping Laurel. Helping was much more satisfying than being helped.

"Welcome to Drama Club," Dr. Drake, the new director, boomed. Danny grinned. Dr. Drake didn't seem to have a problem with projection. And doctor? Pretty impressive for a middle school teacher! "I'm pleased to be with you this year," he said. "As you might have guessed, I retired years ago. I never expected to return to a classroom, although I have stayed active in theater."

Danny noticed Porter nodding in approval. After last year, Porter had become super serious about acting and wanted to learn everything he could. "You need different directors if you're going to improve," he'd said. Danny just wanted to have fun. How would Dr. D feel about spooky Halloween parties, scavenger hunts for props, and things like that? If not a part in a play, Danny thought he'd give Speakeasy a try, if they were allowed to have the scenes and monologue event again. Hannah said he was strict in English. Well, as long as he wasn't too strict here. Danny liked his English teacher and was glad he and Laurel were in the same class. Both of them had received A's on their summer essays.

Making a joke about his name—" before giving you the opportunity to do so"—the director confided that his name was Dr. Donald Drake. "I don't know what my parents were thinking. At least they were somewhat sheepish about it when I decided to earn my PhD."

Most of Drama Club laughed. Good, Porter thought. They're going to give him a chance. He's more formal than what we're used to, but they probably won't tease him about his name. Calling him Dr. D would work. He'd tell the others to spread it around. Then he amended his thought. They'll like him only if we can keep our traditions. That's what everyone wants to know.

"Let me tell you some of my plans for the year," Dr. D said, "and then you can tell me what you expect. Last year, for a number of reasons, you only did one show. A great success, I must say. I came to see it and was most impressed." He stopped to smile at the group and seemed to direct personal looks at Hannah, Porter, and Danny. "I was able to tell many of your strengths and also where improvement was needed." Porter leaned forward. This is what he was hoping to hear.

"What's needed, I feel, is more concentration on the physical aspects of theater: making your whole body work, what to do with your hands, how to gesture effectively, becoming comfortable with walking and sitting on stage." Porter nodded vigorously. This was what was lacking before and what the director in Colorado had pointed out. "So," Dr. D continued, "we're going to go way back in time and learn about Commedia Dell'arte, even making our own masks. Instead of just our faces, we'll rely on other parts of our body to express our feelings. Those masks might come in useful again after the show—during your Halloween party at the castle." Everyone gasped. "Yes, I met with Mr. Markey and Leland Duncan last week. Your Saturday meetings and parties at the castle will continue." Dr. D. grinned. "I imagine that answers most of your questions."

Porter wasn't so sure about mask making, but at least Beth could help him. Concentrating on movement and expression was exactly what he needed. Dr. D might turn out to be as good as the Colorado director and better than Miss Armstrong.

Hannah had been smiling ever since the teacher had looked at her. He likes me, she thought. He saw my performance as Mary Lennox and approved. Phew! He might be pretty cool, after all. In English that morning, he told the class not to worry about that first essay. "You made some mistakes," he told them, "but I might have made bigger ones. I probably shouldn't have restricted the number of words or insisted that your remarks be personal. I do understand that some things are not to be shared with strangers." Hannah crossed her fingers. He might not hold that B minus grade against her, and she had received big fat A's on all her book reports.

"Our first show is called *The Love for Three Oranges*. I realize that you've never heard of it, but it is famous. It's based on an opera of that name and is very funny. Because performances will be before Halloween, auditions will be early next week. Now, are there any questions?"

Immediately, a dozen hands were in the air. Most of the questions Hannah could predict. When would Drama Club meetings be held at the castle? Would there be a Speakeasy? Could they go on theater trips? Dr. Drake either said yes or that he wasn't sure but would get back to them — all very satisfactory. Then there was one last question. Hannah was surprised to see Laurel's left arm in the air.

"Yes?"

"I know the opera," Laurel said. "I love opera — all music, really — but I'm not sure how much I can do with movement." She pointed to her arm, back in the sling she used whenever she became too tired or in too much pain. Hannah thought it might be hurting her because of the long day at school.

"Well, that's a surprise! A seventh-grade girl who likes opera. Your name is Laurel, right? You were the singer in *The Secret Garden*. How about assisting me on the show, and we'll come up with a song for you. I believe in making use of the talents that present themselves."

She cares too much, Hannah thought. Laurel's joyful reaction was almost heartbreaking. Danny had noticed, too and looked concerned. Last year Kammy needed help. This year it would be Laurel. Middle school can be so complicated, Hannah thought, not for the first time.

HANNAH AND PORTER WALKED TO the castle. Normally, Danny would have been with them, but he had an early-morning swim meet and would see them there. Hannah was pleased. It was ages since she and Porter had been alone, just the two of them. Awkward, but things would get back to normal soon—she hoped. "I was thinking of nominating you for president," she said.

Porter laughed. "That's exactly what I was thinking, right this moment about you. Thanks for the honor, but I must decline."

"Why? You'd be great."

Porter shrugged. "I guess I'm not the type. Plus, some of the eighth graders don't like it that I skipped seventh grade. Also, Beth was president last year, so it doesn't feel right. How about you? I think you'd be good."

Hannah shook her head. "I think I might like to be something, but not president. I'm not as shy as I used to be, but still . . ."

"Not the type, either, huh?"

They were almost okay again, Hannah thought. Definitely friends, although maybe nothing more. "Then who should we nominate?"

"Someone else will have to do it? What would you like to be? Vice President?"

Hannah thought about it. "No, but maybe secretary would be okay."

"Deal. I'll nominate you for secretary, and then help you after you win."

"If I win."

After walking a distance in comfortable silence, Hannah confided a little about her trip to Germany. "It's a beautiful country, and I'd like to return someday—but maybe alone. At least, not with my mother and whoever her boyfriend is at the time."

"I'm sorry," Porter said. "I mean, about your mom and everything. But you know, the high school has a foreign exchange program. Maybe you can find out about it. I'll ask Beth. She's taking German at CBHS."

What a great idea! It was about time she felt enthusiastic again! "Thanks, Porter. I think I'd like that."

Should he tell her? Porter didn't want to make a huge deal out of it, but it could be serious. Danny? Probably not. He was certain to overreact—to think it was a case for their secret club, the SSC. "Hannah, something kind of weird happened yesterday. I'd like to talk about it, but I'm not ready for anyone else to know."

"Porter?" Hannah looked scared, uncertain.

"Oh, don't worry, you haven't done anything." He was surprised that he knew Hannah well enough to know that she always thought she was to blame. "It's about Laurel and that bully, her sister."

Hannah nodded. "Avery is mean, all right. What happened?"

"Yesterday, I went down the backstairs, so I could get to my locker faster." He'd had plans to meet with Danny and Seth Edwards at Smithy's. He hadn't told Hannah because it was going to be a boy thing. Then both boys had bailed on him, but that was another issue. "Well, Laurel and Avery were on the stairs. Avery really lost it. She was yelling at Laurel, and then she grabbed her arm. I was afraid she was going to push her down the stairs. Avery is strong, especially when she's mad." Porter shuddered, remembering:

Hey, be careful! You'll reinjure Laurel's arm!

Reinjure. Who talks like that? You're full of it! None of your business, Talking Dictionary Nerd!

I said leave her alone! Now!

"Then she shoved Laurel into the corner of the stairwell. Hard, too—Laurel fell. Then Avery started toward me. Maybe she was going to push me downstairs, instead."

"But she didn't. You're okay, right?"

"Saved by Dr. D, who came along, just in time. He wanted to know, of course, what was going on. Avery said I'd just saved Laurel from a careless accident and gave me this phony thank you. I would have told the truth, but Laurel interrupted and said everything was fine and that she wouldn't be so clumsy next time. So what could I say? Dr. D looked suspicious, but he helped Laurel up, and then led us down to the first floor. Avery bolted out of the building, and Laurel whispered thanks and went down the hall, probably to her locker."

"Then you told Dr. D what really happened?"

Porter shook his head. "Maybe I should have. I didn't think fast enough." Actually, he'd been stunned, not sure about what had just happened. "But then Dr. D said something that sounded strange, at the time, that is. He said, 'Who is that girl?' It really sounded like he meant Laurel."

"But he'd already met her in Drama Club."

"Right, but he could have meant Avery. I told him Avery was Laurel's sister and that I had to get to my locker. He just looked puzzled. Now I don't know if I was overreacting."

"You weren't," Hannah said. "For now, let's keep a close watch on Laurel and make sure she knows we're her friends."

They'd reached the castle. "Maybe we should go in the front and see Mr. Markey before we go to the meeting," Porter said. "I haven't seen him since June."

"Me, neither. Good idea."

"You do the honors, Hannah." Hannah grinned, as she rapped the gargoyle doorknocker, just one of the gingerbread castle's many charms.

They expected Leland, of course, but Leland's wife, Janet, looking flustered, opened the door. Odd, Porter thought. Janet was usually calm.

"Oh, hello, dears," Janet said. "Were we expecting you?"

"We came for the Drama Club meeting," Hannah said, "but we got here early. We haven't seen Mr. Markey all summer and thought we could say hi before we went upstairs."

Janet seemed uncertain. "Well, he is resting," she started, when an irritated voice interrupted.

"If someone has come to see me, let them in." Nervously, Porter and Hannah looked at each other. They had never heard Mr. Markey annoyed before.

"Is he all right?" Hannah whispered.

Janet shook her head before leading them into a parlor.

After a brief visit of no more than three minutes, Hannah and Porter started up the stairs to the ballroom. "He's changed so much," Hannah said. "I hardly recognized him. He looks about 150."

Porter nodded but didn't respond. Not that old, of course, but surely in his mid or late nineties. He had a strong feeling that he and his friends had better treasure all happy moments they had left with him.

Laurel bumped into Danny at the back entrance to the castle, where the stairs leading straight up to the ballroom were located. "Oh, I'm glad I don't have to go in alone," she said. "I couldn't get a ride—my parents took Avery to a swim meet—so I'm late."

"Yeah, I saw them there. But we're not that late. Here, let me get the door. It's awfully heavy, especially when it's windy, like today."

Laurel was hoping he wouldn't notice, but Danny was observant, when it came to her, at least. She had tried a different hairdo, one that would cover the left side of her face. The wind refused to cooperate.

"Whoa, that's a nasty bruise! What happened?"

Once inside, Laurel forced her hair back into its camouflaged position. "Oh, nothing much. Just me being clumsy again. Come on, we're late!"

The meeting had come to order, and Dr. D was requesting nominations for officers. Laurel and Danny found seats toward the back. Laurel was hoping no one would notice them, but three people were staring at them: Porter, Hannah, and Dr. D.

"I nominate Seth Edwards for president," Danny said loudly and clearly. Seth looked surprised but pleased. Other members nodded. Seth was a good choice. He was smart, friendly to everyone, and a good actor. He had played the important role of the gardener, Ben Weatherstaff, in last year's *The Secret Garden*. Two other people were nominated—Hannah and Porter, who both declined—so Seth was elected unanimously.

A student Danny didn't know nominated Laurel for vice president. "But I'm only in seventh grade," she whispered to Danny. He assured her he'd help.

"You'll be all set for the top spot next year," he said. Then he was nominated. "Thanks, but sorry." He smiled. "I'm too involved in sports. Besides, I'm going to be Laurel's campaign manager."

Everyone laughed at that. Danny was popular, and his endorsement of Laurel insured that there would be no more nominations. Laurel, too, was elected unanimously.

Lastly, Porter rose and nominated Hannah for the combination secretary/treasurer position. There was very little—if any—money involved in Drama Club, so the office of treasurer was a "just-in-case" job. No one else wanted all the work involved, so Hannah got her wish.

Dr. D led the applause. "I had no idea this would be settled so quickly," he said. "All of your choices seem wise. Perhaps your new officers and I can find a time to meet next week, so they'll be prepared to lead the following meetings."

Beth would be pleased, Danny thought. He'd text her later. That was exactly what she was pushing for last year. Officers running the club, with guidance from the director. Seth would be in charge of the next Drama Club meeting.

Danny expected Janet to show up with refreshments—just like always—but nothing happened. He would have liked some of Janet's cookies, although Gee's donuts would be even better. Darn it! After the swim meet, he'd been hungry, but he'd skipped a snack in order to be here on time.

Next, Dr. D handed out audition information. "I will attempt to give a part to everyone who tries out," he said. "The show is greatly expandable, and gender isn't especially important."

Well, that was good, Danny thought. As usual, there were far more girls than boys, although it wasn't as bad as last year.

"Today," Dr. D continued, "as soon as we're done with the business portion, we'll play some pantomime theater games. Being able to express yourself physically is vital for our first play."

Pantomime? Yes! Danny raised his hand.

"Danny?"

Dr. D knew his name. He guessed that was cool.

"I have an idea. Some of us have a really good friend who goes to Crofts." Dr. D nodded, obviously familiar with the performing arts school in town. "His name is Kurt Brockway, and he used to go to CBMS." Practically everyone there either knew or knew about Kurt and seemed interested. "Last year, Kurt came and gave us a pantomime demonstration. I'll bet he'd come back. He's almost as good as Marcel Marceau!"

Porter raised his hand. "Kurt is my sister's boyfriend. I can ask him. For a Saturday meeting, of course. He couldn't come on a school day."

Dr. D gave his approval. "One last bit of business. Commedia dell'arte takes place outside, so I'm looking for a possible place to hold our show. If you have any suggestions, please let me know. Perhaps at the end of our meeting today."

"But what if it rains?" Hannah blurted.

"It won't," Dr. D said. "I won't allow it."

Everyone cheered. There was no doubt that Dr. D would be popular.

If only there were food, Danny thought. It was not the same without snacks. He wasn't certain when he'd ever been so hungry.

HANNAH STAYED BEHIND A FEW minutes to talk with Dr. D, while Danny waited impatiently. She'd heard Danny's stomach rumbling and guessed the reason. He wasn't the only one who'd noticed the lack of refreshments.

"Dr. D," she began, and then realized that she might have been the first to call him that to his face. But he smiled encouragingly. "Dr. D, I have an idea for an outdoor theater. I'll have to ask my dad to find out for us, though. He's an art teacher at Castle Bluff Community. They've got an outdoor amphitheater there. It's really cool—kind of like one in ancient Greece. Well, like photos I've seen. Not that I've ever been—"

"I understand, Hannah. Go on."

"Well, last year, the sixth and seventh graders started out at Community when our school was being finished, so we got to know the campus. I'll bet they'd let us use it, if they knew the dates and everything. Dad could find out. He could call you, or I could give you his phone number."

Quickly, Dr. D pulled out a card. "Hannah, I can tell already you're going to make a great secretary. And you say he's an art teacher?"

"Yes, he's the head of the department. Oh, I know what you're thinking! You're wondering if he could help us make the masks. I'll ask him. I know he'll agree. This is going to be so much fun!"

Hannah joined Danny, who was definitely cranky. "My stomach thinks my throat is cut," he complained.

"What?"

He laughed, good spirits returning. "Something my Grandpa says a lot.That's what his father used to say. Basically, it just means I'm starving. This was the first time someone didn't pop in with refreshments."

"I know, but something is wrong in the castle, and I'm afraid it's about Mr. Markey." Hannah explained what she and Porter had witnessed. "He looked awful, like he'd aged fifty years since June. And he was crabby!"

"Crabby? Mr. Markey?" Danny shook his head. "I can't imagine that. Did Leland say anything?"

"He wasn't around. Janet let us in, but she seemed really worried. Do you know how old Mr. Markey is?"

Again, Danny shook his head. "No idea. Pretty old, though. I'll ask Kylie. She's the closest to him. She'll find out what's going on. Now, let's go as fast as we can to Smithy's. Two milkshakes coming up. My treat!" That would blow Danny's allowance for the week, but he didn't care!

Porter learned that Laurel lived in the general direction of his house and offered to walk with her. Maybe he could learn more about what was going on with her sister. Avery had been a year ahead of him in school when the family first moved to Castle Bluff. She was such a brat at East Elementary that practically the whole school celebrated when she headed for middle school. Back then, sixth graders were in the grade school. The main thing he remembered about Laurel was that she was a good singer. He guessed he'd start with that.

"I've known Avery for a while," he said, "but I don't think I really met you until *Secret Garden*. I remember you singing in assemblies and things at East."

Laurel nodded. "I didn't start there until fifth grade, and we didn't have the same teacher. I knew who you were, though."

Porter started. That didn't make sense. The family came to Castle Bluff when Avery was in fourth grade and Porter was in third, but Laurel, who was younger, didn't start at East until fifth grade? He wanted to ask more, but there was a look on her face that said — Uh-uh, no more.

"Are you excited to tell your family about being elected vice president?"

Laurel shook her head. "I think I'll keep it a secret for a while."

Friends were both a blessing and a danger, Laurel thought, at least in her case. A blessing because she needed people who cared about her, who were in her corner. But it might be dangerous if they knew too much. Even though she used the last name Mullen, the adoption wasn't official yet. Officially, she was still in foster care, and the people she called Mom and Dad could send her away any time they wanted. "And they will, if Avery has anything to say about it," she whispered to herself.

Laurel wished she could figure out what she wanted. This was the best foster family she'd had, and she liked Mom and Dad — could even love them if she thought they loved her. But Avery was getting more and more reckless. Even if Mom and Dad didn't recognize it, Avery hated her. No, she wouldn't tell them about being elected vice president. Mom and Dad would pretend to care, and Avery would find a way to ruin it.

If Danny, Hannah, and Porter knew what was going on, they would be sympathetic but couldn't really help. If they told any adults — probably the right thing to do — matters would be worse. She was sure of it. She liked school, especially music class, and she loved Drama Club. She'd stay out of Avery's way and try not to get hurt.

Laurel had brought along her schoolbooks. It was so hard at home, with Avery insisting on using the computer whenever Laurel approached it. Instead, she'd go the library until dinnertime.

But what to tell Porter? "Oops! I forgot I needed to get something from the library. See you tomorrow, Porter." She could feel his eyes watching her as she dashed away.

Danny thought over the events of the day. All in all, a great one, he decided. He'd placed third in the swim meet and was getting stronger and stronger. He laughed as he thought of how humiliated he would have been if he'd placed third in Cross Country this time last year. Now, even walking home from school was a major accomplishment. Last year he'd never thought of himself as being conceited, but maybe he had been — a little.

At dinner, he told Kylie what he'd learned about Mr. Markey. "Porter said he looked really, really old, and Hannah said he was grumpy."

"Oh, dear," Kylie said. "I haven't seen him since his birthday party in July, right before we went to Wisconsin."

"Do you know how old he is, dear?" Mom asked.

"Leland told Brad that he's ninety-seven." Kylie's boyfriend, Brad, and Leland had always gotten along well.

"You should go see him," Dad said, "but you should call Leland first."

Kylie nodded. "I'll call Brad, too. Maybe we can go tomorrow afternoon."

If Mr. Markey were sick — Danny didn't even want to think the word, "dying" — it could make a huge difference to Drama Club. It had started already with the lack of refreshments. That shouldn't be important, of course, but somehow it was. Would Drama Club even meet at the castle if Mr. Markey weren't there? What would happen to the castle? Who would own it?

Very gloomy thoughts! Another worry was Laurel. Something was terribly wrong. There must be a reason she kept getting hurt. You'd have to be totally clumsy to fall out of Hannah's completed treehouse—her dads had made certain it was safe. And Laurel hadn't explained how she got the bruise on her face. Danny liked her a lot—in a different way than Hannah. Hannah and Porter were his best friends, while Laurel could be, maybe, his girlfriend.

Suddenly, Danny missed the old days of figuring out puzzling things with Porter and Hannah. He missed the SSC—whether they were the Super Sleuths, Super Shits, or Super Surprises. In spite of last year's injury, those times of working together were wonderful. "We need a mystery," he said out loud, before reaching for his phone.

"SSC meeting tomorrow afternoon at 3:00," he texted. "Can you come?"

"Is there a mystery?" Hannah responded.

"Not sure, but we need one."

"I agree," Porter wrote. "I'll be there."

"Me, too," said Hannah.

"**S**O, WHAT SHALL WE CALL ourselves?" Porter asked. "What does the middle S mean now?" The club had gathered in the Kennedy's basement, now that Danny could handle stairs again. "Without a mystery, we're not the sleuths, although we might be the shits. I don't think we're planning any surprises." He grinned at his friends. It was good to be back together.

"I've been thinking about that," Hannah started, just as they heard scratching at the basement door. "I'll get it, Danny." She dashed upstairs to open the door, and then moved quickly as Bingo, followed by Boots, barreled downstairs. Boots looked irate, as only a cat can.

Porter laughed. "Now that the entire club is here, except Betsy, continue Hannah."

"Let's call ourselves the Secret Searchers Club—until we can be sleuths again. We're searching for a mystery to solve."

"Good idea," Danny said. "Mainly, I wanted us to meet and talk. I thought if we shared whatever was bothering us, we could decide if we could do anything about it. Well, you know what I mean."

They nodded. Yes, they knew exactly what he meant.

Hannah started. "I'm kind of upset about Mr. Markey. He looked awful yesterday, didn't he, Porter?"

"It wasn't just that he'd aged a lot," Porter agreed, "but his disposition had changed. He was grumpy. I don't think he wanted to see us. And Janet definitely wasn't herself."

"No refreshments," Danny said glumly.

"Get over that, will you?" Porter continued. "I don't see a mystery in this, though. Nothing for us to do but visit him when he wants us. I don't know how old he is—"

"Ninety-seven. Kylie told us last night at dinner. She and Brad might be at the castle right now."

"I wonder if this will mean anything for Drama Club," Hannah said. "At least we've got good places to rehearse and perform at CBMS now. Not the same, of course."

They were quiet as they contemplated. It was wrong, of course, to be selfish when they were talking about a friend's life, but the castle meant so much to them.

"I talked to Dad about the amphitheater at Community," Hannah continued. "He thinks it's doable and will talk to the administration next week. He also said he was willing to help with mask making."

"Moving on, Searchers," Porter said. "Another thing bothering me big time is Laurel. You might know more than I do, but that incident on the stairs with Avery really upset me. Someone needs to say what we're all thinking."

Danny nodded. "We all think Laurel is being abused, but we don't know what to do about it."

This was serious, Porter thought. In many ways, it was just as serious as Kammy and her murdered grandfather last year. It was just as serious as discovering the identity of Danny's hit and run driver, and possibly more serious than learning that the mysterious prowler was Roe's brother, Mateo.

"We should tell someone," Hannah said, "but I don't know who or if we have enough information yet. Porter always said Avery was an awful bully at East Elementary, and I've heard her say really nasty things about other girls."

"Laurel could have lost her arm when she fell out of your treehouse," Porter said. "Avery was there, right? Did you see what happened?"

Hannah shook her head. "I'd gone inside to get snacks when I heard Laurel screaming. Avery must have come over when I was inside. Laurel was on the ground in terrible pain, and Avery was yelling at her. Something about not letting Laurel join the swim team — that swimming was her thing. She sounded angry, instead of worried. I called for an ambulance. Then things got really confusing, and I forgot about Avery."

"So Avery could have pushed Laurel off the ladder." Danny shook his head. "If that's what happened, Laurel isn't telling. And yesterday, her hair was hiding a bad bruise on her face, but she didn't say how it happened."

Porter added to their odd-things list. "I walked with her after Drama Club yesterday. I said something about not remembering her when they moved to Castle Bluff when I was in third grade and Avery in fourth. Laurel would have been in my class. But she said she didn't start East Elementary until fifth. She's a year younger than Avery. It doesn't make sense." Porter had also thought Dr. D's reaction to Laurel was strange. He decided not to mention that, although he was fairly certain Dr. D wasn't being creepy. Not like that social studies teacher was toward his sister when Beth was in seventh grade. But he didn't want the others to think of that. Dr. D was okay, but Porter didn't think Dr. D meant Avery when he asked, "Who is that girl?" He meant Laurel, even though he already knew who she was.

The basement door opened. "Almost suppertime, gang," yelled Mr. Kennedy. "Anyone staying, come and wash up. If not, away you go."

"Uncle Martin is taking us for pizza," Hannah said. "And I've got to let Betsy out."

"And I've still got homework," Porter said. "Let's meet again soon. For now, we'll keep a look out."

Laurel had had a pleasant Sunday, for once. Avery had been on a sleepover the night before and was allowed to miss church. Laurel went with her parents, and then stayed for a smorgasbord and youth group meeting. Without Avery there to squash her at every turn, Laurel enjoyed feeling that Mom and Dad really were her parents and that the other members of youth group were her friends. In truth, they far preferred her to Avery but wisely kept their distance when the bullying sister was around.

Later at dinner, Avery was on her best behavior. She'd received permission to go on a hike with friends the following weekend and was told she could have a new cell phone. "Laurel can't go because of her arm, and she doesn't need a cell phone yet," was about as bratty as Avery got. She was careful not to get too ugly in front of her parents.

Afterwards, Laurel went to her room, blocking the door with a small dresser, which had become her practice. Her homework was complete, thanks to working at the library after the Drama Club meeting, and she'd checked out some books about mask making. I don't need to make a mask, she thought. I always wear one.

Kylie's eyes were watery and swollen, although she was no longer crying. Mom and Dad knew what was going on, Danny thought, but he'd wait until after dinner to talk with Kylie. He looked at her, and she nodded. They could practically read each other's minds, he thought.

Mom and Dad excused them from washing up, and then Kylie followed Danny to his bedroom, still on the main floor. "I probably should see about reclaiming my room upstairs," he said.

Kylie attempted a smile. "If only so you can send light signals to Hannah next door."

"And let the whole family use the downstairs bathroom again," he added. But it had taken a lot of work to put his handicap quarters together and would take an equal amount of work getting it back to normal. Both Mom and Dad were busy, so he wouldn't push it, for now. "Okay, Kylie, what's wrong? Is it about Mr. Markey?"

Kylie's eyes filled again, but the tears did not fall. "He didn't even know us, Danny. He wasn't happy to see us at all, even though Leland said that right before we came, he wanted us. Leland says that's the way he is a lot of the time now—sort of in and out of things—remembering and not remembering. I'm afraid we're not going to have him much longer."

"Is it Alzheimer's disease?"

"I asked Leland, but he said the doctor wasn't going to bother with a diagnosis—not at Mr. Markey's age. Definitely dementia, but there's no way to treat it. It will only get worse. At least he isn't in pain. He's just very confused."

Danny shook his head. The castle without Mr. Markey—unimaginable!

Then Kylie's cell rang. "Just a second; it's Brad." Kylie stayed in the room, though. The conversation was short. "Brad said Leland called him. Mr. Markey just asked where I was. He couldn't remember that I'd been there. He started to talk about the time he and I danced at the cast party, and then he fell asleep. I think I need to go to my room now." She gave Danny a quick kiss on the cheek—not a usual Kylie thing to do. "I'll keep you up to date on things."

Danny wanted to call Hannah but remembered that she had gone out for supper. "I feel alone," he told Bingo. "Let's go for a walk."

Uncle Martin, who was first cellist in the Chicago Symphony, knew all about *The Love For Three Oranges* and had even played it in a concert. "I'll pick up a CD of the music for you," he said. "The story is silly but fun. I'm sure you'll enjoy it."

Dad laughed. "You may be the only middle schooler who's ever heard of it. I think I'm going to like your Dr. D." Then he explained that mask making was an art. "It can be quite involved, so you'll need to keep yours simple. Perhaps your friend Imani's father would like to help, too." Mr. Jones was an art teacher at Crofts Performing Arts.

It was a fine idea. "Thanks, Dad, and I'd love to hear the music, Uncle Martin. I wonder if there'll be a part in the show for me."

Dad grinned. "Meanwhile, what about your part as secretary/treasurer?"

Hannah nodded. "I've been thinking about that. I'll keep the minutes, of course, and I think I'll take care of tickets for the shows. Maybe I could correspond with Crofts and the high school to see if we can attend their dress rehearsals. Beth did a lot before we finally elected officers last year."

"But you'd like to do more," Dad guessed. "Something that would put your personal stamp on things. Thoughts, Martin? You used to be a theater bigwig back in the day."

"Back in the day is right." Uncle Martin laughed. "Back in the dark ages, my high school drama club had a newsletter that came out once a month. Everyone looked forward to it, and we got a lot of new members that way. It had an editorial, a calendar of important dates, jokes and riddles— even an advice column. It was great fun."

"Sounds perfect," Hannah breathed. "I'd love to do that. What was it called, Uncle Martin?"

"*Stage Directions.* Since it was a million years ago, I see no reason why you couldn't use it, too—if you want to, of course."

"Yes! And an advice column could be really fun. Something like Dear Amy in the Trib, but about theater. If I write it, though, I wouldn't want people to say Dear Hannah. It should be anonymous, maybe mysterious."

"George Spelvin," Dad said, while Uncle Martin looked surprised. "Oh, yes, I've trod the boards in my time, too."

Trod the boards? Hannah shrugged. Most of the time she understood Dad and Uncle Martin—most of the time. "Who is George Spelvin?"

Uncle Martin chuckled. "The anonymous actor, although I suppose you could say Georgia or Georgina. The name is used in programs when you don't want the actor's name revealed."

"Back when I was in junior high," Dad said, "we did an old-fashioned melodrama. The same person played the hero and villain—

they were supposed to be twins, separated at birth. It was very funny. The director told us about the tradition of George Spelvin and used his name in the program to identify the villain."

Dear George Spelvin in a Drama Club newsletter called *Stage Directions*! How lucky she was to have two great dads! "I want to start working on it right away, but I suppose I should run it by Dr. D and the other officers first."

"You could do a mock up," Uncle Martin suggested. "Make one copy and show them how it would look."

"When it's approved," Dad said, "I could run it off at work, in case anyone sees that as an obstacle. Maybe a small number, at first, and then see what happens."

Hannah couldn't wait for them to finish their pizza, so she could go home and get started. "I'll call Porter and ask him to write a question for George Spelvin." She'd tell him not to tell anyone she was George.

"I'm surprised Porter isn't an officer," Uncle Martin said. "He's definitely, well, presidential. Of course, we don't know Seth Edwards."

Hannah nodded. "Porter would be terrific, but he thinks the president should be an eighth grader, and while he is one now because of skipping, he's afraid that some of the eighth graders would resent him. He wants to concentrate on school and acting and not draw attention to himself."

"Wise man," Dad said. "So, let's ask for a doggie box, the bill, and then be on our way. I believe Hannah has exclusive rights to the computer tonight."

This had been such a good day, Hannah thought, ending with this rare time with the Dads. None of them had brought up a serious subject, such as Mr. Markey's health, Laurel's injuries, or Hannah's strong opinion that Porter really didn't want to be her boyfriend. Those serious things must wait for another day.

Scene Six - Drama Club Plans

"COMING HOME RIGHT AFTER SCHOOL, dear?" Mom asked Laurel before heading for work. Dad had left hours before, and Avery always slept until the last possible second, skipping breakfast, consumed only by barbarians, in her opinion. Laurel ate breakfast and walked to school alone. She'd take the school bus in poor weather but wanted to enjoy the nice days for as long as possible. Besides, Avery took the bus, and her friends were almost as snotty as she was.

"I'll get the late activity bus," she answered. "I like doing my homework in the library."

"It's good that grades are important to you. Dad and I are going to one of his company dinners tonight, so you and Avery will need to fend for yourselves." Mom gave Laurel a meaningless pat. "Have a nice day."

Alone with Avery . . . Well, she'd think about that later. After school, she'd go to the first officer's meeting with Dr. D. Afterward, she'd go to the library. Doing homework at home had become impossible. Laurel returned to her room and pulled out some of her allowance savings from a secret hiding place. She didn't want to spend anything for a meal, but a sandwich at the corner deli was a much better option than supper with Avery. Now to leave the house before Sleeping Ugly arose.

They met in Dr. D's classroom. A few of the teachers had their own offices, but Dr. D hadn't been at CBMS long enough to have much merit. He'd pulled some chairs into a circle, though, away from his desk. "Next time," he said, "we'll meet in the Green Room. I learned about it after I'd texted you about coming here."

This was fine, Hannah thought. The old couches in the Green Room were almost too comfy, and they wouldn't be able to resist the soda and candy machines. Besides, the circle of chairs said a lot about Dr. D and the way he'd interact with them.

He asked questions about what had gone well in the past and what they'd like to do in the future. Seth mentioned what a fine time they'd had at the Halloween party at the castle.

When Hannah raised her hand, Dr. D said, "I think we can dispense with hand-raising, Hannah, just as long as you're not interrupting anyone, and you're sticking to the subject. You want to say something about Halloween?"

"Yes, the party last year was wonderful, but I think things might be different now. I saw Mr. Markey on Saturday, and he's not doing well. I think we should have a Halloween party or some other event but maybe here in school. At least we should talk to Leland and Janet about it before we decide anything."

Dr. D nodded. "Thank you, Hannah. Your knowledge of the people in the castle will be helpful. I'll talk to Mr. Duncan soon and get his opinion. Meanwhile, let's think about what we might do instead."

Seth continued. "If we always do the same thing again and it isn't as good, well, it's hard to explain, but maybe it would ruin our memories of the first time. Does that make sense?" The others nodded; they agreed.

"But what else is there?" Laurel asked, her first words since the meeting began.

"I was thinking about when I was young," Seth said. This brought laughs from all and a blush from Seth. "My Cub Scout troop used to go trick-or-treating for UNICEF. We earned a ton of money for children. What if Drama Club went trick-or-treating together for UNICEF? I never see anyone doing that in Castle Bluff anymore."

"UNICEF?" Laurel asked.

"It stands for United Nations International Children's Emergency Fund," Seth said. "They do a lot of good for children around the world, especially those who don't have enough to eat."

Hannah smiled. "I remember now. Children used to come around with cute orange boxes and people would put coins in them. Sometimes trick-or-treaters would do that, instead of asking for candy. Or if they wanted candy, they'd go at a different time. I think it's a great idea, Seth." She'd wanted Porter to be president, but Seth was going to be fine. "What do you think, Dr. D?"

"We should ask the membership on Thursday," he said, "but something like that might be workable. I haven't seen one of those boxes in years. I think I read somewhere that they're collecting digitally now — using scans. Hannah, could you find out more about it?"

Hannah made a note. "If that doesn't work out, maybe we can find out if there's a way we can help children right here in Castle Bluff." She remembered the poor families she'd seen at the West Village Flats.

Laurel raised her hand, and then hastily put it down. Raising her hand was a habit hard to break. "We could help children at the Winter Markey Home," she said. "A lot of those kids are orphans. They don't have families who care about them."

Hannah was surprised by how serious Laurel sounded and by the odd look Dr. D gave her. Maybe Porter was right that the teacher was unusually interested in Laurel. But how would she know about the Markey Home? Hannah didn't know much, other than it was located on the north side of the village and that Mr. Markey's grandmother had started it.

"That might work, Laurel," she said. "Miss Armstrong always talked about Drama Club reaching out and helping the community." And it might be a good way to honor Mr. Markey, she thought. "We'd need to put a notice in the newspaper and pass out flyers."

"And have our moms post on social media," Seth added. "But we'll talk to the club first. That will be near the top of our agenda." He grinned. "My dad taught me that word; he's pretty excited about me being president. Of course, the club members might want to do more for Halloween. Maybe when we're done, we could come back to school, count the money, and have refreshments."

"All good ideas. Anything else?" Dr. D wondered.

Smiling, Hannah held up the mock-up and possible start to the first edition of *Stage Directions*. "I thought something like this might be fun," she said shyly, handing a copy to each person.

Seth reacted first. "Wow! This is great! Dates to save, an editorial about masks."

Dr. D burst out laughing. "Even an advice column. How in the world did you learn about George Spelvin?"

"My dad and uncle told me. It stands for the anonymous actor. Uncle Martin was in a play where an actor played both the hero and the villain. In the program, they listed the villain's name as George Spelvin."

"It's an old, old tradition," Dr. D said approvingly. "Did you write the question and the answer?"

"Just the answer. I had a friend write the question. I thought we could have a newsletter once a month. My dad said he could run it off at work, if we can't do it at school."

"That's very nice of him," Dr. D said, "but I'm sure it wouldn't be a problem to do it here. What do the rest of you think? We don't have to put it before the membership."

"I love it," Laurel said. "You are so smart, Hannah."

"And clever," Seth added.

"I especially like your editorial about masks," Dr. D said. "It will provide an excellent segue into what I want to say about our mask-making activity, commedia dell'arte, and the play. We could really use *Stage Directions* immediately. Could you have it ready for Drama Club this Thursday? I'll send you some dates and a small article about our mask-making workshop and the show, itself. I could run off fifty to seventy copies Thursday morning."

"It will be ready, Dr. D!" Hannah liked her editorial, too. It was about how we all wear masks—put on different faces—for different occasions. Sometimes we wear them until we discover the one that suits us best, the person we really are.

Porter waited for Hannah outside the library, where he had finished a report on how people's activities modify the physical environment. By making a few changes and using different sources, he'd be able to use the report in both science and social studies. Eighth grade was about killing many birds with one stone. He grinned. Better not share that expression with Hannah, he thought. Early in the day, they'd decided to walk Laurel home, in an effort to keep her safe and also to learn more about her. He'd also wanted to find out if the officers liked *Stage Directions*. Writing a question to George Spelvin had been fun. He was almost sorry he hadn't run for president. He shrugged. Seth would be as good, if not better. "Hey, Hannah!" There she was, but where was Laurel?

"Where's Laurel?"

Hannah shrugged. "She ditched us. Said she had to run some errands. I didn't think I should make a big deal of it."

"Oh, well, we tried. Let's go."

Porter was going to Danny's house for supper—right next door to Hannah's. Danny was having a little trouble with algebra, and Porter was a wiz in math—he admitted to himself.

They walked fast because it was getting cold—cold for mid-September. "How did they like *Stage Directions*?" Porter asked eagerly.

"They loved it. Especially George Spelvin."

"I can't wait for other people to start asking questions. How are you going to handle that?"

"Maybe put a question box in the castle and another in the Green Room. If no one responds, I'll ask you again. It's just for fun, really." Hannah then told him about the possible Halloween collection. "We started thinking about UNICEF, but then we thought about collecting to help children in town. Laurel mentioned the Winter Markey Home. She was really intense about it, Porter."

"I wonder why."

"Yeah. So did Dr. D. You might be right about him, Porter. He seems too interested."

Porter nodded. He didn't think Dr. D was a pedophile, but he would talk with Beth about it. Something felt wrong. "I like the idea of doing something for the Markey Home, though."

"Because of Mr. Markey," Hannah said. "I'm a little worried about money. I didn't think we'd be collecting any when I said I'd be treasurer, too. Also, having just three officers doesn't feel like enough. Do you think it's too late to elect a treasurer?"

"I'd be willing to do that," Porter said. "President is too important, but I'll bet no one else wants the job of treasurer."

"I'll call Seth tonight," Hannah said. "I'll ask him to put it on his agenda." She giggled. "That's a new word we learned today."

Danny fumed. "Good thing I'm a boy," he said to Boots. "If I were a girl like you, Boots, I'd quit the swim team."

Boots looked alarmed, as she often did when aroused from a nap. Swim? Water? Me? She seemed to be saying.

Danny laughed. "Sorry, Boots. Go back to sleep. You've cheered me up, but I wish Porter would get here." He knew that his two friends were planning to walk Laurel home and wondered if it would do any good. Unless Laurel moved somewhere far away from Avery, she wouldn't be safe. Maybe not even then. That girl was trouble! He sighed as he gazed at the open algebra book on his desk. All done but the last problem. A killer. He supposed it wouldn't matter if he got one wrong or left it blank, but he'd been working so hard to keep his grades up, and Porter was good at explaining.

He heard the mudroom door slam. Finally, Porter!

"Started your homework yet?" Porter glanced at the almost-completed math page. "Almost done. Good. Hi, Bingo—how ya doing, Boots?" Bingo raised an ear in greeting, and Boots gave a look of disdain. Porter looked more carefully at Danny. "You're almost as grumpy as Boots, pal. What's up?"

"Avery again. She hurt an eighth-grade girl during the meet today, just because the girl was going to beat her."

"Hurt? Who? How?"

"Madison Meade. I don't suppose Maddy's badly hurt, but she could have been. Avery tried to drown her. Really, everyone saw it. One of the coaches dove in and rescued her. Avery has been suspended from the team, at least until the coach talks to her parents."

"How did Avery react?"

"Oh, the usual. She denied doing anything and said Maddy was trying to drown her because she could tell Avery was winning. Actually, it was just the opposite. Avery left in a big huff. My team was next, but everything was ruined. No one had any team spirit left. I was just telling Boots, here, that I'm glad I'm not a girl."

"I take it that Boots wasn't impressed."

Danny grinned. "I woke her up. Did Laurel tell you and Hannah anything?"

Porter shook his head. "No, she didn't come with us. Said she had errands in town. I don't envy her going home to that."

Danny sat back in his desk chair, silent at first. "I thought we might have a mystery," he said. "Well, it is, all right, but not the kind you solve. As much as I'd like to keep our parents out of it, I don't think we can. The coach will try to help, but Avery's parents will take her side and defend her, just like they always do, and Laurel and others will keep on getting hurt."

"I agree. Avery might even make the new swim team at school. I think we should invite Laurel into SSC after all, and insist on her telling us what's going on. But you're right, Danny. We can't handle this one alone. We need our parents' help."

"I'll call for an SSC meeting Saturday afternoon," Danny said, "and I'll ask Hannah to invite Laurel to come."

"Tell her not to mention the club. Now let's look at that math problem."

Laurel finished her homework in the town library. The school one would have been better because of the available tutors, but she was less noticeable here. She packed her books and papers into her backpack and put on her happy mask in order to smile at the head librarian. She must not look confused or sad. Her face must not inspire questions. Gosh, she was hungry! She wished she could go to Smithy's for a hamburger but was afraid someone might notice her eating there alone. What would happen if someone started asking too many questions and discovered the truth? It would be onward to a different foster, or, if she was lucky, back to the Markey Home. She'd be free of Avery and the people who were only pretending to want her for a daughter, but she'd no longer have her Drama Club friends or her music. The problem was she didn't know what she'd have. Better to keep what I know, she thought, even though it's sometimes awful.

She'd stick with her original plan and buy a sandwich at the deli. "I'll have a corned beef on rye, a large pickle, and a small Coke," she told the high school boy who waited on her. She thought she'd seen him around—maybe in a play. Then she took her meal to an empty bench in a park between there and home. Dinnertime. No one was there. Then there was nothing to do but go home. With any luck, Mom and Dad had returned. No, the car wasn't in the driveway or garage. She could see that the light in Avery's room was on. It was too cold to wait outside. Carefully, cautiously on tiptoes, she crept up the back stairway. Safe at last in her room, she barricaded the door. Now if she could just wait until her parents came home before needing the bathroom.

STAGE DIRECTIONS
Castle Bluff Drama Club
September 22

<u>Places Please!</u>

Hello, there! Welcome to Drama Club, probably the coolest club in the whole school. We hope that you'll participate in all of our activities this year. If not, we'll always be glad to see you when you're available. We meet most Thursdays, after school until 5:00, in room 214, our Drama Club sponsor Dr. Drake's classroom. Every other Saturday, we meet from ten till noon in the ballroom at Markey Castle (entrance in the back). Our next meeting there will be September 24.

Stage Directions will be distributed monthly at no charge. In it, you will learn of important dates, upcoming shows, and reasons to laugh and applaud.

Remember, we're always ready to play with you!
Your officers, Seth Edwards, Laurel Mullen, and Hannah Rendina

Excitedly, Hannah watched the boys and girls pore through the first issue of her newsletter. They were giggling at the jokes and riddles, mainly, and seemed excited about Dr. D's information about the mask-making workshop and audition. Hannah didn't think they'd read her editorial about masks, but that was okay. It was somewhat serious, something they might read later. Then she heard, "Who is George Spelvin? Are you going to write to him?"

Ask George Spelvin

Dear George Spelvin,

I really need your advice. A good friend (whom I'll call Fred) and I were up for the same role in a play. Fred got the part, and I got an extra, which actually looks like it will be a lot of fun. The thing is, Fred won't stop bragging about winning over me. What shall I do? I'm considering violence.

Signed: An Extraordinary Extra

Dear X,

You couldn't have consulted a better person. George Spelvin, the anonymous actor, never gets proper recognition. But that's okay because I have become a stage legend. Let's see Fred top that!

Violence? Don't go there! Tell Fred to knock it off, or he'll be shopping for a new friend. Say you like your part, so there! Braggarts seldom go far. With a good attitude, there'll be many plays in your future.

Your friend,

George Spelvin

*Ask George Spelvin! Put your letters of grief into George's Mailbox, which you'll find in Room 214 and at Markey Castle. Letters will be answered in the spirit they're received.

Hannah giggled in delight. She would get started on the next issue that very night, even though she had a whole month before the next issue. She'd talk to Dr. D about that. Perhaps Stage Directions should come out every two weeks at the Thursday meeting. It was a good way of distributing information, especially important dates, and even the cast list and rehearsal schedule. Uncle Martin had played "The Love For Three Oranges" music for her last night. The march was awesome! Hannah was certain Dr. D would use it in the show. She didn't hear a song that Laurel might sing, though. The fancy arias were either wrong for her voice or for men. She shrugged. Not as if she were directing the show. It was Dr. D's problem.

Seth called the meeting to order. First, he had Hannah read the minutes, which wasn't hard because there wasn't a whole lot to say. Then he asked Dr. D for an update on the play. Auditions would be next Wednesday and Thursday, right after school. So soon? Hannah supposed they'd have to be since the show was only a month away.

"Thanks to Hannah's father," Dr. D reported, "we will perform at the amphitheater at Community and hold many of our rehearsals there. I went to see it, and it's perfect. I was afraid it might be too large for us. But it's small, intimate, and actors shouldn't have a problem projecting. Mask making will take place on Saturday afternoons at the castle—I checked with Leland Duncan. Unfortunately, we can't use the school art room because of needing to leave our masks out to dry. The art department will give us the supplies, though. We'll begin making basic ones this Saturday. I know it's late notice and not everyone will be able to attend. Please understand that even if you're not in the cast, you may make a mask. Mr. Rendina and an art teacher from Crofts will assist."

Mr. Jones, Imani's father, Hannah thought. Then Dr. D asked for questions, and there were so many Hannah was afraid they'd take up the whole meeting. Hannah took notes quickly, hoping she'd be able to read her handwriting later. Finally, Seth was back in charge. The next item on his agenda was Halloween. He explained that it was unlikely they'd be able to have a party at the castle again and told them about the officers' ideas about trick-or-treating.

Hannah mentioned her findings about UNICEF. "They don't have those cute orange boxes anymore," she said. "Instead, they use APPS and bar codes and things that confuse me. A lot of us don't even have cell phones, so I don't think that would work for us. Laurel suggested we collect money for the Winter Markey Children's Home. That would help local children and also be a way of thanking Mr. Markey for being so kind to us." Some of the kids looked confused, so Hannah explained that Mr. Markey's grandmother had founded the home, shortly before she died, almost 150 years ago.

Hannah stared at Laurel, hoping she'd have something to add, but Laurel didn't respond. Some of the sixth graders seemed disinterested but probably wouldn't raise any objections. They hadn't been at the Halloween party last year and didn't know how much fun it had been. The way things were going, they'd probably never know Mr. Markey, either. At least not the way Hannah and her friends did.

Drama Club voted to trick-or-treat to collect money for the Markey Home, although not as enthusiastically as the officers might have wished, but they definitely were in favor of returning to the school for a party afterwards. Hannah said she and the other officers would contact the home about how to proceed. Come on, Laurel, she thought. Speak up! It was your idea!

Then Seth brought up Hannah's concerns about being treasurer as well as secretary. What followed was what Porter had expected. Quickly, he became treasurer. No one else wanted the job.

There was just enough time for one theater game. Danny suggested Freeze, the most popular theater game he knew. Then the first Drama Club meeting at school for the year was over. A good beginning, Hannah thought.

When Dr. D said that the mask making would begin at the castle this Saturday afternoon, Danny looked at Porter, and Porter looked at him. Danny knew exactly what Porter was thinking. No SSC meeting! "Sunday," Danny mouthed to Porter. Porter shrugged, and then nodded. Porter would have to check with his parents, Danny thought, and so would Hannah, and, possibly, Laurel. They'd all want to try their hands at making masks, whether or not they were in the play. Danny thought he'd make some kind of monster. He didn't think he'd wear it for Halloween, but it would look great hung on his bedroom wall. He wasn't terrific at art, but it would be fun to try.

Maybe Mr. Markey was doing better than Kylie thought, Danny hoped. After all, Leland had approved of their doing the masks at the castle. Could they end up having a Halloween party there? Better not plan on it. They had all they really needed at their own school now, and they should learn to be happy with that.

Danny could tell Hannah was excited about the reactions to her newsletter. He was almost positive George Spelvin was Hannah. He grabbed a piece of paper from his notebook and dashed off a quick letter to George Spelvin. He grinned. Old George would need to do some research in order to answer his question. Danny already knew the answer, thanks to Kylie. Probably Porter would know, too, because of Beth—but Hannah wouldn't. He would lay it on thick, as Gramps would say. He'd try to disguise his handwriting, just in case.

> **Dear George Spelvin,**
>
> I know you have tons of fans, but I think I'm your greatest. I think you are handsome and charming and have the answers to all questions about theater. One of my friends, a student at Crofts, mentioned using a gobo. I didn't want to say I was too stupid to know what that is, but now I feel inferior. I would be grateful if you would tell me. What the heck is a gobo?
>
> **Your adoring fan,**
> **Anonymous**

Ha! That'll give Hannah something to think about, Danny thought. He couldn't wait to see how she'd answer. He tuned back to the meeting in time to see Laurel's reaction to helping children at the Markey Home. She couldn't have looked less interested. Strange, when it was her idea. Danny liked her a lot. In fact, he thought he'd ask her to the Thanksgiving dance, new this year. But he wished he understood her better.

Porter, too, had been thinking about the Thanksgiving dance. What a ridiculous notion! The school had never had one before. He did not want to go but knew Hannah would expect him to ask her. It would be okay if they'd just go as friends, preferably with a gang. But eighth graders got serious way too soon — in his opinion. Heck, his own sister was nuts about Kurt when she was only in seventh grade, and they were still together. Most seventh graders didn't start dating, though. Maybe he shouldn't have skipped a grade after all. No use worrying about it now. It was still September. It was just that everyone kept talking about it.

Well, he was pleased to be treasurer. It was a job he could do easily while being more informed about Drama Club activities. He'd be able to keep a better watch on Laurel, too. He and Hannah would see her after school at least two days a week. Odd that Laurel hadn't joined in the conversation about the Markey Home. Dr. D had been watching her strangely, too. Most teachers didn't pay much attention to what was going on with students, other than how they were doing academically. He'd ask Beth what she thought.

I wish I'd kept my big mouth shut, Laurel thought. Of course they'd assume I'd be in charge, since I'm the VP, and it was my idea. The other officers had too much to do already. She would avoid the subject as much as possible. Soon, they'd forget she'd ever mentioned it. She would not go to the Markey Home. How could she explain people knowing her? "I used to live here, and I might again." How would that go over? Her friends didn't know she was a foster—that she was supposed to be adopted, but the Mullen family seemed to have changed its mind. I'm a Failed Foster, she thought bitterly, even though she knew that's not what the term actually meant.

Drama Club was almost over, and she didn't want to go home. But today she couldn't use studying at the library as an excuse. Mom said this morning that dinner would be at six sharp, and she said it sharply. It had been a dreadful couple of days. Even though Laurel had left the living room when the coach arrived "to discuss Avery's behavior," Laurel couldn't help overhearing Mom, Dad, and Avery yelling over everything the coach had to say.

"Witnesses saw Avery try to drown the other swimmer," the coach said in a steady voice. He didn't name the witnesses or the swimmer. Avery was certain to seek revenge, and Mom and Dad would never admit their darling daughter would do such a thing. The coach said that in order to stay on the team, Avery must apologize. Like that would happen, Laurel thought.

Finally Avery screeched, "F—your stupid team! I quit!" She dashed upstairs, making enough noise to warn Laurel to rush into her room and barricade the door. She could still hear the voices downstairs, although they were a good deal softer. Probably Mom and Dad were trying to smooth things over, justifying Avery's language. Looking out the window, Laurel saw the coach drive away. No one called her downstairs to dinner. Luckily, she had a box of crackers in a dresser drawer.

And in the morning, Mom insisted they all be home for dinner. No doubt Avery was off the park district swim team and would try to join the new school one. The family would pretend that nothing had happened. Because that was their way.

TEN PEOPLE SHOWED UP TO make masks. Porter thought it was a good turnout, considering the late notice. Dr. D thought so, too. "What we'll be doing is basic," he said, "but very messy. We need to make the forms, and then wait a long time for them to dry thoroughly before we paint them."

"Paint?" Danny asked in alarm. Porter laughed. His friend was a disaster with paint. More paint would end up on him than the mask.

"Don't worry about it, Danny," said Mr. Rendina, Hannah's dad. "Only those who feel comfortable painting will complete the masks. And we'll make a few extra today, just in case some of our efforts fail."

Porter's sister, Beth, Drama Club's former president, came along to help. Porter had talked her into it because she was a super artist, and also because he wanted her to meet Dr. D. He'd told her of his concerns about the teacher's reactions to Laurel. Beth promised to use her famous vibes. Porter had been amused, but those vibes were often right on the mark.

"Will the actors wear masks for the whole play, Dr. Drake?" Beth asked. "It's so soon. Do you think they'll be able to project well enough by then? Sometimes it takes almost a whole year for Castle Bluff theater kids to do that."

Porter, Hannah, and Danny nodded. They thought they'd be okay, but a lot of the kids were brand new to theater.

"It will not take more than a few weeks," Dr. D said. "I guarantee that. But I do see what you mean about masks making projection more difficult. Mr. Rendina and I have been talking about it." Dr. D gestured for Hannah's dad to continue.

Mr. Rendina held up a bunch of dowel rods. "We've decided that our masks will go on sticks," he said. "One of the characters will be a narrator, who will introduce the stock characters when they hold their masks up to their faces. Then once the story begins, the actors will remove their masks and proceed."

Hannah and Danny smiled. That made sense. Porter wasn't happy, though. Wasn't the whole point not to depend on faces to show emotion? To learn to make appropriate gestures?

Dr. D must have guessed his thoughts. "Don't worry, Porter. A few of our early rehearsals will be mimed without speaking or using facial expressions. Anyone who smiles or frowns will have their mouths taped. But, of course, the audience must be able to hear. I wanted the masks worn throughout, but I do see the point."

"The stick method also means that it won't matter if your mask doesn't fit well," Beth continued. "Probably the best method of making them is to apply strips of paper mache directly to your face, but you'd have to leave them there to dry for about three hours." She grinned at their looks of dismay. "Right, we're not that patient. Our way means we can make ones for people who couldn't come today, too." Porter was glad he'd talked Beth into coming. He'd missed her at Drama Club. She'd become a true leader.

Just then a door opened and Beth's friend, Imani, and her father, Mr. Jones, joined them. "Sorry we're late," Mr. Jones said. He and Imani had their arms full of bags and boxes, and the others rushed to help. They laid everything out on the tables set up in the large ballroom.

Danny felt like a little kid making mud pies again. First, though, he had to form a shape out of sculpting mesh. It wasn't as hard as he'd expected, and he was even able to help Hannah with hers. He decided to make an evil spirit or a demon. The script was sure to have one of those. He shrugged. Maybe he'd audition after all—especially if he could be a villain.

Porter helped everyone with face measurements. They didn't need to be completely accurate, but the mask had to look like it could at least go on a face. He used his chin, nose, eyes, and forehead as a guide, and also the distance between ear to ear. Danny drew the shape of his mask and cut it out of paper. It fit fine, whether or not he used a stick. Once the shape was on the mesh, he'd be able to fit it to his face.

"I like it, Danny," Dr. D said. "There's a character in the play like that. I hope you'll **try** out."

"I'm thinking about it," Danny said, shaping the horns and raising the ridges to the side, forming fins. Any play that had a character like this was certain to be fun. His nose twitched suddenly. He sniffed. He knew that smell. Donut holes! Gee was back!

"Careful, Hannah," Beth warned. "Don't stab yourself cutting that mesh. And don't cut out the eyeholes yet. Cutting those will be one of the last things you do."

"Thanks, Beth." Hannah had been hoping to make an extra mask for Laurel, but she found mask making harder than she'd expected. Someone else would have to do it.

But where was Laurel? She hadn't been in school yesterday, either. Neither was Avery. Hannah was sure of that because the bratty girl was in a few of her classes. If only Laurel had a cell phone. She did not feel comfortable calling her house. She could be sick; a lot of flu was going around. Hannah never had the chance to ask Laurel to come to Danny's house. She guessed they'd have their SSC meeting tomorrow without her. They wouldn't get much done, but it would be good to compare notes.

Time to add the messy paper mache strips to the mask. "Yuck!" she said aloud.

"Let me help, Hannah."

"Thanks, Seth." She and Seth had become pretty good friends during *The Secret Garden,* but they hadn't seen much of each other since. It would be fun to work with him on the Drama Club Board.

Laurel gazed at the sparkling lake and sighed. The leaves were changing, and the weather was perfect, but she'd rather be almost anywhere than in Rhineland, Wisconsin with her foster family, trying too hard, pretending everything was fine. Even Avery was attempting to get along. No doubt her parents had had some harsh words to say about her behavior, ones lightened, though, with bribery. Surely they must know by now that things were not okay. Laurel shook her head. How could they not know?

More than anything, Laurel wished she were at the castle. What did her friends think? That she didn't care? Or maybe they didn't care. Probably they didn't even notice she wasn't in school yesterday. She didn't know about it herself until yesterday morning when she was all set to walk to school. Avery had pulled her last-minute stunt, of course. There was no way she'd make it to the bus in time. Laurel waited for her sister to feign illness and plead to stay home. The whole school had probably heard about the swimming meet by then. But Mom was cheerful—at least pretended to be. "Dad just called," she said. "He was able to reserve a cabin for us in Wisconsin. It should be stunning there now. I've called the school to excuse you, and we'll be on our way as soon as Dad comes home. Aren't you thrilled?"

"No school?" Avery shouted. "Hooray!" She attempted to dance around the kitchen with Laurel, until even Mom could see that Laurel was in pain.

"Easy," Mom said, laughing. "Laurel needs that arm. Better get dressed and pack a few things. We don't want to keep Dad waiting."

No they didn't. Laurel thought that Dad in a dark mood was even worse than Avery.

She'd take another long walk around the lake and concentrate on staying out of everyone's way. But oh, she wished she were at the castle! She could be wearing a real mask, rather than this perpetual, imaginary one.

"SO WHAT DO YOU THINK?" Porter asked Beth Saturday evening, while she was waiting for Kurt to arrive for their date. Kurt was driving now, and it was a very big deal! "About Dr. D, I mean."

"I liked him," Beth said. "Of course it would have been easier to tell if I had seen him with Laurel. But I didn't pick up on any bad vibes. Trust your instincts, Porter. You're not paranoid. If something says it isn't right, you can probably trust it. What's bothering you about him?"

"I'm not sure exactly. He watches her a lot, but I don't think it's in a creepy way."

"Maybe he can tell she's unhappy and is wondering how to help."

Porter thought it over. "No, that's not what I'm picking up. It's more like—it's hard to explain. It's more like she reminds him of someone, and he's trying to figure out who. He seems puzzled. Thanks, Beth. You helped me think it through." Most of the time, sisters were okay. Good thing, seeing that he had three of them.

But that was then. Now it was Sunday afternoon, and he was on his way to Danny's house. Danny seemed determined to include the grownups in his concerns. Usually, Porter would think that was wise, but this time he wasn't sure. He hoped they had enough to tell. Hannah had never really talked about what happened in the treehouse. He knew what he'd seen on the stairway and what Avery had been like in elementary school. Danny would talk about the swim team. But what else? He didn't know.

Hannah agreed with Danny. This wasn't a mystery; this was a friend in trouble. Laurel was an abused victim, and her parents, the people who should be protecting her, weren't. She might have felt differently had Laurel been at school Friday or at the castle yesterday afternoon — or had come over here today, or had a cell phone, or . . . Hannah was sure the *ors* could go on and on.

"Uncle Martin is home," she said. "I'll ask him to come over." Dad was meeting some teachers over at Community to prepare for a fall arts festival.

"Just my mom is here," Danny said. "Dad is less emotional, but Mom's okay."

Maybe we could use some emotion, Hannah thought, although she considered Danny's father the best one in the world — next to Dad and Uncle Martin, of course.

"How should we handle this?" Porter wondered.

Hannah shrugged. "All we can do, I think, is say that we're afraid a friend of ours is in trouble, and then tell them what we know. They'll see we're serious. Besides, they've met Laurel before. What about your parents, Porter?"

"Busy. Both are working on a church fundraiser. Kelly and her friend, Marta, are there, too, providing childcare. They're being paid."

"Wow!" Danny said. "I'll bet they're excited. Hope they have more little kids than just Zoe."

"I'll go get Uncle Martin. He was practicing when I left and probably turned off his phone."

"I'll get Mom," Danny said. "But let's meet in the dining room, so she doesn't get distracted by the mess." The condition of the basement was often a bone of contention with Mrs. Kennedy.

"What's wrong?" Mom demanded, as she joined the group at the dining room table. Not a good start, Danny thought. He supposed he should begin.

"We're worried about a friend of ours," he said. "She could be in a lot of trouble, but we don't think we're the right ones to help her, even though we really want to."

"We're in over our heads," Hannah added, using an expression Dad used often.

Mom opened her mouth to say something Danny thought they might regret, but Uncle Martin piped up. "Why don't you tell us, in your own way. Take your time. We'll listen before we offer any advice. I wonder if you're talking about Laurel. I have been worrying about her since the tree fort incident."

"I think Porter should start," Danny said, "because he knows Laurel's sister better than the rest of us do."

"Okay," Porter said, "although I don't know Laurel that well. Danny is the one who thought we should talk to parents. I wasn't sure."

Danny's mother looked surprised. Danny was usually the one who was certain he and his friends could solve all problems.

Porter continued. "Avery was a grade ahead of me in school. I was first aware of her when I was in third grade. Even back then, she was a brat—a spoiled sport about everything. She yelled, swore, and even kicked and punched when she didn't get her own way—especially at recess. I know she was sent to the principal's office a lot. Once a policeman came to school."

"Really?" Danny wondered if Mom was thinking about Dad's good friend, Sergeant Dean Lodge. Mom sometimes thought the officer had too much influence over Dad but seemed to have had a change of heart since Dean had helped with their missing friend last year.

Hannah laughed. "Porter told us that East Elementary practically had a celebration when Avery graduated from East and went to CBMS."

"You went to Smithy's with her once, didn't you?" Danny vaguely remembered the conversation.

Hannah nodded. "A year ago when I was trying to make more friends. Avery invited a group of girls, including me, to go after school. That's when I met Laurel. We hit it off immediately, so I just talked with her. Avery and her friends kept saying awful things about girls they didn't like and made fun of boys they didn't think were cool. I don't think Laurel was there by choice. After that, Avery ignored me, and I never spoke to her again. Honestly, I was afraid she'd find out about you and Dad, Uncle Martin. She is that mean and nosy. Laurel and I became friends because of *The Secret Garden*. We never talked about anything personal, though."

"Anything else, Porter?"

"Two things, but just one for now. Last week, I walked partway home with Laurel. I happened to say that I didn't remember her before we were in fifth grade. Then she said that's when she first came to East. Well, that doesn't make sense—not if Avery started so much earlier. I'll tell you the rest after Hannah tells about what happened in her tree fort. Probably if it weren't for that, we wouldn't have started to put other things together."

"It happened right before I went to Germany," Hannah continued, "but after Uncle Martin had turned the fort into an actual treehouse. It was a Saturday. I went to the library to return some books and bumped into Laurel. I didn't know then that she spends a lot of time there. I invited her to come back here. She borrowed my phone to call home, but no one was there, so she left a message. Well, we were having a great time. She loved playing with Betsy and climbing into the treehouse. I went inside to get some snacks and left Betsy with her. Then I heard a loud voice yelling. At first I wasn't sure who it was. Then I heard kind of a clunk and someone screaming in pain. I ran outside. Avery was at the top of the ladder, and Laurel was on the ground."

"And Betsy was barking in hysterics at the back door," Mrs. Kennedy added. "When I opened it Betsy dashed in and went searching for Bingo and Boots. I ran outside."

"And I called for an ambulance," Hannah said. "Avery kept yapping about how it wasn't her fault — that Laurel was being careless as usual."

"I was at work," Uncle Martin continued, "but Troy heard the noise, too, and helped Laurel until the ambulance arrived. The other girl, whom I found out later was Avery, took off. I assumed she had gone to find Laurel's parents."

Mrs. Kennedy and Hannah nodded. They had assumed the same thing, but in all the confusion hadn't thought much more about Avery. The person that mattered was Laurel, who had finally passed out.

"Hannah, you said that at first you heard someone yelling. Probably Avery. Could you tell what she was saying?" Porter was good at not missing details that might be overlooked.

"It was crazy. Avery was yelling that swimming was her sport and that Laurel could not join the park district swim team."

"And she didn't," Danny said. "Instead, Laurel came close to losing her arm, and Avery went to camp. That's how I entered the picture. I knew Laurel from *Secret Garden*, of course, and when I found out that she would be home all summer, I knew how she felt, so I tried to keep her spirits up. We played board games, talked, and just sort of hung out."

"Were her parents around?" Uncle Martin wondered.

"Her mom was, most of the time. I never met her father. I only went into the house once, to use the bathroom. We always stayed outside or on the porch. The house was kind of weird. Oh, I don't mean scary. Just not real — more like a stage set than someone's home. Nothing seemed out of place. It was too perfect. The only picture I saw was a huge painting over the fireplace of two girls who looked exactly alike. Twins, maybe, but they looked like little Averys."

"Avery would be beautiful if she smiled," Hannah observed.

Danny shrugged. "Maybe. I can't see it. But I really wanted to check out more of that house, so I went upstairs to use the bathroom.

I didn't know that Mrs. Mullen was home." Danny remembered the time he'd done the same thing at Hannah's house — the time he'd seen the photo of Hannah's dad and Uncle Martin in the master bedroom. He had been confused back then about what it meant. "I peeked into one bedroom that was definitely Laurel's. I could tell because of the posters of musicals on the walls. It was just as neat as the downstairs but had more personality. Then I opened a door that had a Do Not Disturb sign on it. I know, Mom, I shouldn't have. It was the messiest room I've seen in my life! I've never been that messy, and I can be pretty bad. That room, definitely Avery's, could be on an episode of Hoarders. And it smelled awful. I closed the door and ran downstairs and almost bumped into Mrs. Mullen. I just said I needed to use the bathroom but couldn't find a downstairs one."

Porter laughed. "So, did you ever go?"

"Nope, I sort of forgot until I got back outside. I didn't stay very long after that."

"Let's move along," Uncle Martin said. "I think we need to clarify what you're actually saying. Your concerns need to be put into simple words."

Danny nodded. "You're right. We've been beating around the bush, as Grandma says. Porter saw Avery grab Laurel's arm when they were going down a back staircase at school. She might have pushed her down if Porter and Dr. D hadn't come along. I saw Laurel with a huge bruise on her face that she was trying to cover with her hair. And Avery was just kicked off the swim team because she was trying to drown another team member." Mom started to interrupt, but he said quickly, "I saw it, Mom, and I wasn't the only one. The coach saved the girl. It happened."

"We might have waited to talk with you," Hannah said. "We'd even planned to invite Laurel over today. We were going to insist she tell us what's going on. But she wasn't in school on Friday, and she didn't come to the mask-making workshop yesterday, and we know she really wanted to go. She doesn't have a cell phone, and we weren't sure about calling her home. And" the tears began—"I'm scared. I don't know what to do."

"I'll say the simple words," Porter said. "We think Laurel is being abused by Avery, and their parents are doing nothing about it. We think things are getting worse and Laurel is in danger."

Silence filled the dining room, as the SSC and adults thought, all considering what to do next. Mrs. Kennedy stood. "I need a cup of coffee," she said. "How about you, Martin?" He nodded, although he looked as if he'd prefer something stronger. "Danny, grab some Cokes. Quick break, and then come back here."

Porter smiled. When Aunt Jane made up her mind to be in charge, there was no one as effective. She had a clear mind and would know a way forward. Under her guidance, they wouldn't do anything to make matters worse.

Back at the table, drinks in hand, dogs taken care of, Mrs. Kennedy began again. "Martin, jump in at anytime," she said. "I know that I often talk too much. First, I want to compliment all of you. That club of yours has always been able to handle just about anything that's come your way. Your success has been remarkable, even though sometimes I've wished you'd come to us sooner. This time, you realized that it might not be wise to go it alone. It was a very grownup thing to do."

"I agree," Uncle Martin said. "I am proud of you, both for recognizing the problem and caring for your friend—and asking for advice."

Porter nodded. That's what they really were asking for. Advice. What to do next?

Jane Kennedy continued. "I don't have any appointments tomorrow. I'll be home all day. Porter and Hannah, you might not see Laurel in school, but Danny, you and she are in the same grade. Make it your business to find out if Laurel is there, even if you have to go to the office to ask. If she's not, please call me as soon as you can. Perhaps at lunchtime when you're allowed to use your phone. The answer to that will help us determine what to do next. I need to talk it over with Dan tonight, and I imagine, Martin, you'd like to fill Troy in."

Martin nodded.

"And I should tell Mom and Dad," Porter said. "Tonight, if they don't get home too late." He'd talk to Beth, too, but he kept that to himself.

"If Laurel isn't in school tomorrow," Danny's mom continued, "Dan and I will contact Sergeant Lodge."

"The police? Oh, I don't know . . ."

"Sergeant Lodge is discreet, Hannah. If the police were called in at East School, they'll have a record of it. Perhaps they've been contacted at other times. We need to learn more about this family before we decide what to do."

Hannah was in bed and on the verge of sleep when the door opened and Dad entered her bedroom. He gathered her into his arms and just held her. "I am so proud of you, Hannah. You are the dearest, most caring person I know."

"Uncle Martin told you," she said, unnecessarily. It was obvious he knew. "You think we're doing the right thing."

"Oh, yes, no question about it. True, we need to act quickly, but we must have as many of the facts as possible. Sergeant Lodge was a wonderful help last year. You remember."

Hannah remembered, all right. She remembered well. "Dad, my two best friends are still Danny and Porter, but I'd really like to have a best girlfriend who doesn't have so many problems. I feel like I'm reliving last year. First Kammy and now Laurel—two friends in terrible danger. It would be nice to have a normal friendship—like Beth and Kylie have."

Dad hugged her again. "Then that is my wish for you. Sleep now, and try to put the scary thoughts in a different bed."

Dad kissed her and left the room. It wasn't long, though, before the door opened again. This time, it was her other dad, Uncle Martin. He didn't say a word. He just sat at her side and held her until he, too, left the room.

Hannah yawned. "I am so lucky," she said.

"I DON'T KNOW HOW YOU can read in the car," Avery said in a whiny voice. "I'd be certain to throw up."

"It doesn't bother me," Laurel said softly. She was just relieved to be going home and was trying to avoid conversation. Avery was in a foul mood because no matter how much she nagged, her parents would not extend the trip. Both said they had to return to work and that Avery and Laurel must go to school. Laurel understood that Avery didn't want to face the music, but she did — real music. Auditions were this week, and Laurel had decided to give them a try after all. Her arm felt much better, and surely there were parts that didn't require a lot of arm movement.

"What are you reading anyway? That book is awfully thick. Trying to impress teacher, are we?" Of course the words were sarcastic, and the voice intentionally cruel, but Laurel had learned not to expect anything different, unless it was worse. Avery hated her — and had from the moment she'd come to live with the Mullens.

Laurel turned the book so that Avery could see the title.

"*David Copperfield*. Never heard of it."

Laurel shrugged and returned to her reading. But Mom had tuned into the conversation. "*David Copperfield*? That's awfully advanced for a seventh grader. Surely you should have picked something more age appropriate."

"Mrs. Arnold said we should stretch ourselves," Laurel said. "She believes that age isn't the same as reading ability."

"Oooh, Mrs. Arnold, the amazing English teacher. Do you have a crush? Are you in love with her?"

"Of course not, Avery. Let me read. It's a good book. I'm enjoying it." Laurel wasn't sure enjoying was the right word, but she certainly identified with the main character.

Mom wasn't through. "It's fine that you have the reading ability, dear." Why did she always sound phony when she said dear? "But I wonder how well you understand what you're reading. That's when age and maturity are important."

"I'll probably read it again someday," Laurel said, hoping that would end the discussion.

But it was Dad who ended it. "This bickering will stop immediately!" he yelled. "I can't take it anymore!" It would have been useless for Laurel to say she hadn't been bickering, so she said nothing. Avery and Mom tried to, but Dad turned up the radio, which was already blasting.

Laurel retreated into her book, even though the volume made it hard to concentrate. Her book report was due this Friday. She'd go to the library every day after school and read, and then stay up late at night. She hoped she hadn't missed much on Friday. She had to get caught up on that, too. Homework wasn't as hard now that she'd given up trying to do it at home.

"It's me, Mom." Danny made the call from the cafeteria. "Everything is okay, but I thought you'd want to know. She was in my math class this morning."

"Did she seem all right?"

"I think so. Hard to tell. It's awfully loud in here, so I can't really talk."

"Later then," Mom said. "Thanks for calling."

That probably meant that Mom and Dad wouldn't contact Sergeant Lodge—at least not yet. Danny didn't know if that was a good thing or not. Physically, Laurel looked okay, but she seemed— what was the word? — withdrawn, maybe. She was seated alone on the other side of the cafe, reading a thick book and picking at her food. He wanted to join her, but the boys he was sitting with would tease him. He turned to them. "So, who's going to try out for the swim team after school?" he asked.

Porter finished his homework in study hall, with fifteen minutes to spare. Two classes to go, and then home. Today, he might even take a nap, unusual for him. Danny had swim tryouts, so he wouldn't be hanging out with him, and he didn't need to do anything for tomorrow's Drama Club officer's meeting. No regular one this week because of auditions. He supposed he was as prepared as he could be. He yawned. He was absolutely beat!

Last night had been a late one. He and Beth talked until eleven when his parents and little sisters finally came home. Then he had to explain why he was still up, and that led to another discussion that lasted until after midnight. Kelly and Zoe were the only ones not howling yawns at breakfast.

"Something is going on that doesn't make sense," Beth had said. "You don't know enough yet. I can add that Brad sold Laurel a sandwich one evening at the deli. It was dinnertime. It does sound as if Laurel is being abused, but I don't understand why she doesn't ask for help. Even I, when I finally used my brains, talked with Kylie and Marla about my suspicions of Mr. Carroll."

"And you told a teacher," Porter added. "Laurel either pretends nothing is wrong or lies about it."

"I guess it's different if you're related to the person hurting you."

Porter nodded. Beth really didn't have any advice, but it always helped to talk with her. They would again, both agreed.

Dad and Mom were shocked. They'd had no idea this was going on. Of course, they hadn't really met Laurel. They just knew her from seeing *The Secret Garden.*

"That lovely, talented girl," Mom said. "Are you sure, Porter?"

He nodded. "Absolutely. I was not imagining what happened on the stairs."

Dad was on the East Elementary School Board, although he thought he'd step down once Kelly went to middle school. "I never met the Mullen family," he said. "I suppose I could enquire about them. The older daughter, Avery, certainly made her mark there. I've heard the horror stories."

"Be very discreet," Mom advised. "I'm glad you told us, Porter. For now, let's let Jane and Hannah's uncle take the lead, since you discussed the matter with them."

And that's how they left it. Porter glanced at the large clock on the classroom wall, just before the bell rang. He gathered his books. "Two more periods to go," he whispered.

Hannah passed Laurel in the hall. "Hey," she called out, "we missed you Saturday. Were you sick?"

Laurel shook her head. "We went out of town for the weekend. Got to hurry. Don't want to be late."

"Wait! Can I see you after school."

"Can't. Have to study in the library."

And Laurel was gone.

Strange, Hannah thought. That wasn't very friendly, and Laurel normally was. But if Hannah was going to help, she'd have to be nosy. Another person was going to the library, not just to study. She and Laurel were going to talk.

But when Hannah arrived in the library, Laurel wasn't there. "Haven't seen her," the librarian said. "She used to come regularly."

That was weird. Hannah thought Laurel did her homework there practically everyday. She wondered what to do next. Should she take the bus? She'd rather not. The ride took so long, and the weather was nice, although predictions were for rain later. Danny had swim tryouts, and she hadn't seen Porter. She started off alone, and then came to a sudden stop. What if Laurel meant the town library? Laurel had no reason to lie. What if Hannah had just assumed she meant the school's? "I'll go there," she decided.

Hannah started up the steep steps of the old brick library just as the sky began to cloud over. "Goodbye, nice weather," she said, reaching into her jacket pocket. Quickly, she sent Dad a text. "At library in town. Didn't expect it to rain so soon. Can u get me when u leave?"

"5:30," Dad texted back.

That would work, although Betsy might have made a mess by then. If Laurel weren't there, Hannah would just read. "Whoa! Here it comes!" She dashed inside just as the cloud burst.

In a back corner in the adult section, not an area favored by teens because of the lack of coffee, soda, and snack machines, Hannah finally found Laurel. "Phew," she said, sitting across from the startled girl. "I've been looking everywhere for you."

"Hannah, what are you doing here?"

"Well, you said you'd be in the library, so I thought you meant the one at school. Then I decided to try here."

"But why? What do you want?"

"For one thing, I'd like to know why you're being so unfriendly all of a sudden. I thought we were friends."

Laurel looked down. "We are. I'm sorry. I've just had a lot on my mind."

"Well, so have Danny, Porter, and I. And a lot of those things have been about you."

"I'm okay," Laurel muttered.

"No, you're not. You're in trouble, and you need to let us help you."

"I don't know what you're talking about."

"Stop it, Laurel. We know that Avery is hurting you. She's a bully; everyone knows that. Porter saw her grab your arm, which was bad enough. He thinks she would have pushed you down the stairs if he and Dr. D hadn't come along. Danny saw the bruise on your face. He also saw Avery try to drown a girl. For your own safety, you've got to admit it!"

Laurel shrugged. "I'm okay. Avery can be a little rough sometimes, that's all. No big deal." Then she stood. "I think I'd better go home."

Hannah shook her head. "You haven't looked out the window lately, have you? It's pouring out there, and the temperature has really dropped. My dad is coming at 5:30; he'll give you a ride. Sit down, Laurel. Do your homework. I won't say anything more."

Laurel sat, and the two stared at each other until Laurel nodded and retreated into *David Copperfield*.

"Boy, your English teacher is going to love you!" Then, startled by Laurel's angry look, Hannah said, "Sorry, didn't mean anything."

Hannah opened her math book. It was hopeless. Laurel was not going to confide in her. I'll call Mr. Kennedy tonight, she decided. I think he should call Sergeant Lodge—and soon!

HANNAH HIT *SEND*, AND AWAY went the second edition of *Stage Directions*. Hopefully, Dr. D would have a chance to print it before auditions tomorrow. For sure, it would be ready for read-through at the castle Saturday morning. They would find out their parts Friday afternoon, after the two afternoons of auditions they were to attend both times. Dr. D might have callbacks on Friday, but he was hoping not to. Thus, Drama Club and theater were consuming Hannah's entire week, and she was working as hard as possible in her study halls and lunch periods. She wondered if Dr. D would quit making Drama Club a priority once rehearsals began. Danny's sister Kylie had told Hannah that when she was in eighth grade, Drama Club came to a halt during their *Mouse That Roared* rehearsals. Hannah would try to keep that from happening. After all, they had officers now.

She'd been surprised to find two questions in the "Ask George Spelvin" box. She read the one about gobos first. Someone was trying to trick her, she thought, giggling. We'll see about that! It probably wasn't Porter because he'd written the last one. She didn't think Laurel had that much of a sense of humor, at least not lately. Danny, Seth, or even Dr. D were her guesses. Of course, she didn't know what a gobo was, but a quick call to Beth, with a promise of secrecy, supplied an answer, which she wrote to her "adoring fan."

Dear Anonymous (if that's your real name),

How lucky you are to have consulted me. I, a genius who knows all things theatrical, can make you a gobo knower. A gobo is a round metal disc with a design etched into it that can be projected onto the

stage by a light. Gobos can contain varieties of designs, such as clouds, trees, or even the name of your play or school. You can order them from technical theater catalogues, most online. So, that's a gobo, Anonymous. No need to feel inferior anymore.

Your friend,
George Spelvin

Then she opened the other note. She had no idea who wrote it but didn't think it was an officer. She'd put the gobo answer aside for another issue. This letter was timely and belonged in a newsletter concerned with auditions. The question was serious, but the writer still kept it amusing. As secretary, she needed to get to know some of the new kids. This writer, especially, could be worth knowing.

Dear Mr. George Spelvin,

I am your biggest fan. (Really, I'm huge!) I even shaved my dog so he has the same haircut as you. (Bald!) Oh, wise one, I have a problem. I don't know what to do at auditions. I always get so nervous. I'd love to be cast, but I'm really afraid to try. Got any advice?

Sincerely, Petey Peterson

Dear P.P.,

Consider giving yourself a stage name, please. After all, Judy Garland's real name was Frances Gumm, and John Wayne's name was Marion Morrison. It's not too early to consider your future. Now, where were we? Oh, right! Actually, I've never auditioned because once the director hears my name, I'm automatically given a part, although a secretive one.

But I've never allowed my lack of experience to prevent me from offering expert advice.

First, make sure you show up on time and remember what play you're auditioning for. That's important. Suppose you audition for Macbeth, but the play being cast is Little Red Riding Hood. Right off, you have a serious problem. Next, dress sensibly. Never show up for an audition wearing a costume. If you're wearing a peasant dress, with your hair in pigtails, the director will think you're trying too hard. If you have audition material, practice in front of family or friends. Try to relax and remained focused. If it's a cold audition, bribe the director. Well, another problem solved by Super George!

Your friend,
George Spelvin.

P.S. Did I say I was a mister? Can you really tell these days? What's in a name?

Uncle Martin had roared with laughter when Hannah had showed him that.

Seth wrote the editorial, which sounded a little pretentious, but Dad said that was the way editorials were supposed to sound. Seth wrote about the importance of keeping up your grades once rehearsals began, and he talked about the tutors available in the school library, each afternoon after school. Like they'd have time to go to the library once rehearsals started. Hannah shrugged. Seth was the president and had a right to his own editorial.

Dr. D listed the entire rehearsal schedule, important, especially to those who did sports. Hannah could imagine Danny poring over it, figuring out if he could be in the play and swim. He was excited about being picked for Castle Bluff Middle School's first swim team. Their practices would be at 7:00 every morning before school. Hannah shuddered. Cold and wet so early in the day? Not for her!

Hannah wrote about trick-or-treating to benefit the children living at the Winter Markey Home and the party at school afterwards. She had to find time to go to the home but didn't want to go alone. Laurel should go; it was her idea. Hannah would try asking her again. Porter was a possibility, too, now that he was treasurer. That made sense, since they'd be collecting money. Beth had told her that theater could take over your life, if you let it. Yep, that was starting to happen.

Danny set the alarm, determined to fall asleep early. Tomorrow would be a long, long day. Swimming at seven, classes, and then auditions at school. *The Love For Three Oranges* sounded totally ridiculous but fun. Tomorrow, Dr. D would have them do pantomime exercises. Those who'd been in Drama Club last year should be good at that. Then they'd get some short monologues to practice for Thursday. They didn't have to memorize them, so that shouldn't be a problem. The rehearsal schedule versus the swimming one would work, although he'd have to fill every moment of the day to keep it all together. He was close to being scared when he remembered this time last year. He'd been running, certain to take a first at the Cross Country meet when his whole world fell apart. But somehow he got through it, and today he was okay. "I am so lucky," he breathed.

The Laurel problem was out of their hands, at least for this week. Hannah had talked to his dad about contacting Sergeant Lodge. Danny and Porter agreed, after hearing how Hannah had tried to get Laurel to open up. Porter had suggested talking to his counselor at school, and the grownups thought that was a good idea. "If only nothing bad happens before anyone can do anything," he said to Bingo and Boots, snuggling next to him.

Porter grabbed Danny and insisted they be partners in the mirrors game. They had been partners before and were good at it. He ignored Hannah who had been looking at him hopefully. He was relieved when he saw her pick Laurel. A better choice, he thought. Hannah understood about Laurel's arm and would make things easier for her. He saw Hannah pretend to brush her teeth, and was pleased to see Laurel grin. That was the first time he'd seen her happy in ages, he thought. "Let's nail this, Danny," he said, and pretended to vigorously wash his face. Danny was his reflection and just managed not to crack up when Porter took an imaginary Q-tip to dig into his ears. Porter knew very well what a real doctor would say about that.

Next Dr. D had them pass a face. They all stood in a circle, expressionless, faces blank. Then one person made a face to the person to the right, who pretended to take the face, change it, and pass it to the next one. Each face had to be slightly different. No one waiting a turn was allowed to show any emotion.

The next activity pleased Danny — an imaginary swimming meet. "I'll win this, even without water," he told Porter. Danny realized that Dr. D was looking for big movements and that it would be too difficult for Laurel. He crossed over to her and whispered, "Just get off to the side and pretend to tread water," he said.

Laurel giggled. "Thanks, Danny. Great idea!" Dr. D watched approvingly. Evidently, he was looking for teamwork as well as good pantomime. Porter thought Danny had won his swimming meet in a different way.

Porter and Danny both enjoyed the imaginary Tug-of-War. Porter thought he could actually see the rope and was reminded of a boy named Joe's pantomime last year, in which he could almost see the water Joe was drinking from a water fountain. Laurel skipped Tug-of-War but participated in jump rope, even Double Dutch, which she could never do in real life.

That was the best part of pantomime, Porter thought, as he hit a home run in a mimed baseball game. You could be a winner in something you'd be lousy at in gym class. His favorite activity, though, concerned body language. Each person took a slip of paper and then expressed whatever emotion was written there, just using arms and legs and adding facial expressions. He thought that he and Hannah were best at that.

The time passed quickly. Dr. D signaled them to sit, before distributing stapled packs of monologues. "Choose one to read tomorrow," he said. "I'm giving it out at the last moment on purpose. I do not want you to memorize. But when you practice tonight, think about how you can use your body as well as words."

Porter couldn't wait to go through them. He was grateful he'd completed his homework. Working on the monologue was all he wanted to do that night.

Five o'clock. Laurel frowned. She had to go home, but if she tried to use the computer, Avery was sure to claim it. She'd finished reading *David Copperfield* but needed to write the report, due tomorrow. Her teacher preferred it typed. Well, she'd write it in her best handwriting and get to school early tomorrow. Then, if a computer were free in the library, she'd type it then. Don't worry about it, she told herself. It might be easier to talk to her teachers about not having a computer at home. Some kids checked out chrome books from the library, but Laurel was afraid Avery might damage it.

She'd had a good time at auditions. It was fun. She was happy. How rare that emotion was. Once rehearsals became daily, she might have to talk to Mom and Dad about her schedule. She hadn't even told them about being Vice President of Drama Club. True, she rarely came straight home from school, so it might be okay. Last year, Mom and Dad seemed proud that she was in *The Secret Garden*. Not proud enough to come to a performance, of course, but they hadn't minded her doing it. They attended practically all of Avery's activities, but they loved her, while—Stop! She scolded. This was a good day. Go home, eat dinner, write your report, and then work on your monologue. That, at least, will be fun!

Scene Twelve - A Very Strange Play

HANNAH READ THE SYNOPSIS OF the play again. She shrugged. It sounded really stupid, but Dr. D had said it would. A clown welcomes the audience and promises them a wonderful performance. The clown's name is Pantaloon, and some of the actors—extras—portray audience members, in what becomes a play within a play. Pantaloon narrates, does tricks, and recites awful rhymes. A fun part that could be played by either a boy or girl. Another character, the King, is worried about his son, the Prince, who never smiles or laughs or is happy about anything. Pantaloon suggests that the King send for Truffaldino, the court jester. After all, making people laugh is his job. Truffaldino is ordered to produce a show that will amuse everyone, including the Prince. Chelio the Wizard, though, is worried that Fata Morgana, the witch, will ruin Truffaldino's show. Chelio goes deep into the forest to talk to Fata Morgana, to convince her to leave the group alone. Fat chance! Fata Morgana thrives on causing confusion. She ignores Chelio and dashes off to do her evil deeds.

So far, sounds like a lot of other fairy tales I've read, Hannah thought. Maybe they borrow from each other.

In the play, Truffaldino's show is a hit with everyone who attends, except for the Prince. Fata Morgana enters, determined to end the proceedings, but she slips on her foolishly high-heeled shoes and falls flat on the stage, exposing her silly, striped knickers. She might have saved face, if the Prince hadn't chosen that moment to roar with laughter. Enraged, Fata Morgana casts her spell. She tells the Prince that he is in love with three oranges and must go to a far-away desert to find them. The witch's personal monster enters with a pair of bellows and blows the Prince and Truffaldino on their way.

By reading ahead, Hannah saw that there would be three princesses inside the oranges. She hoped she wouldn't be one of them. They seemed to come at the very end and didn't look like big parts, although she didn't have access to the script. She looked into the mirror. Yeah, that was the problem. She looked like every director's dream of a princess. What might she try instead? Looking through the audition material, one part popped out. Fata Morgana, the Witch! After all, in the Narnia movies, the White Witch, Jadis, was a blonde.

Hannah practiced. First, she borrowed Dad's ratty old bathrobe and covered her hair completely with a gray woolen winter cap. She glowered at herself in the mirror until a mean expression appeared. Her eyes were angry and her mouth cruel. *How dare you laugh at Fata Morgana?* She didn't scream. That sounded silly, rather than evil. Instead, she kept her voice low, almost a hiss, and her face expressionless. But she followed with nonsense curses that she made sound sinister. Finally, she allowed her voice to screech. *I command you to fall in love with three oranges!*

That's what she would do, and if Dr. D wanted her to be a princess, she guessed that a princess she'd be. "But mean would be much more fun," she said.

Laurel was undecided. None of the parts seemed right for her. Dr. D said she'd be given a song to sing. She hoped he'd remember. She guessed she'd try for a Princess, although she was afraid they'd be too physical. There were three princesses, each trapped in a paper mache orange. Could she do that? Because of Truffaldino's greed, two princesses die horrible deaths. Laurel imagined that Dr. D would play the death scenes up big, making them as wild and theatrical as possible. The last princess manages to live but not without awful things happening to her first. Oh, well, she'd audition for the winning princess, Ninetta. Dr. D would decide if it were the right role for her.

Just as Hannah had done, Laurel faced her bedroom mirror. *Yes, I will marry you, as soon as you find me a drink of water. But look at me! I'm covered with orange skins, and my dress is ruined. Find me the most beautiful gown that was ever seen, and we will be wed.* Ninetta is beautiful until Fata Morgana turns her into an ugly hag (a reverse Beauty and the Beast?). How would Dr. D make that happen? Laurel vowed not to be on the costume committee.

She'd completed her homework, the *David Copperfield* report, written so neatly that she didn't think Mrs. Arnold would object to it not being typed. Just in case, she would include a note explaining that she seldom had the use of a computer at home. Laurel was tired. She'd go to school early to avoid Avery, but she did not want to deal with the typos she'd make by doing a rush job on a computer. She wanted and deserved a good grade.

She opened the door and peered down the hall. "Coast is clear," she whispered, before dashing to the bathroom.

In spite of the mask he'd made, Danny didn't want to be the monster. Being Pantaloon, the clown, would be more fun. Danny had a vision of what his costume might look He was pretty good at gymnastic-type tricks. His physical therapist, Sid, would help him there. It would not do to reinjure his legs. Thanks to swimming and bar work, his arms were amazingly strong. He thought he could walk on his hands. Pantaloon was probably on stage in the very beginning and ending of the play and wouldn't have as many rehearsals as some of the others. Danny hoped to medal in some of the swimming events — get a blue ribbon — or whatever they did. It was less thrilling than running, but it was safer for now. As Sid said, just being able to walk had been a long journey back, and nothing must spoil it.

Go through the monologue a few times, he told himself. Then take a quick walk with Bingo, and then a video game or ten before lights out.

Gather around, everyone, for the most exciting, energetic, entertaining play you've ever seen. Presenting The Love For Three Oranges! If you quiet down and behave yourselves, as a respectful audience should, you will soon meet our dreadfully worried and sad King. Perhaps you can lift his spirits by cheering when he comes on stage.

It was a super part, Danny thought.

Porter thought the play had great possibilities. He wished he could read the script, though. He'd looked online but couldn't find one. Someone named Carlo Gozzi wrote the original play. In Italian? He shrugged. Sounded Italian. If it were in public domain, Dr. D might have adapted it. From what he could see of the synopsis and monologues, Prince was the male lead. Strange that King and Prince didn't have names. Most of the other characters had.

Well, lead or not, Porter didn't want to be Prince. It was likely that Hannah would be cast as Ninetta, the princess Prince ends up marrying. That would make sense because Hannah was the prettiest girl in Drama Club, if not the whole school. He did not want to be cast as a romantic twosome with Hannah, even though Prince was a terrific part. He and Hannah had returned to being great friends, now that she'd stopped insinuating they should be more. Porter did not want a girlfriend.

Shaking off the worrying thought, he returned to the audition material. What other parts might interest him. King wasn't challenging enough, and Pantaloon was a narrator part—a gymnastic narrator. Not right for Porter. The Wizard could be fun, but it wasn't very meaty. A girl could play Truffaldino, but Porter thought Dr. D would go with a boy. Truffaldino was a lead, who tried to be helpful but often failed. He made a huge mistake when he got so thirsty he opened the oranges. Pretending to die of thirst as he traveled through the desert with Prince might help Porter's mime skills, too. Yes, he'd try for Truffaldino.

Who cares about oranges? We'll never find any in the desert. You can't really be in love with them, and how could you marry all three, anyway? Please, my good Prince, let's leave this wasted place before we die of unquenched thirst. What? You're going to sleep now? How can you sleep in this furnace? I shall soon be buried alive if I don't find water!

He'd do fine, Porter thought, but it would be Dr. D's decision. He hoped there wouldn't be callbacks on Friday. He and Hannah needed to go over to the Markey Home. Did the Home need money? He'd always heard they were pretty well off.

He wondered if Beth were home or at her rehearsal at the high school. He wanted to ask her if she knew how Mr. Markey was doing and to just catch up. Now that she was in high school, they didn't talk as much. A knock at his door interrupted his musings. Beth, he thought. What a coincidence! "Come in."

But it was Kelly. "Are you busy?" she asked nervously.

"No, I'm all done. You need anything?"

"Yes." Her eyes filled. "My homework! I don't get it! It's hard math. Mom doesn't understand it, either, and Dad isn't home."

Porter smiled. Kelly was growing up fast. Next year she'd be in sixth grade at the middle school while he'd be in high school. "Let's go downstairs and spread out on the kitchen table. We'll figure it out together, and a snack might help, too."

Scene Thirteen - Cast List and a Hike

TOWARD THE END OF LAST period Friday, Vice Principal Mrs. Abbott gave the final announcements for the day. "The Cast List for *The Love For Three Oranges* has been posted outside the office. Congratulations to everyone who auditioned. Whether or not you made the cast, we are proud that you tried. You will receive your scripts at 10:00 tomorrow morning at the Castle. Lunch will be provided for those staying to work on masks. Have a lovely weekend, and we'll see you back here, alert and ready to learn, on Monday."

Everyone liked Mrs. A., Hannah thought. Kylie had told her that vice principals weren't always so nice.

No callbacks meant that she and Porter would hike over to the Winter Markey Home after school. It was a long walk, but the weather had turned unexpectedly warm. They'd be fine, and Dad said he'd drive them home once they texted they were ready. She'd tried again to ask Laurel to come but wasn't surprised when she refused. Laurel was friendlier, though, and continued to pretend all was well.

Trying for a look of indifference after the bell rang, Hannah headed slowly for the office, where she found a smallish crowd. Not a lot of people had auditioned. Hannah was fairly certain they'd all get something.

Castle Bluff Middle School Theater Presents
THE LOVE FOR THREE ORANGES

<u>Cast</u> (in order of appearance)
Pantaloon - Danny Kennedy
Pantalette - Laurel Mullen
King - Timothy Howard

Prince - Seth Edwards
Truffaldino, the Jester - Porter Walters
Chelio, the Wizard - Stephen Boulder
Fata Morgana - Hannah Rendina
Pet Monster - Perry Hill
*The Mad Cook - Joe Pappas
*Princess 1 - Kendra Yu
*Princess 2 - Sarah Barkley
Princess 3 (Ninetta) - Carol Tennant
Ugly Princess - Georgia Spelvin
*The Rat - Joe Pappas
Townspeople - *Kendra Yu, *Sarah Barkley, Julia
Burke, Bill Lawrence, Kevin McCloud
Additional Clowns - Les Finke, Katur Patel,
Maggie Jo Morgan, Luanne Holt

* Indicates more than one role.

Hannah pinched herself. "It worked," she whispered. "I convinced Dr. D that I could be mean." A new seventh grader would play Princess Ninetta. Hannah didn't know her yet, but she was certainly pretty.

She laughed when she saw Georgia Spelvin listed. "Thanks, Dr. D." Ugly Princess and Princess Ninetta were the same person. Dr. D could have given a different person the part, but then some poor girl would have to be called Ugly. Better that the beautiful Carol had the part. Hannah, as Fata Morgana, would cast a spell making Ninetta ugly. The Rat was also the beautiful princess, but Dr. D might have thought the transformation too difficult. Most of the townspeople and clowns were sixth graders. That made sense, Hannah thought. Laurel was a character named Pantalette, a part that wasn't listed or included in the monologues. She remembered Dr. D's promise of a singing part for Laurel. Maybe he invented Pantalette just so that could happen.

A great cast, Hannah decided, and she couldn't wait till tomorrow. They all had to work hard if they were going to perform before Halloween. Rehearsals would be everyday. Goodbye, Drama Club! Oh, well, not her problem. Meanwhile, she had to find Porter, so they could make their way to the Winter Markey Home for Children.

Laurel shrugged. Who was Pantalette? Sounded like something you'd wear when you had your period. She hoped she wouldn't get teased. Avery would, of course, but she hadn't paid much attention to her lately. Mainly, she brooded in her disgusting room. Word of her actions on the park district swim team had gotten around, and she had not been picked for the new swim team at the middle school. Mom and Dad were fighting it, but Laurel didn't think the swim coaches would change their minds. Avery developed a bad reputation wherever she went. She still had a few nasty buddies, but most of them had dropped her. Hanging around with Avery meant trouble for them, too. Laurel wished Mom and Dad would stop defending her and try to fix whatever was wrong. One of the main things wrong was her—Laurel. Avery did not want to be her sister. If Laurel had the guts, she'd go with Hannah and Porter to the Markey Home and talk to someone. But what if they sent her to another foster home? What was that old saying? Something about you're better off with the devil you know? What if the next place was even worse? At least here, she had her friends and theater and music.

No callbacks meant she'd work at the library and stay there as long as possible.

"Hooray!" Danny shouted, not much caring who heard him. After all, school was over. He would hardly get into trouble for being excited about a part in a play. He was Pantaloon, the part he wanted. He bet his costume would be terrific. Tomorrow, he'd get the script, and then stay for lunch to work on masks. He wouldn't paint but would be willing to make masks for other people. The messy part was fun! He laughed out loud. He guessed the painting part would be messy, too, if he were doing it.

Probably he and Laurel would be partners in the play—Pantaloon and Pantalette. She wouldn't be able to do any tricks, of course. Did Dr. D know about his leg injuries? No matter. He and Sid would figure out what he could do safely.

He didn't know the sixth-grade cast members, except for the few that had gone to Saint Joe's, but he did know Sarah, Kendra, Steve, Joe, and Perry. They were all on Cross Country last year. The schedules definitely conflicted. Would they drop Cross Country? That was weird. Maybe the rumor about no one liking the new coach was true. If so, that really was too bad. He would still be on Cross Country—if he hadn't gone after a little dog chasing a Frisbee. Almost a year ago. So much had changed!

Porter and Hannah met on the school's front steps. "Congratulations!" both yelled at once.

"Looks like we both got what we wanted," Porter said. "I was certain you'd be Nanetta, until I heard your Fata Morgana audition. I never knew you could be mean."

"It's called acting," Hannah said smugly. "I wanted to play something different. Mary Lennox was often unpleasant, but she was never evil."

Porter agreed. "She was still the sweet heroine. You don't want to be typecast."

"I guess not, although I'm not sure what that means. Does it mean always getting the same kind of part because of the way you look?"

Porter shrugged. "I suppose it can, but the director I had in Colorado said it usually meant becoming famous for a particular kind of part and directors not being able to imagine your doing anything else."

"Oh, I get it. Kind of like Daniel Radcliffe worrying that everyone would always expect him to play Harry Potter, so he took off his clothes in a play. That showed them!"

Porter grinned. "I guess it did. Well, let's go. It's getting cold."

"We'll walk fast. How long will it take?"

"Maybe twenty minutes—half an hour. Not bad, but I'm not sure how to approach things once we get there."

"Well, I called, so the woman in charge knows we're coming. She seemed a little confused about what we want to do but said we could figure it out together."

"I wish UNICEF still had boxes," Porter said. "It would be so much easier."

"I wish we could have another Halloween party at the castle. That was the best party I ever went to."

"Except for walking Kammy home afterwards," Porter said. Both of them grew quiet, remembering.

"That was almost a year ago. I wonder how she's doing."

"Did you ever hear from her again?"

Hannah shook her head. "I didn't really expect to, even though Mr. Markey said she could always consider the castle her home."

"Mr. Markey. I wonder if we'll see him tomorrow."

"And Leland. Do you think Mr. Markey is going to die, Porter?"

"Yes," Porter said. He refused to say more. He didn't want to talk about it. He didn't want to think about it. Beth brought it up almost every night at dinner, and Danny said that Kylie was doing the same. Both girls were terribly worried about Mr. Markey, Leland, Janet, Drama Club, the castle—well, everything. He supposed he was, too.

"Oh, we're here," breathed Hannah. "I didn't expect it to be so beautiful. It's just the way I imagined Misselthwaite Manor. A huge mansion, with miles and miles of lawn and trees that reach the sky."

Porter grinned. "Well, at least a couple of acres and the tallest trees in Castle Bluff. I can imagine Mary and Dickon running around and playing hoops."

"With Colin all better, of course. *Three Oranges* will be fun, but I don't think any play will ever be as good as *The Secret Garden*, do you?"

"Nope," Porter said, but not for the reasons Hannah had. *The Secret Garden* was when he finally realized that his passion was theater, especially acting. He'd never known before where his interests truly lay. And *The Secret Garden* was when Hannah knew that she belonged in Castle Bluff and that she had friends who liked and appreciated her for the person she was. "Let's go inside," he said.

They walked up the sturdy staircase, and then Hannah rang the doorbell. "I think Winter Markey must have been inspired by the castle when she had this built."

"Probably. We should find out how old the castle is. I don't know, do you?"

They waited, endlessly, it seemed. Porter wondered if they'd made a mistake in coming. Finally, a tired-looking woman, holding a dishcloth, opened the door. She seemed friendly enough—just frustrated.

"I'm sorry. I was working in the kitchen and didn't hear the doorbell." Although she didn't say it wasn't her job to tend to the door, Porter thought she might be thinking it. "How may I help you?"

"We're from Castle Bluff Middle School's Drama Club," Hannah said. "We have an appointment with Mrs. Duncan."

Porter gave a start. Hannah hadn't said who they were going to see. Duncan was Leland's last name. Could be a relative, although he didn't suppose the name was that unusual.

The woman wiped her hands. "Come right in." Porter and Hannah followed her down a long hall until they reached a door.

"Come right in," another voice echoed.

Inside, sitting on a flowered chair opposite a matching couch, sat an elderly woman with white permed hair and a generous amount of face makeup. "Come sit down," she said, indicating the couch. "My nephew has told me about you."

Nephew! "Are you Leland's aunt?" Porter asked. Hannah stared at him. She hadn't made the connection.

Mrs. Duncan, whose first name was Winifred, chuckled. "I suspect you didn't know I existed. Leland has always been foolishly private, although your group has loosened him up a bit." She smiled warmly. "And dear Janet, of course. Now, how may I help you?"

Exactly what the woman with the dishcloth had said. Were they related? Or, Porter let his imagination run wild, clones? They seemed to parrot each other.

Hannah explained that their club wanted to do something different Halloween night. "Last year we had a terrific party at the castle, but we've decided not to this year because of Mr. Markey's health." She figured that Leland's grandmother must know about that.

Mrs. Duncan nodded sadly while Hannah continued to tell her about the club's plans to collect money for the United Nations International Children's Emergency Fund. "But they don't have the little orange boxes anymore. Everything is digital, and most of our members can't do that."

"I remember when my Girl Scout troop used to participate," Mrs. Duncan said.

Hannah continued. "Then someone thought about the Markey Home and how collecting money to help the children here would be a way to honor Mr. Markey."

Mrs. Duncan sighed. "Well, it's a fine idea, to be sure, but there are all kinds of legalities involved — grants and other things. Most of our children come from very difficult backgrounds. Some are, you might say, in hiding. Many have parents who are not able to take care of them now. Some of the children are hopeful and others fearful." Hannah nodded. She couldn't help but think of Kammy.

"Occasionally, youngsters come who are orphaned and later fostered or adopted. One of our fosters goes to your school. For their protection, we keep a low profile and avoid all publicity and press coverage. So, I'm afraid I have to say no to your very generous and worthy offer." She watched their disappointed faces for a few seconds, and then said, "Come with me. I have an idea."

They climbed to the second floor of the mansion. Porter thought it was strangely quiet for a children's home. "Where is everyone?" he asked.

Mrs. Duncan laughed. "Shortly before you came, it wasn't so quiet. The children are outside playing or in their rooms doing their homework. Soon they'll be in for our simple supper. Our main meal each day is at 12:30. Makes life a little easier for my sister. We truly need more live-in help."

The woman with the dishtowel was Mrs. Duncan's sister and also related to Leland. Funny, he'd never thought of Leland having a family, or Mr. Markey, either, for that matter.

In a dramatic fashion, Mrs. Duncan flung open two wide doors and turned on the overhead lights. "What do you think of this?" she asked.

Hannah stared. "It's awesome!" Not as grand as the ballroom at Markey Castle or the new, efficient auditorium at CBMS, with its large stage, raked seating, and new light and sound boards, but a spacious, lovely room with a small stage at one end.

"It's very nice," Porter said, although he wondered what the woman had in mind.

Mrs. Duncan seemed to sense his uncertainty. "We have a few youngsters—about your age—who would love a Drama Club program. No one here has the time or qualifications to run one. I heard about your event at the castle last year. What if you hold your party here Halloween night? I think it best that just your club members come. Our middle school-age youngsters, who are interested, would attend, and you and your director could teach them some of your theater games. No money would be involved. Both your group and our staff would provide refreshments. What do you think?"

"I'd love it," Hannah exclaimed. "Thank you, Mrs. Duncan!"

Porter nodded. "It's a great idea. We'll have to get permission, but we are meeting at the castle tomorrow and can talk to our director, Dr. Drake, then."

"And as soon as he says yes," Hannah said excitedly— certain that Dr. D would; in fact she'd text him as soon as they left— "I'll email everyone in Drama Club. I know they'll like this idea much, much better!"

Porter was thoughtful as they waited for a ride from Mr. Rendina.

"Don't you like the idea, Porter?"

"It's terrific. I was just thinking about how everything is changing."

"For good or bad?"

He shook his head. "Either, both, I don't know. Beth complained about that last year, and I'm beginning to see what she meant. New friends have entered, and maybe new places, as well. The castle is still important, but I have a feeling this place will be, too."

"Oh, here's Dad!"

Scene Fourteen - Read-through and a Reunion

QUICKLY, LAUREL OPENED HER SCRIPT and started highlighting her lines. Her part looked terrific! Both she and Danny would be a narrative team, both clowns. He'd do the clown acts and most of the speaking, and she'd do some speaking and all of the singing. The lyrics of one song were especially fun. Pantalette kept echoing in song what Pantaloon had just said, causing him to become more and more irate. A humming sound filled the ballroom as the cast looked through their scripts and mumbled comments.

The first thing that happened after Dr. D had passed them out, though, was a huge gasp—at least from those who recognized a certain name. *The Outrageous Love for Three Oranges* had been adapted by Anna Armstrong, the adapter and director of *The Secret Garden*. How wonderful that she hadn't forgotten them! She'd even dedicated the script: "For my dear friends, the theater students of Castle Bluff Middle School." And it was going to be published! Hooray for Miss Armstrong!

They were about to start their first read-through when Leland Duncan entered. Was something wrong? Many of them were expecting that grim news might come at any time. No, Leland was smiling as he approached Dr. D and whispered to him. Leland nodded to Hannah and Danny before he left again. Those who knew Leland began to buzz among themselves.

Dr. D gestured for quiet. He rarely used words to command their attention. "Cast, before we begin, we've received an invitation. Good news for many of you. Mr. Markey is feeling well enough to see us downstairs for a few minutes." The seventh and eighth graders cheered while those in sixth seemed puzzled.

"We won't stay long because we don't want to tire him out, and we do have work here."

Work? Laurel thought. This is play, and the only bright spot in my life!

Mr. Markey did not look great, Danny thought, but better than Hannah had described. Maybe Porter and Beth were wrong. Maybe Mr. Markey would be well again soon. Danny bet he would live to be one hundred!

"What a fine thing to have company again," Mr. Markey said, his voice shaky, but his smile as wide and his eyes almost as twinkly as ever. Hannah had immediately crossed to his wheelchair and given him a hug. Danny wanted to and probably would have if others hadn't been around. "Leland and I were just saying how much we missed seeing you. Danny and Porter, I don't see those sisters of yours. Why aren't they here?"

"They're in high school now, Mr. Markey, so they aren't in our Drama Club anymore," Danny said.

"We'll tell them that you were asking for them," Porter added.

"You do that," Mr. Markey said. "Tell them to come see me soon. Tell . . ." He seemed confused, as if he were trying to remember their names.

Leland's wife, Janet, seated next to Mr. Markey, assured him. "They'll tell Kylie and Beth." Then she added, "Mr. Markey just wanted to say how proud he is of what you're doing."

All of the students looked puzzled. Proud? What had they done?

"Oh, dear," Dr. D said. "I'm afraid they don't know about it yet. Hannah and Porter found out yesterday, and Hannah texted me last night."

"I am sorry," Janet said, embarrassed. "I had no idea."

"I'm sure it's not a problem," Dr. D said. "Hannah and Porter, suppose you tell the group about your trip yesterday."

Danny knew because Hannah had told him last night. He'd act surprised, though. After all, he wasn't on Drama Board.

Quickly, they related all that had happened at the Winter Markey Home, although they didn't say much about why a fundraiser wouldn't work. That might draw attention to the home, as Mrs. Duncan had said. "We really liked your aunt, Leland," Hannah said.

Leland smiled shyly. "She liked you, too."

A real Halloween party at an old mansion? Yes, Drama Club definitely approved. And it would be challenging and fun to teach their favorite theater games to new kids.

"Will we have time to prepare?" Seth asked. "Rehearsals are going to put an end to Drama Club, aren't they?" The rest of Drama Board nodded. Danny knew they had been worrying about the same thing.

Dr. D looked sheepish. "I've been thinking about that. Yes, we do need lots of rehearsals if we're going to pull off this show before Halloween. I went over to Community and asked if we could change the date until a few weeks later. They mentioned weather. That's the problem, of course."

Danny raised his hand. "Couldn't the Drama Board meet after rehearsals on Saturday instead of on Tuesday? They're all in the play. Maybe a small committee could plan the party. I volunteer to head that. We could meet at my house on Sunday afternoons. Then, since our Thursday rehearsals will be at school, we could have a short Drama Club meeting right before the rehearsal; it wouldn't have to take long. I say we stick with our original performance date."

The others applauded, liking Danny's suggestion, and Dr. D looked relieved.

"I must say, you are all fine children," Mr. Markey said. "I think I might need to rest now."

Leland and Janet gestured for the group, seated on the rug, to rise and return upstairs. Danny might have been the only one to notice that Laurel was not thrilled by the news. In fact, she looked miserable.

But Porter had noticed, too, of course. He noticed most things. Laurel's reaction to having a Halloween party at the Winter Markey Home was weird. After all, she was the one who'd suggested collecting money. He thought he might be missing something—something he'd heard but didn't remember. Maybe it would come to him later. He'd check with Hannah, but he didn't think she'd even looked at Laurel. Hannah was thrilled by the way everything was going—the play, the party prospect, and seeing Mr. Markey again. All those things were wonderful, of course, but Porter had also watched Leland. Leland didn't think Mr. Markey was getting better. Leland probably loved Mr. Markey more than anyone, and Leland was worried.

I'll talk to Beth tonight, he told himself. *I'll tell her to call Kylie and say they need to get over here fast.*

Porter put all problems aside as they started read-through. His part suited his needs perfectly. It was much more challenging than Dickon, his part in *The Secret Garden*, even though it was smaller. He wished he could talk to Mr. Webster, his director in Colorado, about it. Truffaldino had to demonstrate practically every emotion possible; he was humble, proud, angry, penitent, sad—nothing was ever the same. The lines weren't difficult, but the antics would be more demanding than calisthenics in gym class. Hannah and Danny were happy, too, and Laurel, no longer looking like the scared girl she'd been downstairs, glowed. Seth was the perfect, handsome prince. Yes, Dr. D was good at casting. That was certainly a relief. Even the sixth-grade extras felt valued as they laughed, cheered, and jeered together.

In character, he began to wail. *Poor Truffaldino! I shouldn't have to face this. I'm only a simple court jester. My only job is to make people laugh. I am a stranger to sadness and death. The Prince is royalty and, thus, must have the power to save himself. I'm leaving now and soon shall forget everything that happened today!*

A few sixth graders started to applaud, but Dr. D held up his hand to stop them. He wouldn't stop the audience, though. The play was going to be great!

I hate happy endings, Hannah announced, in her role of Fata Morgana. *I must conjure up a scheme to stop any future attempts at merrymaking.* Hannah was reaching the end of her lines, almost without giggling. Pretending to be mean was so much fun!

Soon, the King gave the closing line of the play, *I do like a happy ending*.

Then Pantaloon and Pantalette thanked both the pretend and real audiences for coming. The play was very short, which was a good thing, considering the amount of time they had and all that was involved technically.

"Next Saturday, we'll meet at the amphitheater at Community. Please have all lines learned by that time." If Dr. D was surprised by the looks coming his way, he pretended not to notice.

Only one week to learn their lines? Before the blocking even began? Hannah shook her head. Miss Armstrong always said that lines and blocking should be learned together. She saw Porter smiling at her. Then she remembered him saying that directors often have very different ways of doing things and that actors needed to adjust and follow directions. Hannah shrugged. Miss Armstrong's method made more sense. Good thing her homework was done. She knew exactly what she'd be doing tonight.

But now, sandwiches and soda, provided by Dr. D, and then returning to mask making and painting. She was glad Dad, Beth, Imani, and Mr. Jones planned to help. Hannah wasn't confident about painting masks but thought she'd help construct the three giant paper mache oranges. Those she could paint!

Scene Fifteen - More About Laurel

A LAST-MINUTE CALL FOR swim practice meant that Danny couldn't remain at the castle to work on masks. In some ways, he was disappointed, but he figured he wouldn't be much use there anyway. Swimming might help clear his head. He really hoped he hadn't taken on too much. Only one week to learn his lines? And without knowing that would happen, he'd volunteered to organize the Halloween party. He could not afford to get behind in his schoolwork as he had last year, but he did not want to give up anything! Oh, well, sometimes his best ideas came to him when he was swimming. He'd figure it out.

He wondered why the masks were necessary, even though they'd add a lot to the show. In his opinion, the biggest challenge would be costumes. Could Dr. D be planning to rent them? Had he ever met Gee, Kurt's grandma? She was a wiz at sewing—as well as making the best donut holes in the world!

A good swim practice did the trick. In fact, not even thinking about swimming resulted in his fastest time ever. He'd be ready for the early-morning meet next Saturday, but man he'd be tired for rehearsal at Community. One lap at a time, he told himself. Try to do what Mom always insists: "Use your time wisely."

Mom should talk. She was back to booking the family for too many activities. He'd have it out with her, as Kylie once did. Yes, he'd go to church and then to his grandparents for dinner, but he needed to be home on Sunday afternoons, for a few weeks anyway, to plan the party and maybe hold an SSC meeting. Worrying about Laurel seemed to be on hold.

He checked his phone for the time. Maybe the mask people would be home by now. He'd make some phone calls and form his committee. Porter and Hannah, of course, because they'd gone to the Home. Maybe Laurel because she'd started the whole thing. Who else? A couple of the new sixth graders, just to be fair. Too large a committee would mean they wouldn't get anything done. He'd had another idea during one of his laps. He would call Kurt and Joe from last year to see if they were free. Both of them were wonderful at leading theater games and pantomimes. Yeah, Joe was a show-off, but Beth said he'd calmed down and that he and Imani were dating. That was weird. Perhaps Joe had discovered that someone's race didn't matter after all.

Back home, Mom greeted him with, "Oh, good. Please set the table, dear. We're having company."

Danny sighed. So much for homework, phone calls, and learning lines! He'd send Porter a quick text, asking him to call Kurt and Joe. Hannah, as secretary of Drama Club, had all the cast's contact info. He'd ask her to pick two sixth graders and ask them to be on the committee. Two o'clock tomorrow afternoon, right here. Danny opened the silverware drawer. Guests on a Saturday night were unusual in the Kennedy household. "Who's coming?" he asked.

"Oh, it will be informal. Dean Lodge and his new wife, Rebecca."

Sergeant Lodge? That was different! Maybe they'd learn more about Laurel.

"And," Mom added, "I've asked Porter to come, too."

"Really?"

"Hannah will be over later for dessert."

"Mom?"

His mother smiled mischievously. "I'm sure Rebecca will help me clean up and prepare dessert. It will give us a chance to become better acquainted. Then you, Hannah, and Porter can talk with Dad and Dean in private. I understand they have some information about your friend, Laurel."

Danny shook his head, wondering if he'd ever figure Mom out. But why try? Instead, he gave her a hug.

Laurel had stayed behind to talk with Dr. D. "I think I can learn my spoken lines in time," she said, "but I don't know about the songs. I could memorize the lyrics, but it would be easier if I knew the music." She didn't mention that the music would determine the rhythm of the lyrics. She wondered how much he knew about music but was afraid of insulting him.

Dr. D laughed. "Don't worry, Laurel. I know your situation is different. Let me see your schedule." He took a pen from his shirt pocket. "Instead of going to rehearsal on these dates"—he marked them off—"go to Miss Raynor's room. She's your music teacher, correct?" Laurel nodded. Miss. Raynor was new and her favorite teacher this year. "She'll have all of your music and will work with you on your songs. Will that help?"

"Yes, that will be perfect, Dr. D."

"Laurel, I keep meaning to ask you something."

Oh, no, Laurel thought, on guard. He's going to ask me about the time Avery tried to push me down the stairs. She didn't respond, didn't encourage him to continue.

"I just—I—you remind me of someone I once knew. Did you ever live in Des Moines, Iowa?"

She shook her head. "No, sorry." Actually, she had no idea if she had. She had lived in so many places they'd all become a blur.

"No, I'm sorry. You look like someone I knew there. Laurel was her favorite name. Well, it's getting late. Better run along home now. I'm glad that you'll be able to work with Miss Raynor."

Laurel headed down the back stairs but could feel Dr. D watching her. He watched her often but not, she thought, in a creepy way. She knew creepy—too well. Something had happened in Dr. D's past that made him sad. She knew sad, too.

She could go home. Mom and Dad were taking Avery somewhere—Laurel didn't know where—but she preferred studying in the library. The librarians knew her and were helpful. Math, a report for English, and then working on her lines. Most of her part was singing, so learning her dialogue should come easily.

But what in the world was she going to do about the Halloween party? Why had she ever mentioned Markey Home? She couldn't go there, but no one would understand why not.

Porter accepted Aunt Jane's dinner invitation but explained he could not stay overnight. "Danny and I have tons of homework." He didn't add that Danny was also hosting a meeting in the Kennedy basement the very next day. Danny might not have informed his mother yet.

After receiving Danny's text, Porter followed orders and sent texts to both Kurt and Joe. Joe responded immediately, saying he'd be delighted and was grateful for the opportunity. He asked if Imani could come, too. Porter shrugged. Beth seemed to be correct in saying Joe had changed. Imani would be a welcome addition. Another text. Oh, too bad. It was from Kurt to remind him that Crofts was having its annual Halloween dance and that he'd invited Beth. "Another time," Kurt said.

Truffaldino (Porter) nailed a few more pages of lines before heading over to the Kennedys. He should have turned down Aunt Jane's invitation, but something in her voice said his presence was important.

Meanwhile, Gramps was ill again and might go back to the hospital. Fingers crossed, of course, but Porter wondered how much more his poor body could stand. It might have been a mistake for his grandparents to move to Colorado last year. Porter sighed, certain his grandmother needed him. He felt overwhelmed by too many things happening, including having his heart in two places at once.

"Sergeant Lodge is going to tell us more about Laurel," Hannah told Dad. "I want to hear, and also I don't. I think I'm a little scared."

Dad nodded. "I don't blame you. I wonder how much he'll be able to say, though. Martin and I wish we could go with you; you'll have to fill us in later."

Dad and Uncle Martin were going to Libertyville to see friends in a Community Theater musical. The friends would be disappointed if they cancelled. Also, Hannah thought, Dad and Uncle Martin deserved a date night.

She gave Dad a quick kiss. "Have a great time," she said, before heading next door.

Dessert was apple pie, with ice cream or Cool Whip on top. Mrs. Kennedy was a terrific baker. The adults had coffee. Then Danny's mom suggested that Mrs. Lodge help her clear the table and enjoy a little "girl talk" while the rest convened in the living room. Hannah guessed that Mrs. Kennedy would hear later what happened from her husband. She didn't know how much Mrs. Lodge knew. For sure, the sergeant's wife didn't know Laurel at all.

Hannah sat next to Danny and tried to avoid looking at Porter. A funny thing had happened, and she wasn't certain how to talk to him about it, or if it was necessary. Seth had walked her home after the mask-making workshop and asked her if she wanted to go to the movies with him sometime—and, even though it wasn't for a long time, to the Thanksgiving dance. She'd assumed that Porter would get around to asking her, although she'd probably end up asking him by suggesting that Danny go, too. But this was a real date invitation. Seth wanted her to go with him, and Porter would need to be nagged. So Hannah accepted. Somehow, she doubted that Porter would even care. Seth had become a good friend, and they would have fun. No dance would ever be as wonderful as last year's Valentine/Birthday one, but a lot of that was due to getting Betsy for a present. Thanksgiving was a funny time to have a dance, but that was what the Student Council had decided upon, perhaps thinking that Halloween and Christmas were too full of activities.

Sergeant Lodge and Mr. Kennedy refreshed their coffee, and then Sergeant Lodge began. "You kids were correct asking Dan to contact me, so well done. I wish I could tell you everything I've learned, but much of it is privileged. I can tell you that DCFS is involved."

"DCFS?" Danny asked.

"Department of Children and Family Services," Porter said. "They are in charge of making sure that children at risk are safe."

"And most times they succeed," Dean Lodge said. "Usually the only time you hear about them is when someone botches the job, which is why they have a poor reputation."

"So they already knew about Laurel," Danny's dad said. "What about Avery?"

"Complaints have been made about Avery for years—mainly from school and neighbors. The police have quite a file on her. The problem is that her parents excel at casting doubts and making excuses."

Danny nodded. "That's what happened at the swim meet. She didn't get away with it that time."

"But the parents are suing the park district," Sergeant Lodge said. "Also, Maddy's parents are suing the Mullens. It's a big mess. Perhaps I shouldn't have revealed that."

Hannah wasn't surprised. "But you said the DCFS already knew about Laurel, as if it didn't have anything to do with Avery. I don't understand."

"Right." Sergeant Lodge paused. "Here's where it gets tricky. Please, anything I tell you is in confidence. You must not tell anyone. Talk about it among yourselves, help your friend however you can, but don't reveal it to anyone else."

"Except Dad and Uncle Martin," Hannah said. "I won't keep anything from them."

Mr. Kennedy nodded. "And Porter's parents. That's different. They've been a part of this. We promise, Dean."

"Then okay. At least two families have tragic stories—I don't know which is worse. Starting with Laurel, no one seems to know anything about her real family."

"What?" Three young voices chimed.

"Laurel is using the last name, Mullen, but she hasn't been adopted officially. Mr. and Mrs. Mullen were planning to, but then for some reason put it on hold. She's been in and out of foster care most of her life. At the time the Mullens decided to foster her, with the plan to adopt, she was living at the Winter Markey Home."

"So that's what's going on," Hannah blurted. "That's why she knows about the Home but doesn't want to go there—even for a party. She's afraid we'll find out when people there recognize her."

"And they would!" Porter exclaimed. "That's what I couldn't remember. Mrs. Duncan said that one of the former Home kids goes to our school. She must have meant Laurel."

"There could be others," Mr. Kennedy said. "But why, Dean, do you think the Mullens changed their minds?"

"I don't know for certain, but I imagine it's because of the way Avery is behaving. They probably know it's not working, but pride or fear of being judged is keeping them from admitting it."

"Avery hates Laurel," Danny said. "I think I'm glad they're not really sisters."

Hannah nodded. "I hope DCFS figures out it's not safe for Laurel to live with them."

Sergeant Lodge sighed. "Even though it won't be Laurel's decision, I'm not sure she'd agree with you, Hannah. From what I've determined, she wants a home, even if it's less than perfect. Her record shows several disastrous placements."

Mr. Kennedy moved the conversation along. "You said there were two sad stories."

"Yes, and I doubt anyone outside the family knows it. When did the Mullens come to Castle Bluff, Porter?"

"I was in third grade, and Avery was in fourth. But Laurel didn't come to East until fifth. I was surprised when I found out Laurel hadn't come the same time as Avery. I thought I'd just never noticed her. She is pretty quiet."

"What happened was a tragedy," Dean Lodge said. "Avery had a twin sister—identical, in fact. Shortly before the Mullens moved to Castle Bluff, Avery's twin, Ashley, died."

"Oh, my God! Did Avery kill her?"

The sergeant almost laughed. "No, Danny, she did not. But it was awful. Ashley had a rare, genetic disease. It took several years to progress, but she simply wasted away until she died. The family, especially Avery, was devastated."

"And they decided to replace Avery's twin with another girl?" Mr. Kennedy shook his head.

"Poor Avery." It was the first time Hannah had ever felt sorry for the unpleasant girl.

"And poor Laurel," Danny said.

L ATE THAT NIGHT — LATE, CONSIDERING that it was almost nine and Laurel had no idea where they'd been — the front door opened, and in came Mom, Dad, and Avery. Mom looked frazzled, and Dad enraged. Avery was in tears as she dashed upstairs. Soon, Laurel heard Avery's bedroom door slam. Whatever had happened did not concern her. Mom and Dad would not welcome her questioning. "Goodnight," she whispered, and followed Avery up the stairs.

She lay on her bed, barely holding back her own tears. As scary as an unknown future seemed, it was time to face the truth. She did not fit into this family, maybe not any family. No one really loved her. "My friends like me," she whispered, "but if I weren't here, they'd forget about me soon enough." When she got older, she might consider finding her real family, or at least find out who they were. She had to have come from somewhere.

Loud crying persisted in the next room. Whatever had happened? Usually tantrums meant Avery hadn't gotten her own way, but this felt different. Laurel almost felt sorry for her, even though she was a mean bully. Imagine losing your twin sister, and then having your parents try to replace her almost right away. Well, Laurel couldn't imagine having a sister or parents who loved her, but she did understand unhappiness. Avery was desperately sad, and it came out as mean and vindictive.

Laurel left her room and knocked softly on Avery's door.

"What?"

Laurel stepped cautiously inside. "Can I help?"

"You? Oh, go away. You're the problem. I hate you!

"I know you do. I'm sorry. This isn't my fault, you know, but I will go—permanently—as soon as possible."

At that, Avery sat up in bed and stared at her. Laurel couldn't read her expression—hateful, fearful, confused, so many different emotions.

But there it was. Avery had said the words, "I hate you." And Avery was not a petulant little girl, lashing out at her parents when she didn't get her own way. She was thirteen and in eighth grade. The words could never be unsaid. Laurel wished she had a cell phone. She wanted to talk to someone right now. Instead, she would wait until the morning and call Hannah. She'd get herself invited to that planning committee, and then attend the Halloween party. It was time to seek help at the Markey Home. They had always been kind to her, she reflected. It was just that she wanted a real home—a real family. Most of all, she wished she could stay with her friends at Castle Bluff Middle School. But that no longer seemed possible.

Hannah answered her cell phone. Only nine o'clock. She never got calls that early on a Sunday morning. She hadn't even bothered to go downstairs yet, even though Betsy was becoming seriously dismayed and had started making "I gotta go" noises.

"Oh, hi, Laurel!" Hannah hadn't thought about what it would be like talking to her again. Definitely weird, after learning more about her. "What's up?"

"Nothing much. I just wondered if I could join the planning committee after all. I found out I can go to the Halloween party, although I will need a ride."

Hannah shivered. Laurel must have decided to return to the Markey home—to stay? Hannah didn't know what to wish for. Certainly Laurel would be safer away from the Mullens' home. But she'd miss her friend, and what about the play?

"I'm sure finding you a ride will be easy," she said. "My dad will probably take us. And, yeah, we'd love to have you on the committee." Well, basically, Danny was in charge, but he'd be fine with having Laurel there. "This afternoon at Danny's house, and some of us are staying after to work on lines."

"That would be great," Laurel said. "See you then, Hannah. Thanks."

"It's not fair!" Hannah struggled into jeans, sweatshirt, and boots. "Last year I lost Kammy. Is it happening again?"

Betsy, assuming the question was directed to her, gave a quick bark before heading for the bedroom door.

"Right you are, Betsy. First things first." Betsy took that as her cue to take the lead in charging downstairs.

I could talk to Dad and Uncle Martin about having Laurel live here, she thought. They could foster her. No, Hannah shook her head. Dad and Uncle Martin wouldn't want the scrutiny that DCFS or some other group might give them. Better that the Rendina family continue to stay very private. Discreet was the word Uncle Martin would use.

A good romp with Betsy, breakfast prepared by Uncle Martin, homework, and lines — that was the plan. She wanted to be done with everything before going to Danny's. Oh, and she'd also start thinking about the next edition of *Stage Directions*. Maybe she should text Seth to see if he would write an editorial. Would he be in church now, like Danny? She didn't know much about Seth. It would be a good idea to learn more. Hannah sighed. Her brain was overstuffed. She was doing too much. She shrugged. She could handle it. She'd always made things work before.

Hannah finished the last math problem, just as a text from Danny arrived. Could she come early? She shouldn't, of course, but Danny must need help. "I'll be there soon." But she felt as if she'd forgotten something. She shrugged again. "Mustn't be important."

Danny looked around the basement. Chips, pretzels, and cold sodas on the bar, comfy chairs in a circle, and a broom and vacuum cleaner close by, so his guests would help clean up. Angering Mom by leaving a mess would be stupid. Danny was excited. This was his first time having a gathering like this, a planning party. Kylie had had them for years. He remembered when she used to host line-learning parties. That's exactly what he'd be doing as soon as they finished planning for Halloween. True, they couldn't have an SSC meeting, especially with Laurel coming. But that was okay, for now. In a sense, their conversation with Sergeant Lodge last night had been an SSC meeting. There wasn't more to say. Danny shivered. Today, he didn't even want to think about Laurel's situation.

He sat on a bar stool and began making a list of what they needed to decide. Invitations, food, games. Mainly, who would do what? He texted Hannah. "Could you come early?"

With some reluctance, Porter headed to Danny's wondering what was wrong with him. His sister's friend, Priyanka, would say he had a foreboding. Pri had inherited a sixth sense from her great-grandmother. Nonsense, of course, but Beth swore that Priyanka was usually right. Porter tried to shake off the feeling that something awful was about to happen. Something about Gramps, perhaps? That was more than possible, and certainly, all of them were waiting for something dreadful to happen to Laurel, but the police and DCFS were on the case, and there was little he could do about it.

Everyone was buzzing about the Thanksgiving dance, more than a month away. He supposed he should ask Hannah, as she and his friends expected. Maybe they could make it a threesome again—best friends, Danny, Hannah, and himself. Yes, he'd been skipped to eighth grade, but that didn't mean he felt mature inside. Socially, he felt younger than Danny, who would probably ask Laurel. He sighed.

Get it over with, he told himself. Ask Hannah. It's only one night, and he did not want to hurt her feelings.

The party planning was a cinch, Danny decided, thanks to the committee dividing the responsibilities. The sixth graders volunteered to reach out to all members about bringing cookies. Danny, personally, planned to talk with Gee. Seth would coordinate with Dr. D. Porter volunteered to talk with Joe and Imani and to make final arrangements with Mrs. Duncan at the home. Hannah would work with Laurel on invitations and handling the R.S.V.Ps. They all agreed that costumes would add to the fun.

To Danny's relief, the party plans would not take up much of his time after all. His homework was complete, and he'd made a good start at projects that were due at the end of the week. A tiring week ahead, what with swimming practice early every morning, but he'd manage. He'd run lines with Laurel as soon as she was finished working with Hannah. In fact, he was going to ask Laurel to the Thanksgiving dance. Yes, life was going his way.

Porter worked with Seth on the desert scene. Actually, most of his lines were with Seth. The play was very short. Porter doubted the running time was more than forty-five minutes, and an intermission would not be necessary. Dr. D was not crazy. They could do this with a short rehearsal period. He wondered what they'd do about costumes. If he were the director, he'd rely on the masks to identify the characters, and then let the actors figure out their own costumes. There were plenty of likely choices in the costume cage at school. Should he say something to Dr. D? Probably not a good idea. So far, it looked as if the director had everything all planned.

"Let's run it again," Seth said.

"Forget the three oranges," Porter said, as Truffaldino. *"We must leave this inferno while we still can. Soon the sun will scorch me to a blackened crisp. These oranges are not worth our lives."*

"Abandon my beloved oranges, Truffaldino? I know you're a jester, but if this is an example of your jesting, you need to find a different occupation. I am overcome with fatigue. Therefore, I will nap now, and when I awaken, I alone will decide our next step."

"There, what do you think?" Hannah asked with a flourish, handing the invitation to Laurel.

Boo!

A Halloween Happening for Drama Club Members

Games, Prizes, Treats

At the Winter Markey Home for Children

Lane Court, Castle Bluff

Halloween night from 7:00 – 10:00

Come in Costume!

Please get permission from your significant adults

before sending an rsvp to Hannah Rendina!

221-536-2000

Transportation problems? Let Hannah know!

"It's perfect. If you can print a copy, Hannah, I can run off more at school tomorrow."

"Great! We make a good team." Hannah knew that Laurel didn't have access to a printer at home. It seemed to her that Laurel didn't have much of anything at home.

"Shall we work on lines now? I'm solid, but if you need help . . ."

Laurel shook her head. "I can't do much more until I meet with Miss Raynor."

"Then help me with *Stage Directions*. I've got Seth's editorial about the play, and I suppose I could include another Dear George Spelvin letter, but I don't know what else to put."

"The party invitation," Laurel suggested. "You can't ever have too many announcements. Lots of kids will misplace or lose their copies right away."

"Sad, but true. Anything else? The edition will be short, but it will be better than nothing at all."

Shyly, Laurel handed Hannah a sheet of paper. "I don't know if this would work, but I like writing silly poems. Everyone loves George Spelvin, so they might like this, too.

Hannah read and laughed at the same time.

DENTAL ISSUES AND A PUMPKIN

By a Certain Pathetic Poet

About two weeks ago,

Head attached to a vine,

I sat in a pumpkin patch:

A place that was mine.

A three-year-old ran up to me

With very smelly toes.

Plucked me up with sticky fingers,

Probably from his nose.

They took me home in a van
And parked me on a mat.
Gave me exactly four blunt teeth
On my head, a hat.

They shoved me out on the porch –
Then squirrel sashayed up to me.
Took a bite – Oh! Ow! Ouch!
I got a cavity.

Three teeth left, lookin' fine –
Things still goin' my way.
Football struck another tooth.
That was not my day!

The oldest kid picked me up
To show me to her friends.
Stuck a pencil in number 3 -
Alas, a bitter end.

One tooth left, kinda scary,
Youngest kicked it out.
Now I'm just a Jack-o-lantern
With a boring, ugly mouth.

"Laurel, this is terrific! Yes, we'll definitely print this! You are so talented! I like the idea of your being anonymous, too, but you're not pathetic. Let me think of something else . . . I've got it! We'll call you our Prolific, Poetic Prodigy."

Laurel giggled. "I'm not sure what that means, but it sounds terrific."

"And write more poems. It would be fun if we printed one each time."

"Okay, I'd love to. I've got one that might work after the play and Halloween."

Neither girl knew the other was thinking the same thing. Would Laurel still be at Castle Bluff Middle School after the Halloween party?

As far as Hannah was concerned, all *Stage Directions* needed now was a final typing. The next edition would be ready Tuesday.

"Hannah," Danny called out suddenly. "Don't you have your phone? Your Dad has been trying to call you. He finally called me."

"Oh, I turned it off." Hannah checked. Yes, he'd called three times. "Dad? Anything wrong?"

"Hannah, do you have Betsy?"

"No, she's in her playroom."

"She isn't anywhere in the house, and when I got home, the back door was wide open!"

Two LONG DREARY WEEKS FOLLOWED. Hannah, Danny, and their friends searched everywhere possible. After contacting the police and animal control, they plastered posters, offered a reward, and trudged from house to house, but no one had spotted the tiny Labradoodle. Hannah was broken-hearted and blamed herself, of course. Somehow, she must have been very careless.

"Try to remember," Danny and Porter had asked her many times.

Well, she couldn't exactly. The main thing she recalled before heading for Danny's that day was a feeling of being overwhelmed, thinking she'd forgotten something important. Was that something Betsy? Had she left her outside in her haste to pick up her Drama Club bag and rush to obey Danny's urgent request? No, of course she didn't blame Danny for calling her. He had no way of knowing she was flustered from doing too much.

"Maybe I forgot to bring her back inside," she said.

Porter shook his head. "That wouldn't explain why the backdoor was open and some of Betsy's things are missing."

Betsy's leash and a small bag of dog food were also gone. The only comfort Hannah had was the hope that Betsy wasn't lying injured or cold somewhere. It seemed obvious that she had been kidnapped. Betsy was valuable, as well as adorable.

And through it all, of course, rehearsals continued, every single day, even Saturdays and Sundays. When it all became too intense, Dad and Uncle Matthew went searching, as did Danny's parents. Everyone was concerned about the little dog. The only good thing about it, Hannah reflected, was that she was having an easy time making Fata Morgana super mean. She was furious at whoever had done this to Betsy—and her. In fact, she hated that person even more than she'd ever hated Mom's boyfriends! The horrible dog kidnapper had even taken away Hannah's joy about the play, now less than a week away.

"I know, Bingo, it's really hard." Danny tried to soothe his dog, as well as Boots, now almost a full-grown cat. Both animals seemed aware that something was missing, although Danny wasn't certain they knew it was Betsy. He thought they probably did, though. Boots, especially, was smart. "I'm sure we'll find Betsy any day now." Danny received looks that told him clearly they knew he was lying. Well, maybe not lying exactly, but at least that he was treating them like little kids who couldn't handle the truth. "Okay," he said. "The truth is I don't know, but it's too soon to give up."

Bingo gave a short bark before jumping onto his bed and turning around three times before curling up for a snooze. Uncharacteristically, Boots joined him, snuggling close, perhaps for comfort. Danny though they might be picking up on everyone's tensions. Not much he could do about that.

"Coming, Dad," he yelled, responding to his father's demand. Danny grabbed his amazing costume—orange and white pants, a wide ruffled orange tunic with big black buttons, and a long, sailboat-shaped hat, also orange and white with a black button. The colors would be perfect for Halloween, but the cast had agreed not to use the costumes again. Besides, some of them were rented. Danny's costume had been made by Gee and would be stored in CBMS's costume cage, probably forever, he thought. He was pleased that he didn't have to wear much makeup—just circles of red on his cheeks and black circles around his eyes. He'd just received his first crop of zits and was not pleased.

"All set?" Dad was waiting in the car. Danny hopped into the back. Hannah was sitting in front, obviously just finishing a crying spell.

"Hannah?"

"I'm okay, Danny. Just had a bad moment. Don't worry. I'll put the play first at rehearsal."

He nodded. "I know you will. You're going to be great. I can't wait to see you in your costume. Dress rehearsal, and we're only having one, so it's really important!"

Hannah's costume was black and flowing, of course. What distinguished it from normal witch's attire were the green stripes in the cape. And instead of a pointed hat, she wore a green wig, covered in plastic black spiders. Gee had also made the costume, but they purchased the wig online. She was also carrying Pantalette's costume because Laurel had said she wasn't sure how she was getting to rehearsal. Hannah thought that was true, although perhaps only half true. It was likely Laurel was afraid to keep the costume in her house—because of Avery.

"I know the rehearsal is important. I just wish . . ."

"Me, too." Danny was starting to feel weepy, himself. This would never do.

Mr. Kennedy started the car. "Now, as I just told Hannah, after I drop you off at Community, I'm going to meet up with Sergeant Lodge for breakfast, and we're going to brainstorm what we might do next about Betsy, and, well . . ."

Danny thought Dad might be about to say "Laurel" but didn't want to add another worry. One problem at a time, he thought.

"You're sure you don't mind walking?" Mom asked Porter at breakfast. "I had planned on taking you, but Kelly spent the night at Marta's, and Dad had an emergency at work."

"And Zoe is sick," Porter finished. "It's okay, Mom. The sun is shining, and it's not too cold. My costume is a little bulky, but I'll be fine. I thought I'd stop off at Laurel's. She won't have a ride, either. I'll walk with her."

"Yes, that poor girl." Mom was off in her thoughts, leaving Porter to finish his breakfast and grab his costume, wallet, and cell phone. It was going to be a long, long weekend. Rehearsals until 5:00 today, and then two performances tomorrow. There were still some technical details to work out, but he thought they'd be ready.

In truth, Porter would be pleased to "put the show to bed," as Miss Armstrong used to say. Worrying about the show and schoolwork and Laurel and, most of all, the missing Betsy had been hard on him and his friends. For the first time ever, he was behind in English, although he knew he'd catch up once the weekend was over. Every spare minute he wasn't rehearsing, he had been searching for Betsy. He kind of agreed with Dad. Betsy must have been stolen by someone who was long gone or who had sold her to someone who lived in a different town. It was such a shabby, cruel thing to do! He did not want to know anyone who would do anything like that.

Jacket, cap, gloves, costume—he was all set for the long trek to Community. Soon he would become Truffaldino and forget about the trials and concerns of Porter Walters.

Laurel, too, was about to leave the house, although she didn't share her reasons with Mrs. Mullen, as she now thought of the foster mother. "A Drama Club activity," was all Laurel said. What was she afraid of? Not being allowed to participate, when the show was tomorrow? Surely, the Mullens wouldn't want that kind of scrutiny from school authorities or DCFS. But there was always Avery.

Avery slept until at least noon on Saturdays, and Mr. Mullen was out of town. Life was always easier when he was. Rage seemed to have taken over lately, and he was angry — without apparent reason — with everyone.

Mrs. Mullen was picking at her eggs and sipping coffee. Laurel put on a phony smile. "I'll see you later, Mom. Hope you have a good day."

"Oh, thanks . . ." was the vague reply. "Oh, before you go, Laurel, please check the shed. I'm wondering if a raccoon or a squirrel or something is trapped inside. I got another call from a neighbor complaining about scratching and whining noises. The shed is closer to their house than ours. I don't see why they didn't bother to look. Such a nuisance! Hope it isn't a fox."

"I'll see," Laurel said. "Probably a raccoon, or maybe," she shuddered, "rats." But Mrs. Mullen had picked up the newspaper and seemed to disappear.

Laurel put on her boots and stuck her shoes in a bag. The shed was located way in the back of their one-acre property. It was bound to be swampy. Just what she didn't need before a long day of rehearsing. "Good thing Hannah has my costume," she thought. She cheered herself up by singing a favorite song from the show.

As she approached the old shed that should have been torn down when the Mullens bought the property, she could hear what the neighbors had complained about. An unbearably sad crying or whining. She didn't think she'd ever heard a raccoon or squirrel cry before. It was more like a —

"Oh, no! No, Avery, you didn't!" The shed door was padlocked — a new padlock. Laurel shook the door, and the cry grew louder. Then she heard a feeble attempt at a bark. She rushed to a window and pulled back the weeds covering it. The window was too dirty for her to look inside, but she didn't need to. "Betsy," she called out as loud as she dared. "I'll get help right now!"

Should she risk going back in the house to use the phone? Better not. She'd go to Porter's. It was early. His parents probably hadn't taken him to rehearsal yet. They'd call for help, both for Betsy and her.

Not even trusting the safety of reaching the sidewalk through the Mullens' property, she crossed into the neighbor's yard, and there, approaching her house, was Porter!

"Hey, Laurel," Porter greeted. "I thought we could walk to rehearsal together. What are you doing here? Why, what's wrong?"

"Porter, I have never been so happy to see anyone in my life! It's Betsy! I've found her!" Quickly, Laurel explained what had happened. "What should we do?"

"Hold this." Porter held out his costume, and then grabbed his cell. "Let's walk just a bit, so no one in your house spots us." He hit one of his most frequently used contact numbers. "Danny," he said excitedly. "Laurel found Betsy. Where are you now? Great! Okay. Tell your Dad to come down Laurel's street and stop when you see us. We're on the sidewalk a few houses east of her house. Yes, tell him. I'll wait."

"What?" Laurel demanded.

"Mr. Kennedy is driving Danny and Hannah to the rehearsal. Danny is telling him now."

"Yeah, I'm here, Danny. Good idea. You're right. It's that serious. See you soon."

"Porter?"

"They're coming now. Mr. Kennedy is calling Sergeant Lodge and Hannah's dad."

"Oh, no!"

"Don't worry, Laurel. Nothing bad will happen to you. I promise."

There's no way you can promise that, Porter, Laurel thought, but she said instead, "I hope Betsy is okay."

Sergeant Lodge rang the doorbell. Next to him stood Mr. Kennedy. Behind, shaking, arms around each other were Hannah and Laurel. Hannah's dad and Uncle Martin were on their way. Porter pulled

Danny to the foot of the driveway, and they composed a text to send to Dr. D. Sure, they'd all be late for dress rehearsal, but perhaps Danny and Porter could go soon, if they got a ride. There were certain to be a lot of technical details to put together before the actual rehearsal began.

Hannah couldn't tell if she was excited or scared. Excited because Betsy had been found — scared because she didn't know if Betsy was okay. Maybe locked in a cold shed for two weeks? She could tell, though, that Laurel was terrified.

"Don't be afraid, Laurel," she soothed. "We're all here for you." Laurel smiled, but Hannah didn't think her words meant much.

"I could just open the door," Laurel said.

Hannah shook her head. "No, it needs to be official."

Finally, Mrs. Mullen came to the door. "What?" Then she stared at the group. "What in the world?"

Sergeant Lodge showed his credentials. "Ma'am, we have a report that a stolen dog may be locked in your shed."

"Nonsense. You checked earlier, didn't you, Laurel? What are you doing here? I thought you had a school activity." Laurel didn't answer, and Hannah held her closer.

Sergeant Lodge continued, although it was obvious Mr. Kennedy wanted to chime in. "The shed door is padlocked, and it must be removed at once."

Mrs. Mullen looked haughty. "And I suppose you have a warrant?"

Mr. Kennedy sighed loudly. His friend, Dean Lodge, didn't have children, but he did. "Do you really want to take it that far, Grace? We're talking about kids here. A warrant will mean police reports and a request to a judge on a Saturday. We'd get the warrant, but possibly not until Monday or Tuesday. This would cause an innocent little dog to suffer longer and more police attention on Avery."

"Avery?" Mrs. Mullen squeaked.

"Get her now, Mrs. Mullen," Sergeant Lodge demanded.

Mrs. Mullen nodded. "I'm sure it's all a big mistake, but all right. Laurel go upstairs and get your sister."

Laurel shook her head. "I can't," she whispered.

Seeing her dad walk up the driveway gave Hannah courage. "She's afraid Avery will hurt her," she said. "Avery stole my dog, and Laurel is afraid you'll pretend she didn't and that Avery will get away with it, just like she always does."

"Why, you!"

"Get her now, Mrs. Mullen, or I will." Sergeant Lodge was back in charge.

"Very well." Nose in the air, Avery's mother closed the front door, presumably intending to obey orders.

Quickly, Porter requested that one of the adults drive Danny and him to Community. "We can explain more why Hannah and Laurel will be late. The show is tomorrow. At least Danny can do some of the narrator parts, and I can do scenes with Seth."

Danny grumbled. Next to Hannah, he loved Betsy the most. He wanted to see it through. But Porter was right, and he agreed that Hannah's uncle could take them.

"And bring back a bolt cutter," Mr. Kennedy told Martin.

"Wait!" Laurel's voice was shrill. "This is taking too long. Go to the back. They might have gone out the back door!"

They looked at each other. Might Mrs. Mullen try to make matters worse by covering for her daughter? Yes, that was possible. Leading the way, Sergeant Lodge and Mr. Kennedy rushed to the backyard, where they discovered Avery unlocking the padlock, with her mother standing by.

"Well, we tried," said Sergeant Lodge. "We tried to make this as unofficial as possible, but you weren't interested. Ma'am, you and your daughter will come to the station with me. Mr. Rendina, do you wish to press charges?"

"Unfortunately, yes," Hannah's dad said.

Hannah, not able to wait a minute longer, pushed Avery aside and entered the shed. Huddled into a corner, next to empty food and water bowls was her shivering, frightened little Betsy. She cuddled her inside her coat and took her outside, where she glared at Avery. "I feel sorry for you," she said. "You must be miserable, so full of hate!"

Scene Eighteen - Drop off Your Baggage!

IN A COMMUNITY COLLEGE CLASSROOM, Drama Club's makeshift *Green Room*, Dr. D passed out small paper bags on which each person's name was printed, with slips of paper and golf pencils inside. "While you did fine on both dress rehearsals yesterday, many of you had a difficult day. Some of that stress no doubt remains. You're carrying a lot of baggage. Today, you owe it to all of us and your audience to free yourself of that, so that you can give your very best to this show. We've all worked too hard to let anything prevent that. Now, what I'd like you to do is write down whatever baggage you're still carrying and put it into your paper bag. Then please toss it into this bin." Dr. D held up a large wastebasket. "Then your baggage — your worries — will be gone for a few hours. If you want to pick it up after the final performance, you may. If not, the custodian will remove it with the other trash."

Don't leave your baggage here, missy! The words exploded in Laurel's head. When and where had she heard those words before? She could hear a man saying them. Not to her, but to a woman. Dr. D's instructions had brought it back to her. A real memory from when she was very young, but that was all. The voice hadn't been mean, exactly, just very firm. Whatever baggage the woman had wanted to leave would not be allowed. Unbidden, a few more memories popped up. The woman was angry, and she grabbed Laurel's hand and pulled her out the door. Laurel tripped and started to fall, but the woman kept on pulling. My knees hurt, Laurel remembered. I was very small, and she hurt me. One more memory. *Wait!* The man had pleaded. *Come back!* He had sounded frightened.

"Laurel." A voice from the present, one belonging to Danny. "If you're going to write anything, better do it now."

"Right. Thanks!" She didn't have time to write down all that was bothering her. "Who am I, and what's going to happen to me next?" She thrust the questions into her paper bag and threw it into the bin.

She knew she'd been dreadful in the two dress rehearsals yesterday, but her friends said it was amazing she got through them at all, and that they hadn't been much better. She'd performed automatically, robotically, without any energy. What was the expression? Phoning it in. That was it. She was phoning in her part. On automatic pilot. Not really acting at all. Today would be different because she had dropped off her baggage.

At the shed yesterday, right after Sergeant Lodge had said he was taking Mrs. Mullen and Avery to the station, she'd blurted out, "What about me?" She had started to feel totally invisible—and meaningless.

"Right." Hannah's Dad had taken over. "Martin, please take Laurel, Danny, and Porter to their dress rehearsal."

"Dress rehearsal?" screeched Mrs. Mullen. "What dress rehearsal?"

"For the play these youngsters are in tomorrow," Mr. Rendina answered.

"Why didn't I know about it? I should be there."

"Why?" Laurel had asked softly. "You never bothered to come to *The Secret Garden*. You knew about that, and I had a lead."

"We'll sort it out later," Mr. Kennedy said. "Laurel, you'll stay with Kylie and Danny at our house, until we can figure out what's next for you. Troy, you and Hannah will want to take Betsy to the emergency vet. At the very least, she's dehydrated. Then please take Hannah to her rehearsal, and then join Dean—Sergeant Lodge—and me at the station."

Danny started to protest that he should go to the vet's, too, but his father threw him a look. He shut up. As Sergeant Lodge had told Dad many times, he should have been a cop.

Danny didn't have much garbage to write about. All he wanted to do was get the day over so he could go back to his real life. Drama Club, especially this play, had consumed too much of it. "Betsy, Laurel, and a D on my math test," was the best he could do. Tomorrow, he'd talk to his math teacher about how to do better. It was the first poor grade he'd received this year. Unlike last year, he cared now.

Porter could help, but he'd been every bit as busy as Danny. Porter seemed to have a lot on his mind that he was unwilling to share. Danny shrugged. Of course, Porter had never been much of a talker.

Time to get into character. His whole family was coming to both performances. He was so lucky to have them. Poor Laurel would have no one. Dad and Mom had insisted she stay with them until things were sorted out, but none of them knew what would happen to her. They didn't even know what would happen to the Mullens.

You've dropped your baggage, he told himself. Concentrate on your first line. Make the audience happy they're here.

Betsy is not baggage, Hannah thought, but she is my main worry right now. The vet would call tomorrow with an update. Betsy was severely dehydrated and malnourished. A few days more, she wouldn't have made it. Hannah gave a mental thanks to the neighbors who had complained about the noise. She couldn't really thank Mrs. Mullen, who had told Laurel to check it out, but thank goodness she had. It looked as if Avery had just dumped all of the dog food she'd stolen—not that large a bag—and had left a few bowls of water. After locking Betsy into the shed, Avery had never even gone back to check on her. Dad said that at the station Avery blamed the dog for being so greedy and not rationing her food. Animal cruelty was just one of the charges against her, as well as theft and breaking and entering. Avery was a horrible person!

But Dad also said that Avery called out for her sister Ashley and began to cry. "Imagine, trying to replace a dead child—especially so soon," Dad said. The main reason he pressed charges was so Avery and, perhaps, the whole family would get help. "They can't keep sweeping things under the rug," he said. Hannah wasn't sure what a rug had to do with it, but she got the point.

She looked into a mirror. She looked mean and vengeful. A perfect role for a day like this, she thought.

Porter was the only one of the group who had done well during dress rehearsal. Theater was like that for him. Whether it was a rehearsal or a performance, nothing else mattered. The rest of the world went away. Maybe that's why theater should be my future, he thought. I think there will be many times the world will need to go away. He supposed he should write down his main worry, the baggage he definitely would pick up again. No way would he chance anyone reading it. "I think I might be gay," he wrote, before heading to the amphitheater.

Prokofiev's March began over the loudspeaker, and Danny, as Pantaloon, marched around the arena, arms swaying as if he were conducting an imaginary orchestra. Then, grandly, he gestured for the music to stop. *Gather around, everyone! You are about to see The Love for Three Oranges!*

Pantalette pranced in and pushed him out of the way. *Why three oranges?* she sang. *Why not five apples, or two figs, or a dozen tangerines?* Laurel's voice almost made the silly song sound like grand opera as she trilled while Pantaloon became more and more frustrated. The entire cast responded to their high spirits, and the audience roared!

Scene Nineteen - Halloween Happiness and Heartache

IN A CORNER OF THE auditorium of the Winter Markey Home, Mermaid Hannah and Witch Imani watched Joe MacCracken entertain the delighted young residents with his very best pantomimes. Laurel—once Mullen, now last name unknown—was among them. Hannah crossed her fingers, hoping they'd have a chance to talk. She appreciated the opportunity to catch up with Imani, though. "You and Joe," she said. "Are you two, like, serious?"

Imani grinned. "Well, we're seriously having a good time, and seriously good friends. But serious like Kylie and Brad or Beth and Kurt? Probably not."

"I've never seen anyone change so much. He doesn't even look like the Joe I remember. He's just happy and not trying to impress anyone. I used to think he was a borderline racist."

Imani shook her head. "No borderline about it."

"What happened?"

"Well, you, and Castle Bluff, and Beth, and my family, and so many different things. I think he started to change at the Valentine's Day dance when Eric came over from the high school to be my date and Brad, Priyanka's. Then he saw how you cared about what Kammy was going through. I saw the expression on his face during the show when you added that line and told her you'd never forget her."

"I didn't think other people would notice, except Miss Armstrong." Hannah had been worried the director would be annoyed she'd added a line to her play.

"Lots of people noticed. And Joe is really impressed with my family, especially Dad because he teaches at Crofts. Joe wants to go there, but his father won't let him."

"Because?"

Imani shrugged. "Not manly enough, I guess. Too liberal. Too many—"

"Gays?"

"Yeah, but that's not the word he uses. I can't stand the man. Joe and his mom aren't getting along with him, either. Hannah, none of my business, but I sometimes wonder if Porter— Oops! Joe wants me to do a mime with him."

Hannah waved. "Later." She was saved from saying, "Sometimes I wonder, too," although she probably wouldn't have.

What a strange week it had been, ending finally with the Halloween party. The play seemed an eternity ago, not less than a week. Without Hannah knowing it was coming, Laurel returned to the Markey Home on Monday, the day after the show. Although Mr. Kennedy drove her, Danny didn't seem to know anything, either. All they'd heard afterwards was that Laurel would not be returning to Castle Bluff Middle School. Here at the Halloween party, Hannah hadn't been able to say more than "Hi." Laurel was sitting with a few other Markey Home residents, as if she and Hannah had never been friends. Avery hadn't returned to school, either. No one seemed to know what would happen next.

Obviously, Laurel didn't show up for the Drama Club officers' meeting on Tuesday. Dr. D demanded answers, and Hannah, Danny, and Porter told him what they knew, advising Seth to keep it private. Dr. D was visibly upset, Hannah thought. He said they would not replace their vice president until they learned more. The Drama Club meeting Thursday had been a big nothing. Just a discussion about the play, last-minute thoughts about the party, and theater games.

The party was a huge success, even though Hannah wasn't feeling it. So different from last year at the castle when she realized that people liked her and that she finally belonged. She tuned in to Joe announcing that everyone should pick a partner for the mirror game! Thinking of Imani's reminder of how she'd been able to say goodbye to Kammy, Hannah bolted to her feet, almost tripping on her stupid mermaid tail. She was determined to grab Laurel before anyone else had a chance! She knew exactly how they could communicate—without any words at all!

The mirror game! Any other game would be preferable, Laurel thought. She wouldn't be able to avoid looking Hannah right in the eyes.

"I'll lead," Hannah told her. Laurel shrugged. Whatever.

At first, Hannah kept it funny—so funny Laurel had to force herself to keep from laughing, especially when Hannah stuck an imaginary eyebrow pencil into her eye while ineptly trying to apply makeup. Laurel followed the best she could, inaudibly howling in pain and then removing lipstick from her teeth after Hannah's hand shook holding the imaginary tube of lipstick. Hannah was good, Laurel thought, almost certain the lipstick was a flaming red. She didn't think they would win the game—she was a half-step behind Hannah—but she was having fun. Something rare these days!

She only knew a few of the girls remaining at the Markey Home. One, Shaila Lee, might become a good friend. Shaila had been sympathetic, sorry that things hadn't worked out for Laurel. Shaila wasn't an orphan; she had two parents who couldn't or wouldn't take care of her and had signed her over to the state. Laurel figured that Shaila's position was worse than hers, but she said she was used to it. Shaila had even convinced her to come to the party. "If you don't, your friends will think you've dumped them," she'd said. "That wouldn't be fair."

So here she was, back at Markey's, almost as if she'd never left, going to school in a class with kids of all ages and abilities. Here, she was almost a scholar in comparison.

The only time she'd left the grounds was when Sergeant Lodge had taken her over to the Mullens' house to pack up her belongings.

He seemed surprised by how little she owned—mainly clothes. She didn't care about them, but she was pleased to have her theater programs, a few photographs and notes, and mementos from her time at CBMS. The Mullens hadn't been home, and Laurel had no idea what was happening to any of them. Sergeant Lodge didn't say, and she didn't ask.

Back to the mirror game. Hannah had grown serious. She waved, smiled, winked, and blew kisses. Even with the dialogue wordless, Laurel knew what Hannah was saying. They were still friends, and Hannah was still there for her.

Danny and Porter also were partners. When it came to the mirror game, they were an unbeatable team. Danny wondered when others would catch on that they were sort of cheating by using agreed-upon codes. Danny was leading today, and he held out two fingers on his left hand. That meant he was going to do stretching exercises to his left. Thus, Porter would have to stretch to the right. The two fingers also indicated what would follow. Last year, they had developed a well-oiled routine, which varied somewhat when Danny was wheelchair bound. It started as a fun way for him to exercise with Porter's help. Now it was their secret. Danny supposed he should feel guilty, but he didn't. He was certain they'd win again tonight, and he tried to guess what the prize would be. A full-sized Butterfingers, he hoped.

He had noticed Hannah choosing Laurel. He wondered if he'd have a chance to talk to her. Should he still invite her to the Thanksgiving dance? He didn't think there was a rule about not asking someone from another school, if you could consider the Markey Home a school. But he didn't know what the Home's rules might be. It was a mess all around. Maybe he'd just go with a gang of friends and hold off on this whole dating thing. Coming back here must be so hard on Laurel, but at least she was safe now. Dad didn't know what was going on with—the case. The case, Danny called it, because that's exactly what it was.

Porter noticed Joe watching them and grinning. He's caught on, Porter thought, wondering if Joe would say anything. Fine by him. At first it was fun, tricking everyone. But it was cheating; not the kind of thing he believed in at all. He hoped Joe would name another team the winner.

The party was successful, he thought. The Markey kids were having a great time, except maybe Laurel, although she seemed to be warming up to Hannah. He wasn't sure he'd ever felt so sorry for anyone. Well, maybe Kammy last year. It was a tie. Both girls had been thoroughly screwed over by adults who were supposed to take care of them. Kammy had disappeared from their lives, but Laurel was right here, right now. Porter wondered if there were ways they could still help her. Keeping a Drama Club connection with the Home might be a possibility. He would bring it up with Dr. D and the other officers on Tuesday.

Porter shook his head, causing Danny to look annoyed. That movement hadn't been planned. But Porter had been thinking about something else. Between games, he had overheard Dr. D asking Mrs. Duncan if they could talk privately in her office. About Laurel? Well, maybe in a way. Perhaps, he, too, had been wondering if they might continue to offer Drama Club activities to the Home.

"Okay, that's it!" Joe announced suddenly. "Cars are lining up outside, so it's time to announce the winning team. First, I want to thank Danny and the Drama Club officers for inviting Imani and me to lead this tonight. We had a great time. You guys are all talented. I hope Drama Club and the Markey Home will continue to find ways to work together."

Unbelievable that this was the same pretentious, bigoted kid Porter had known last year. Of course, Joe hadn't given Imani many chances to shine, but still . . .

Joe continued. "As usual, the amazing team of Danny and Porter gave the most polished performance, but Imani and I are going with a new duo. The most entertaining, enjoyable team was Hannah and Laurel! You two were so much fun to watch. I think you demonstrated every emotion possible."

Everyone cheered while Hannah and Laurel hugged. "Darn," Danny whispered in Porter's ear. "I was practically tasting that Butterfingers." But Porter could tell Danny didn't mean it. He was grinning from ear to ear.

Teeth brushed, in pajamas, Danny patted the bed for Bingo and Boots to join him when he heard the doorbell ring. He looked at his clock. 11:30 — much too late for visitors. He probably wouldn't have heard the bell if his room were still upstairs. Pushing Boots and Bingo aside, he went to the front door. Hesitantly — perhaps he should have called Mom or Dad — he opened the door.

"Leland? Brad?" Leland's eyes were wet with tears, and Brad looked grim. It could mean only one thing. "Come in," Danny said. "I'll get Kylie."

INTERMISSION - REMEMBERING A FRIEND

PORTER THOUGHT THIS WAS FAR MORE religious than the actual funeral had been. Instead of a funeral director talking about a man he didn't know and a pianist playing solemn music Mr. Markey wouldn't have liked, people who loved him had gathered in a circle in the castle's ballroom. Beatles music, Mr. Markey's favorite, played softly on a CD player, and delicious smells were coming from the kitchen. As soon as they finished saying goodbye to their friend, they would enjoy a lovely lunch. True, it was a sad occasion, but it was also joyful—a true memorial service. Porter wasn't always grateful his family belonged to a church, but he was today. Funerals led by strangers must never happen to those he loved.

Just about everyone who had known Mr. Markey from Drama Club was there, even Roe, Miss Armstrong, and Robbie. There were a few sad faces, but the only one crying was Gee, and Porter didn't think it was because of chopping onions for lunch. Beth's boyfriend, Kurt, had told her he thought his grandmother was in love with Mr. Markey. Not the way the rest of them loved him, but real, serious love.

People were starting to share stories about Mr. Markey. Porter hadn't known him as well as some of the others, so he'd just listen.

"I'd like to tell you about the first time we met Mr. Markey," Kylie said. "I'll never forget what he said first. 'Who is it Leland? Do we have company?'" Leland smiled, remembering. "When Leland told him we were looking for props, Mr. Markey said, 'A play? How splendid!'"

"And then he invited you for lunch." Leland chuckled. "I was not pleased. Little did I know that our lives would change for the better."

Beth continued the story. "Do you remember how hard it was to sit on those antique chairs while balancing plates on our laps? I was so worried that Kurt was going to dump his whole meal on the oriental rug."

"Me?" Kurt shouted. Everyone laughed before the room grew quiet again.

Kylie's eyes welled up, causing Brad to put his arm around her. "Most of all I remember when he asked me to dance at our cast party. I told him that my camp scholarship was only conditional, and he said—Beth and Brad mouthed the words as Kylie spoke—'So what in life isn't?'"

Porter wished his relationship with Mr. Markey had been stronger. He guessed, though, he was fortunate to have known him at all.

Hannah raised her hand, hoping she could tell her story without breaking down. "As some of you know, my grandparents kind of disowned me along with my dads. When I first met Mr. Markey, I decided he was my new grandfather, or maybe a great-grandfather. He was so kind and supportive."

"You said you thought you were in love," Beth said.

"Yes, that's the way it was. And he said I could visit anytime I wanted to. I wish I had more often." Other students nodded, agreeing with Hannah. "I got to know him when we had all the problems with Kammy. He wanted her to stay at the castle, even though, for her own protection, it wasn't possible." Hannah didn't add that Leland and Janet wouldn't have allowed that because they felt Kammy had betrayed them.

Perhaps sensing an untactful moment, Beth added quickly, "Mr. Markey was so funny when he thought the castle was haunted. He said it was about time that the castle had a haunt of its own." She shook her head. "Then he said helping an unhappy girl was more important than having a castle ghost."

Danny couldn't think of anything to say. He'd always liked the old man, but he hadn't known him the way Kylie, Beth, and Hannah had. He doubted that any of the others would speak. But then, to his surprise, Marla Gray raised her hand. Marla and Kylie were good friends now, but they hadn't always been.

"My eighth-grade year was almost a disaster," Marla reminded them. "I was an awful person back then. I was unhappy with my family, and I took it out on everyone, especially Roe Santos. I am grateful she finally forgave me. The three people who helped me most to forgive myself were Gee, Beth, and Mr. Markey. Mr. Markey never judged anyone. He loved and accepted us as we were. I will think of him every day for the rest of my life."

Oh, gosh! Danny thought of Avery. What if someone had helped her the way they did Marla? He hoped someone would end this on an upbeat note, or he would need a tissue, too. Besides, he was becoming seriously hungry. Then Leland came to the rescue.

Leland stood, obviously controlling his emotions. "Marla, I think you gave the most accurate description I've ever heard of Mr. Markey. He never judged but valued us— just as we were. He rescued me when I was a young man and kept me with him ever since then. I never called him by his first name, Harold, but he was the dearest friend I've ever had." Then he pulled a folded, legal-looking paper from his pocket. "I'm sure that in spite of your sorrow, many of you are wondering what will happen next—about the castle and your place in it." He opened the paper. "I want you to know that Mr. Markey has left the castle and all of its contents to me. Janet and I will live here for the rest of our lives. There is an important stipulation, though. Jointly, Kylie Kennedy and I now own the ballroom, with its adjacent kitchen." The room exploded into an acapella gasp. "Mr. Markey hopes that Kylie will manage Castle Bluff Middle Theater's usage of the ballroom for as long as she is able. Drama Club may continue to meet and perform right here."

Applauding at the end of a memorial service might be odd, Danny thought, but this time it was absolutely the right thing to do.

ACT TWO – Removing the Mask

Behind every mask there is a face, and behind that a story.
— Marty Rubin

Scene One - Come Ye Thankful!

KELLY WALTERS BURST INTO THE kitchen and threw her arms around her mother. Then she allowed herself to cry. "Mom, it's terrible!"

Porter, who had been having a rare chat with his mother, stopped in mid-sentence—the conversation about Grams' letter over. What now? More drama? He grabbed a box of tissues from the counter.

Beth, looking sheepish, followed her sister. "Sorry," she said. "I guess I didn't do a very good job explaining."

"I guess you didn't." Mom led Kelly to her chair. "I'm sure whatever is wrong can be figured out. Give your sister a tissue, Porter, and I'll pour some lemonade."

"It's too cold," Kelly complained, sniffling but recovering. "Hot chocolate would be better."

"I'll make it," Beth offered. "This is my fault. Not what happened, but the way I told Kelly."

Porter didn't think Beth had ever made Kelly cry before. There was nothing he could do but pat her shoulder and offer more tissues. Finally, the hot chocolate was ready, as was a plate of sugar cookies. Nothing like sugar to bring Kelly back to normal.

"Now, Beth, tell us simply. And, Kelly, do try to stay calm, dear."

"Well, I found out today that the Grays are moving, and I made the mistake of blurting it out to Kelly."

"Marta is leaving! Right away! To Idaho!" Kelly began to wail again. "I don't even know where that is."

"I'll show you on a map," Porter said, academics as usual coming to his rescue. "It's far away, but it's still in our country, and you can get there by plane."

Kelly, normally responding to Porter, was somewhat mollified.

"My goodness," their mother said, "this does seem rather sudden. What happened, Beth?"

"I don't have all the details. I do know they're in danger of losing their home. Mrs. Gray has a job now, but she doesn't make much, and Mr. Gray isn't giving them anything, not that he has anything. They're going to live with Marla and Marta's grandmother in Idaho Falls. Mrs. Gray and her friend there are going to open a dress shop. Marla thinks it's a good idea. She'll work there after school. They need to get away from the stigma of Mr. Gray."

Kelly put down her half-eaten cookie. "Stigma?"

"Not important," Mom said. "Things like that happen all the time. You'll call and text, Kelly. Maybe we'll take a family trip out there someday."

Fat chance, Porter thought. His family and others had done everything they could to help the Grays, but Mrs. Gray remained cold and distant. The family trip would not happen, and Kelly would get over the loss eventually, but she needed something to cheer her up right now. "You can have a farewell party for Marta!" he exclaimed. "I need to finish talking with Mom, and then I'll help you plan it, Kelly."

Kelly beamed. "Oh, she'd love that!"

Beth stood. "Grab some cookies, Kelly. You and I will plan two surprise parties — one for Marta and another one for Marla. Thanks for the idea, Porter, but this is a girl thing. We'll make sure they know we'll miss them and will see them again!" Cookies in hand, the two dashed from the room.

"Phew!" Porter said.

His mother laughed. "Rescued from being involved in a 'girl thing.' I'm sorry for Kelly, of course, but I think it's just as well the Grays are leaving — for them and for us."

Mom still didn't completely believe that Marla had changed, but Porter did not want to talk about it. When he did, he'd tell Mom what

Marla had said at Mr. Markey's memorial service. "Back to Grams' letter," he said.

"Right. Well, what do you think? Your grandfather is back in the hospital, and Grams doesn't want to be alone. She realizes it would be too hard on all of us to go, but she wonders if you could. It's totally up to you, of course."

"Wish I could, but Thanksgiving break isn't very long. I'd get there, and then have to come right back."

Mom nodded. "True, but your grades are perfect. What if you left next week and returned the Sunday or Monday after Thanksgiving? You could ask your teachers to give you some advance assignments."

Porter thought it over. "And I'd take my laptop. I'll do it!"

A trip away was what he needed. Time to think, to avoid the Thanksgiving dance, and maybe see Peter again. No, that must not happen, but the rest would be great.

Mom looked relieved. She did not get along well with her mother-in-law. She was always polite, of course—painfully so. It was partly a matter of personalities, but mainly Mom was well aware that Dad's parents had wanted him to marry someone else. Mom would have more than enough drama right here. Once the farewell party was over and Marta Gray was gone, Kelly would still be difficult. Suddenly, he had an idea!

"Mom, Grams said she'd pay for my ticket. Could we buy one for Kelly? She could go with me. I'd help her with school."

Porter found himself engulfed in his mother's arms. "Porter," she said, "what a fine idea!"

"Oh, no! That's terrible!" Hannah recovered quickly. This shouldn't be about her. "Seth, I am so sorry. You sound awful!" And her words sounded awful, she thought. "Don't worry about me. Just get better soon!"

"Thanks, Hannah," Seth croaked. There was nothing else to say.

Hannah looked longingly at her festive, three-tiered skirt waiting on the bed. She would not be going to the Thanksgiving dance after all and might never have a chance to wear the skirt. The CBMS Student Council was determined to have a square dance and had asked members of a senior citizen group to teach the students—at the dance itself. Hannah had gagged, along with her friends. She'd hoped for a new dress she could wear all winter, not something to wear just once. Also an outfit for a square dance would be impossible to find. Then Gee came to the rescue. "Buy me the material, and I'll make skirts for all you girls. In fact, you can help me sew them. All you'll need to do is find a top."

This offer inspired an old-fashioned sewing bee at Gee's house. Hannah's lilac gingham skirt with white ruffles was gorgeous. Hannah thought she probably could make a skirt all by herself if she had a sewing machine. Maybe she could drop the idea into Dad's ear—a hint for a Christmas present. Uncle Martin had purchased the lilac peasant blouse that was perfect with the skirt. Everything was set—until it wasn't.

"Darn!" Hannah said to Betsy, who was attempting to nap. "I really want to go." She and Seth had purchased their own tickets, so she could—but alone? Porter would have been her first choice, of course, but he was in Colorado with his grandmother. Hannah sighed. It wasn't fair! She grabbed her cell. "I'll call Danny," she told Betsy.

"Do-si-do! Hey, Hannah, this is fun!"

Danny had just decided not to bother with the square dance when Hannah called. "So, will you go with me?" she asked.

Danny hemmed and hawed until Hannah pleaded, "Gee made me a square dancing outfit. Her feelings will be hurt if I don't use it. Honestly, it's not like I really care about a square dance. Please, Danny!"

He gave in. Hannah was his friend. Besides, it would not do to upset Castle Bluff's finest donut hole maker. "Okay, Hannah, I'll go. But Gee didn't make me an outfit. What should I wear?"

"Oh, anything. Maybe a pair of jeans and a flannel shirt."

"That's easy enough. How do we get there?"

Hannah explained that her dad and uncle weren't home and that Seth's mom had planned to take them. "We could walk."

"Dad's home," Danny said. "I'll ask him."

Soon they were on their way, listening to Mr. Kennedy's tales of when square dancing was required in schools. He laughed at Danny and Hannah's bewildered looks. "We hated it," he said. "I suppose teachers thought it would help us learn etiquette without having to do much, well, personal touching. You should have a good time, though, since it's not required and just for fun."

Fun was right, Danny thought. In fact, it was a riot. Everyone was a beginner, and it didn't matter if you had a date. People without partners were matched up quickly, whether or not they were placed with a boy or a girl. Even some of the boys were dancing together, which Danny thought was a riot. If Porter were here, he'd ask him to dance.

"Promenade, all!" the caller cried out. Oops! Danny stopped himself when he discovered he was headed in the wrong direction.

During a snack break—cookies shaped like turkeys, small bags of popcorn, and glasses of cider—he and Hannah had a chance to chat. "Seems strange without Porter here," he said.

"I was thinking the same thing," Hannah admitted. "I know he wanted to help his grandmother, but still—"

"Still," Danny agreed. "He didn't want to come to the dance, but he might have enjoyed this. And I was going to stay home. It's mean of me to be glad Seth got sick, but—"

"But," Hannah concluded. "It's nice not thinking about being on a date. Oh, they're starting up again. What do you say, Dapper Dan?"

Danny stood. "Time to bump into people!"

The dance would end at ten. Since there was nothing to do but dance, talk, and eat, the Student Council decided to keep it short. Let people have a good time, and then go home. But a little after nine, Danny, Hannah, and a few other students noticed that something had changed.

"Danny, isn't that Sergeant Lodge, your dad's friend?"

Danny stared. "Yes, and he's not alone." Other police officers had entered the room, and a few were guarding the door.

Dr. Stewart, the principal, looking worried, took the caller's microphone and asked for silence. It took a few minutes for the less observant students to notice the policemen. Something had happened. Something major.

"Please listen carefully," Dr. Stewart said. Danny wasn't sure he'd ever heard the principal's voice before. It was usually the vice principal who made the PA announcements. "The police and I believe that everything is okay, but someone called them and reported a problem. The police have searched the school and have not discovered anything dangerous. To be on the safe side, though, we would like you to reach your parents, or whoever brought you here, to ask them to pick you up. The police will escort a few people at a time to the locker rooms where you've hung your coats, and then from the building. We thank the Student Council for sponsoring such a fine event. Perhaps we can do this again sometime."

Danny could tell that whatever had happened was serious, even though Dr. Stewart was trying to make light of it. He reached for his phone and then remembered. "Hannah, my phone is in my jacket pocket in the boys' locker room.. Do you have yours?"

Hannah nodded. "It's okay. I'll make the call."

Dad might have been the first to arrive. Danny had a hunch Sergeant Lodge had notified him when he saw Danny and Hannah. Outside, Danny could see the line of cars, and then a few students at a time being brought from the school. It was orderly, but people looked scared.

"Dad, do you know what happened?"

"Most likely a prank, but the police couldn't take a chance. Someone called them and reported a shooter in the building. Not 9-1-1, as you might suspect, but the police directly."

"Gosh!"

"Are they sure it was a prank?" Hannah asked.

"No," Mr. Kennedy said, "but they wanted everyone out of the school before they searched more thoroughly. It looks as if everyone is safe, so let's put it behind us for now. Did you have a good time?"

"Yes," Hannah said faintly.

Danny echoed her, but it was hard to think of the fun now. Shooters in schools were something they worried about every single day. It happened once a few towns south of Castle Bluff. It could happen anywhere — even in Castle Bluff Middle School.

As he was about to go to bed, Danny decided to text Porter to tell him what had happened. He had forgotten to remove his phone from his jacket, presently hanging in the mudroom. He crept down the back stairway to get it. Rats! Kylie and Brad were in the kitchen; he could smell the popcorn. Well, it didn't matter. He grabbed his phone.

What? A call? Who from? The police! The emergency call to the police had been made from his phone! Danny rushed into the kitchen. "Kylie, Brad, I need your help. Now!"

"Pssst, Laurel, wait up! He's here again!"

Laurel stopped. The two girls would sit together at the Thanksgiving assembly. Laurel was somewhat excited because she was going to sing a solo, but mostly she was sad. Last year at this time she was at the Castle Bluff Middle School assembly and was starting to give up on the idea that the Mullens would be her forever family. But at least she had lots of friends. Here, she just had Shaila, and while she appreciated her, it just wasn't the same.

"Hey, Shaila, who's here?"

"That Drama Club teacher from your old school. I keep seeing him around."

"Dr. D? That is strange. Maybe he's still trying to convince Mrs. Duncan to let us have a club here."

"Maybe, but that doesn't explain why he'd be coming to our Thanksgiving assembly."

Laurel shrugged. She liked Dr. D, but something about him made her uneasy. He reminded her of something or someone, but she didn't know if the slip of memory was good or bad. Shaila was right. His presence at the assembly today explained nothing.

Once again, Laurel felt as if her former life had disappeared. It was as if she'd never lived with the Mullens or had friends in Castle Bluff. She didn't know what was happening with Avery. Had Hannah's dad charged Avery and her family? Could they go to jail? She wondered if Hannah and Danny had even tried to contact her. Maybe she'd also disappeared for them. By now, they must have picked someone else to be vice president of Drama Club. They'd pretend the office had never been hers. All Laurel's life had been this way—a new facility or a new family or a new whatever—never look back. Best not to get too close to Shaila. Eventually, she would lose her, too.

Academically, Laurel was now number one. From struggling at Castle Bluff, she was tops at the Markey Home. A lot of that was to her credit, she supposed. All of that studying at the library in order to keep parts in plays had paid off. No plays here, but Mrs. Hill, the music teacher, almost made up for it. She was even better than Miss Raynor.

Shaila nudged her. "Come on, Laurel. You're too quiet—even for you. What are you thinking about?"

Laurel smiled. "Oh, not much, I guess. Just that I might want to be a music teacher when I grow up."

Shaila shook her head. "No, you're too talented for that. You'll be on stage performing."

Laurel doubted that either would happen. She'd just continue to coast from one brand new life to another, letting the past one drift away. Meanwhile, Shaila, who would probably be here until she aged out of the system, needed a friend. Laurel might as well be that friend for as long as she could.

In the auditorium, Mrs. Duncan and a few teachers gave some Thanksgiving-type prayers, and the junior choir, consisting of the youngest children, sang some cute songs about turkeys and pilgrims. One of the songs reminded Laurel of the poem she had written for *Stage Directions*. Probably Hannah had tossed it.

Then it was time for Laurel's solo, an old Thanksgiving hymn Mrs. Hill had taught her. Laurel wasn't nervous exactly. She loved to sing, and she did want to please Mrs. Hill.

> *Come, ye thankful people, come,*
> *Raise the song of harvest home.*
> *All is safely gathered in,*
> *Ere the winter storms begin.*
> *God our Maker doth provide*
> *For our wants to be supplied;*
> *Come to God's own temple, come,*
> *Raise the song of harvest home.*

Laurel sang all of the verses — it was a long song. Surely just one or two verses would be enough, but Mrs. Hill had insisted. "You must give them time to really listen," she'd said. It wasn't difficult to sing, not at all fancy, just kind of soothing. And it was good to be protected in this cocoon of a home, all wants supplied, safe from Avery's cruelty, but this life didn't feel quite real. As her song came to an end, Laurel allowed herself to really look at the audience. A few of the older adults seemed close to tears. Perhaps they remembered the hymn from their own childhoods.

One of those adults was Dr. D. He wasn't crying, but he looked absolutely brokenhearted. Suddenly, Laurel seemed to hear a loud, angry voice. *Don't leave your baggage here, missy!* Shaken, Laurel returned to her seat next to Shaila.

Scene Two - To Be Determined

"I'll call Dean immediately!" Danny thought they should wait until morning, but Kylie had insisted they rouse their parents out of bed. Mr. Kennedy was in charge until Sergeant Dean Lodge arrived and took over. They convened in the living room, except for Brad, who decided to drive home.

"So you left your phone in your jacket pocket, Danny? Why was that?" The policeman's voice was firm.

Kylie was right, Danny thought. It was good they'd reacted immediately. Sergeant Lodge might be his dad's friend, but he was also a deadly serious cop.

"Well, I only needed it to let Dad know when we wanted a ride home. And the jeans I was wearing were too tight to fit a phone in my back pocket. The pocket in my jacket is deep and has a zipper. I thought it was safe."

"And you hung it in the boys' locker room."

Danny nodded. "Yes, that's what we were told to do. And I never went back there—not until we had to leave the building. Honest, Sergeant Lodge!"

"Just getting a clear picture, Danny. Did you leave the gym at all during the dance—like to go to the bathroom?"

"No. Hannah and I were either dancing or eating. I was just thinking about going to the bathroom when the police arrived. Then I kind of forgot about it."

"Understandable," Dad said.

Danny thought everyone believed him, but he still felt awful. Calling in a fake threat was a terrible thing to do, and it would be even worse if someone was trying to frame him. That would make it personal.

"Did anyone know the phone was in your jacket pocket?" Mom asked.

Danny shook his head. "I don't see how. I set it on mute and stuck it in my pocket before I left the house. Hannah didn't even know."

"We'll talk to Hannah tomorrow," Sergeant Lodge said. "And I imagine both of you will be questioned at school on Monday. It was definitely a prank, but a serious one."

"What about in the locker room?" Kylie wondered. "Did anything seem wrong? Was there anyone there who might not have liked you?"

Was there anyone, period, who didn't like him? Danny didn't think so. He was pretty popular. He supposed someone might not care for him, but enough to do something as mean as that?

"I don't think so," he said slowly. "I wasn't really paying attention to anyone. I just hung up my jacket and went into the gym."

"Nothing else?" It was like a TV cop show. Danny wondered how many times he'd be asked the same questions.

"No, nothing." He paused, thinking. "Oh, wait! When it was time to go, I had trouble finding my jacket. I don't think it was in the same place where I'd hung it, but I thought I just wasn't remembering correctly. I had been in a rush."

Sergeant Lodge sighed. "I don't think we can do anything more tonight. It's good that you called me. I will need to take your phone, though, Danny."

"That's okay," Danny said. There wasn't anything personal on it. It was too late to call Porter tonight anyway.

Sergeant Lodge left soon after.

"Bedtime for all," Danny's mom said.

"Don't worry about it, son," Dad said. "I'm sure it will all work out."

Whatever came next was TBD, Danny thought. He knew he was innocent, and he thought everyone would believe him. But it felt weird, wrong. Did someone at school hate him? That much? He'd suspect Avery—if she were a boy, and if she'd been at the dance. He didn't think she even attended CBMS now.

Hannah was enjoying breakfast with Dad and Uncle Martin and giving them the highs and the lows of the dance when the police called.

"Sergeant Lodge and another officer are coming over to ask you some questions," Dad said.

"Me? I don't know anything."

Uncle Martin patted her hand. "They're probably questioning everyone who was at the dance. Don't worry, dear."

Well, Uncle Martin was only partly right. She had no need to worry about herself—she wasn't in trouble. The only students being questioned were those who might know something. She backed up Danny all the way, of course. He had been with her the entire time. He had never left the gym and had done nothing wrong. But as soon as the police left, she headed next door. No one home. That figured. Very little stopped the Kennedys from going to church. She'd call Porter, as she'd been longing to do ever since he'd left for Colorado. And then, just maybe, she'd walk over to the Markey Home and try to see Laurel.

Porter waited with Kelly in Grams' living room. One of her neighbors was taking them on the famous Pikes Peak Cog Railway. Kelly was thrilled, and Porter pleased to see her happy, although he didn't care about the railway trip. Here, in Manitou Springs, winter had come already, and he didn't wish to rush it. Snow, wind, cold would last a long time once he got back home. But it was good to get away. Grams definitely needed them, at least for lifting her spirits. Gramps was back in the hospital, and Porter feared it wouldn't be long before they attended another service. What would Grams do then? Porter shrugged. It was too soon to talk about it. Kelly's sighs took him away from sad thoughts. "I'm sure they'll be here soon," he said.

"I know. I was just thinking about Marta."

Kelly had cheered up more than she would have at home, but she was still sad, no matter how much her family had assured her it was for the best. "It's not best for me," Kelly had insisted. "I'm just devastated!" Porter smiled, remembering her reaction.

"She's your best friend, and you'll miss her," Porter soothed for at least the hundredth time. "But you will see her again. Beth is already working on it."

"But I won't see her every single day." Kelly resumed gazing out the window.

Porter shrugged. His sister, Beth, was sad, too, about losing Marla, but she understood the Grays' reasoning. Castle Bluff *was* too expensive, but that was only one factor. The family needed to be away from the constant reminders of all Mr. Gray had done. "A fresh start for all of us," Marla had told Beth. "You'll come and visit us." Beth agreed and had started to plan and save. Beth could be pretty determined. Maybe it would happen.

The doorbell rang. "Yes!" Kelly screeched.

"Pikes Peak, here we come!" No, Porter didn't really want to go, but he preferred it to the Thanksgiving dance in middle school. He pictured Hannah and Seth together. He guessed that bothered him a little, but not as much as it should have.

The route up the mountain was thrilling, and the smiles and occasional shrieks from Kelly made the train trip worthwhile. And the view from the top was spectacular!

"This was where the poet, Katharine Lee Bates, got the idea for her poem, *America the Beautiful*," Porter said, and smiled when Kelly started to sing it.

Porter breathed in the pure, cold air and felt his head clear, too. Look at this beautiful country, he told himself. Your problems are so small. In fact, you don't even know if you have problems. You're just afraid you might. Take one step at a time. You'll be home soon, you've done all your schoolwork, and Dr. D will tell us about the new play. You need to stay focused on good grades and the fact you want to be an actor someday. He hadn't seen Peter, and that was okay. He would forget all about Peter. Way too complicated for someone not quite thirteen.

"Porter, do you have change? I want to look through that?" Kelly pointed to a viewer telescope for tourists. Porter inserted the amount needed, just as his phone rang.

It was Hannah. In a way it was a good time since Kelly was occupied, but Porter didn't really want to talk. But he didn't want to be rude, either. "Hannah, hi! I can't talk now because I'm on top of Pikes Peak. How about I call you back tonight?"

"Pikes Peak, wow! I'll text you about what's going on, so you can think about it. We can talk when you get home."

Hmmm, so she didn't want to talk about her date. He waited while the text came in; it was a long one. Porter scanned it, and then read it more carefully. No date. Seth was sick. She went with Danny. Then she wrote about the dance's abrupt ending and the part Danny's phone had played. Porter didn't like it one bit. Of course Danny wasn't guilty, but the news would get out quickly, and some people would blame Danny. Why? Because that's the way people were.

"SSC meeting a.s.a.p." he texted back.

"I agree," Hannah replied.

Laurel's homework was done, but Shaila was trying to finish up a huge project. Laurel was alone, bored, with no ideas of what to do. So what would you do if you were back with the Mullens? she asked herself. Trying to stay out of Avery's way, was the only thing she could come up with. That life had been only a few weeks ago, but already it seemed like years. Of course she might have written poetry or thought about what play would be next or— She shook her head. No question about it. She'd have a ton of schoolwork, and it wouldn't be easy.

She shrugged. It was a nice day, and snow was predicted for later in the week. She'd walk around the grounds. By herself, of course, but maybe something would interest her. She grabbed a jacket and left out the front door. And there, coming up the walk, was Hannah!

"Hannah, what are you doing here?"

Hannah laughed. "I came to see you, of course, but I didn't think it would be so easy. It's like you were waiting for me."

Anxiously, Laurel looked back at the building. No one was around. "Well, maybe I was without knowing it. No one ever came to see me here before. I don't know what the rules are."

"I don't want to get you into trouble," Hannah said. "Should we go inside and ask?"

Laurel shook her head. "They might say no, but what could they do, anyway? Kick me out? Let's go for a walk."

"Uh, okay. If you're sure."

Quickly, they walked out of sight of the house. Laurel guessed she was happy to see Hannah. After all, Hannah wouldn't have come if she had decided not to be friends anymore, but she doubted the teachers or Mrs. Duncan would allow them to just wander around outside. Mrs. Duncan was pretty strict.

"So I guess the dance was last night," Laurel said. "Did you have a good time with Seth?"

Hannah laughed. "I had a very good time but with Danny, not Seth."

"You had a date with Danny?" Laurel didn't like the sound of that. She was pretty sure he was going to ask her until—Oh, well, it hardly mattered now. She wouldn't have been able to go.

Perhaps Hannah guessed what Laurel was thinking. "Not a date. Seth got sick, practically at the last minute, and Porter is in Colorado. So I called Danny. He'd decided not to go, but I had a fancy outfit, so, well, it just happened. It wasn't a date, Laurel. Danny is, like, my best friend."

Laurel nodded. "I wouldn't have been allowed to go even if Danny had asked me. Too bad about Seth, but you had fun, right?"

They had reached a bench in a grove of trees—an excellent spot for a private conversation. Although maybe a bit chilly.

"It was great, until—" The whole story pored out.

"Hannah, that's awful! Are you sure Avery wasn't there? I wouldn't put it past her to go after my friends."

Hannah shook her head. "It wasn't Avery. She never came back to school. I don't know if the family is even in Castle Bluff. No one is talking about it, and Mr. Kennedy won't even tell Danny anything. It's all hush-hush. Besides, Danny's phone was in the boys' locker room."

Laurel nodded. "I don't think even Avery would have the nerve to go in there."

"The problem now is I'm worried people might think Danny is guilty, but I swear, Laurel, he was with me the entire time."

"And Danny would never do such a thing. You don't have to convince me, Hannah. So what are you going to do?"

"Figure out who did it—with Porter and Danny's help, of course."

"But it might have been random. Just some idiot checking pockets and coming up with the idea—because he was mean or thought it was funny."

"That's true," Hannah said. "I wish you could help us learn the truth."

"I do, too, but unless he does something else, something directed at Danny, you might never find out."

Hannah nodded. "I hope Danny and I can talk later today. They went to church and then to the grandparents for dinner. Just like always."

Laurel stood. "It's getting cold. I'd better go inside before I'm missed."

"Is it going okay? Being here, I mean?"

Laurel shrugged. "It's okay. Everyone is nice, although Shaila is my only friend. I miss you and Drama Club, but I don't have to worry about Avery hurting me. At least, I don't think I do. I wish I knew where she was."

"I think Dr. D is trying to get Mrs. Duncan to agree to let us come here sometimes for Drama Club events."

"Well, he sure comes here a lot now. I should go back, Hannah, but I'm really glad you came."

"I'll come back whenever I can. Let's try for every Sunday afternoon about this time. Don't expect me if the weather is awful. I'll just go to the bench and wait. If you don't show up, I'll go home again."

"And if you don't show up, I'll go back inside." Laurel gave Hannah a quick hug. "Thanks, Hannah!"

"Wait! One more thing. Your copy of *Stage Directions*."

"My poem! You printed my poem!"

"Right. And no one knows it's yours. If you keep writing them, I'll keep printing them. You're still our vice president, you know."

They heard voices. "Quick, Hannah, sneak out this back path. I'm glad you came, and I hope I see you next week!"

Laurel raced back to the house. Maybe this time, she wasn't going to lose her friends.

Scene Three - Too Many Unknowns

A N EASY START TO THE week, Laurel thought. Almost too easy, plus no homework. Shaila could use her help, but the students were not allowed to help each other. Laurel shrugged. That didn't make sense to her, unless they were afraid of cheating. Slowly, she walked back to her room, not sure of what she would do once she got there. She looked out the second story hall window. The first snow, and she could see the little kids romping around for pure joy. Only a small part of her wanted to join them. The main part did not want to be cold and wet. She hoped snow wouldn't prevent Hannah from returning next Sunday. Sure, she meant to, but things were bound to come up. Laurel must try to guard herself against disappointment.

But Hannah had included Laurel's poem in *Stage Directions* and said she'd print more. That's what Laurel would do in the few hours before supper. She'd write another poem! Maybe about snow and how it can affect theater. A little funny, a little serious—she couldn't wait to get started.

A note on Laurel's door put her plan on hold. Mrs. Duncan wanted to see her as soon as her classes were over. Oh, no! Someone must have reported seeing Hannah yesterday. True, Laurel wouldn't get kicked out of the Markey Home, but she was certain to be told Hannah couldn't come anymore. Goodbye, Hannah. Goodbye, snow poem. Guess she'd better get it over with. She plopped her books onto her bed and wearily returned downstairs, this time to Mrs. Duncan's office.

Mrs. Duncan was smiling, so perhaps Laurel wasn't in trouble after all. There was even a plate of cookies on the table between the two chairs Mrs. Duncan always used for private chats. "Sit down, dear. Have a cookie."

Laurel sat, picked up a cookie, and nibbled. Mrs. Duncan was friendly, but what did she want?

"You've had a difficult month, Laurel." Mrs. Duncan sounded unsure. "I wondered how you're settling in."

"Okay," Laurel said.

"I'm sure coming back here was hard."

Laurel nodded. "I was sad things didn't work out, but I guess I'm used to it."

"Perhaps it won't be for long."

What? Did they plan to move her again so soon? "No!" she shouted, forgetting that she'd promised herself to stay calm. "Please," she said quietly. "I'm tired of . . ."

Mrs. Duncan nodded. "I understand. I shouldn't have said that. Really, I was just trying to make you feel better. We don't know of any placements coming up, and if something does, we'll help you make the decision, and it will be yours."

"Okay," Laurel said. "I miss my school and friends, but I am safer here."

"We're trying to pull your story together. That is, where you were and what happened to you before you came here the first time. We have the names and addresses of some of your various foster families, but that's about it. You've slipped through a few cracks, but we'll continue to find answers."

"We?"

Mrs. Duncan laughed. "*The Royal We*. I mean your teachers and me. Sometimes people come here inquiring about our children. Perhaps a relative of theirs is missing. It helps if we have information. Could you share some of your early memories?"

Weird. No one had asked her that before. "I don't remember much," she said. "Usually, people want me to forget what happened before—to move on, to start fresh. That's what they always say."

There was always some reason for a new placement, and it had never had anything to do with her. *Don't leave your baggage here, missy!* That was a very early memory, but it was unpleasant, and she did not want to share it.

"Well, it's getting close to suppertime. Suppose you think about it, and we'll talk again someday soon. And feel free to ask anything. It's not right that you know so little about your past or your future. Let's try to change that."

Laurel stood. "Okay. Thanks, Mrs. Duncan." Actually, she was more interested in the present. Should she ask about Drama Club and why Dr. D was around so much? No, that might draw attention to Hannah. That was their secret, for now.

It wasn't until Wednesday that the SSC finally met. Hannah had been truly frustrated. For some reason, Danny wasn't available on Sunday or even Monday. Hannah considered that mysterious. And Porter didn't get home from Colorado until late Monday night, so she didn't even see him until the Drama Club officers met on Tuesday after school.

Seth had brought up the subject of Laurel. "We don't have a vice president now," he said. "Any thoughts on that?"

Hannah did. Lots! But she decided to wait to hear what others had to say.

"I could do it," Porter said. "It doesn't look as if money is going to be an issue after all." That was true. Since raising money for the Markey Home never materialized, it was unlikely the club would be dealing with it for the rest of the year.

"That makes sense," Seth said. "If I get sick again, like I did last weekend, someone needs to take over the meeting. Hannah, what do you think?"

"Well, I really miss Laurel, and I wish we had another girl officer. But I'm not sure who that would be." The same old story! Every time

Hannah thought she had a best girlfriend, the friend disappeared. "Porter would make a good V.P., and he's right about the lack of money." Then she had a thought. This was a good time to ask. "Dr. D, what about doing theater with the Markey Home? Have you found out anything?"

Dr. D seemed uncomfortable, Hannah thought. At least he didn't answer right away. "Well, I have had a few meetings with Mrs. Duncan," he said. "We've been talking about possibilities. I suggested meeting at the castle on Saturdays. Might work, but Mrs. Duncan isn't certain the Markey Home board would allow the kids to come here."

"But if they did," Hannah added excitedly, "we could have our officers' meeting right before Drama Club, and Laurel could still be vice president."

"Well, every other Saturday, perhaps. But we may be a long way from that. How about we declare Porter our 'acting vice president,' until we know for certain what will happen?"

On that they agreed. Then Porter asked about the next shows. Dr. D said he was still working out details with Leland and Kylie, but he hoped they would do a couple of one-acts at the castle.

"No main play?" Seth asked.

"Oh, yes," Dr. D answered, "but it will be in the spring this year. The new music teacher has decided to skip the musical."

Hannah thought that probably made sense. The new teacher, Miss Raynor, seemed to be doing a fine job but probably wanted to get the feel of things before tackling something as hard as a musical. Of their friends, only Laurel would have cared about that. Hannah sighed, and the meeting was over.

Danny had finished his homework in study hall, so he was free to head over to Hannah's. She had made it clear that an SSC meeting was necessary. He wasn't sure why. He hoped it wasn't about what happened at the dance. He'd followed his parents and school counselor's advice and kept a "low profile." He hadn't talked with anyone, including Hannah. Fortunately, he hadn't heard so much as a whisper about it at school.

The police seemed to think it was a random, though dangerous, prank, although he still didn't have his phone back. Once he did, he didn't think he'd take it to school again. Yes, it might have been a joke—someone just going through all the jackets in search of whatever. But what if it were intentional? What if someone was out to get him? Danny didn't want to talk or even think about it. He hoped the SSC meeting, to be held in Hannah's basement, was about something else.

Normally, gatherings were at Danny's, with its comfortable couches and fridge filled with sodas. But it was off limits this week. Kylie was planning a huge surprise 16th birthday party for Brad this Saturday night. According to Kylie, Brad didn't have a clue what was coming. All he knew was he had been invited to the Kennedys' for dinner.

Danny was fine with this. He liked Kylie's boyfriend, but Hannah's basement was creepy. Oh, well, didn't matter. They probably wouldn't be there long.

As soon as they were gathered around an old circular table, Porter began. "We haven't had a good talk in ages. I thought—well, Hannah and I did—that we should."

"Okay, yeah, but you said it would be an SSC meeting. If all we're doing is hanging out, we could be upstairs in the kitchen."

"Actually, I think this is a perfect place for us to meet—dark and definitely mysterious. I think it should be SSC headquarters. But Danny, you sound defensive. What's going on?"

"Nothing," Danny said.

"Right. Why don't I believe that?" Porter continued. "Hannah contacted me on Sunday about what happened at the dance, but then my plane was delayed, so I didn't get home until late Monday night."

"And," Hannah added, "I haven't been able to talk to you since it happened. I've tried every day, but you haven't been around, and you haven't answered your phone. So I agree with Porter. What's going on?"

Danny shuffled his feet, and then took a long gulp from his can of Coke. "The police haven't given back my phone, but okay, I guess I have been a little weird. It just feels so strange thinking that someone might be out to get me. Nothing like that has ever happened before."

"Well, get us up to date," Hannah said. "What do the police think? They talked to me, but the only thing I could say was that you were with me the whole time."

"They think, or at least they say, that it was probably a random prank, but that I should keep a low profile and not talk to anyone about it."

"That does not include us," Porter said, annoyed. "We're your friends. Of course we need to know what's happening. Don't you remember what happened to Roe when she was in 7th grade? Someone was definitely out to get her, and it might have worked if her friends hadn't solved the mystery."

"I know. I'm sorry. I should have talked to you. But I haven't heard anything about it at school, so I guess I'm okay."

"No one spreading rumors is a good thing," Hannah said. "Maybe it was just random. Someone with an odd sense of humor searched through pockets in the boys' locker room and found your phone." She chuckled. "Laurel thinks it sounds like something Avery would do."

"Laurel?" Both boys said.

"Oh, right. I went to the Markey Home on Sunday afternoon."

"They let you see her? Porter said.

"Not exactly." Hannah explained the circumstances. "And I'm going to try to see her every Sunday."

"Let's hope you don't get caught," Porter said. "One of us in trouble is enough."

"I'm not," Danny started, but stopped when he saw the look on Porter's face. Porter was only teasing. His friends knew he'd done nothing wrong.

"Just in case," Porter said, "let's keep our eyes open. And Danny, watch your back. After school, stay with us as much as possible. There's no reason why you can't come to our Drama Club officers' meetings. Do your homework. Listen. Whatever."

Danny nodded. "I guess I feel better. Anything else? Another mystery would be nice."

"Just Laurel, as usual," Hannah said. "Dr. D has been hanging around a lot, and she's wondering why. He's probably trying to figure out a way Drama Club can connect with the home, like he said."

"Still, it's odd," Porter said. "Anything else?"

"I told Laurel what happened to you, Danny, and that's when she said it sounded like Avery."

"Right. If Avery were a boy and went into the boys' locker room." Danny shook his head. "No, this time Avery had nothing to do with it. Our only mystery, other than who did it, is was it random or directed at me?"

Porter ended the meeting. "Maybe it wouldn't hurt for us to find out what happened to Avery, though. I'll go by her house and see if I can tell if anyone is living there."

Scene Four – Fun in Basements

DANNY HADN'T EXPECTED TO BE excited about Brad's surprise birthday party, but this was going to be fun. Right before dessert, he would announce that he had to go to Hannah's because Porter would be there to help him and Hannah with math. Mom had baked an extra pie for them. No way was he going to miss dessert!

Going to Hannah's was not a lie, although the math part was. Before heading there, Danny would stand at the Kennedy's backdoor and escort the party-goers downstairs to the basement. He would not attend the party that was strictly for high school friends.

Danny was certain Brad had no idea what was about to happen. Dinner was in the dining room, with the kitchen door closed firmly, although Danny had posted a quiet sign on the back door. Steak, salad, baked potatoes—an elegant feast for a Saturday night! Normally, the family scrounged the fridge for leftovers. First, Brad opened his presents: a gift certificate to Smithy's from his parents and Danny (well, Danny signed the card) and a new wallet with her photo in it from Kylie.

Then, of course, questions, which seemed to be the only way adults communicated with teens:

Dad: *Are you in any plays, Brad?*
Brad: *No, I haven't had time because of my jobs.*
Dad: *Oh, right. You have two now, correct?*
Brad: *Yes, I'm still working for Leland, and I serve suppers at the Deli.*
Mom: *Don't overdo it. You don't want to fall behind on your grades.*
Brad: *I know. That's why I'm skipping extracurricular activities.*

It was just small talk. Mom and Dad knew Brad's family was having a hard time and that Brad planned to put himself through college. The questions were something to say. If they were hanging out in the living room playing board games, they'd relax. There was just something about dinner in the formal dining room.

"How are your brothers and sisters doing?" Mom asked. Brad had a huge family, and his parents had almost split up last year.

"Better, thanks, except for Nick. He's in sixth at CBMS. Do you know him, Danny?"

Danny shook his head. "Sorry. We must not be doing the same stuff." He and Nick Michaels hadn't attended the same elementary school.

Brad sighed. "The only stuff Nick seems to be doing is failing his classes and getting into trouble."

Silence filled the room. Not exactly birthdayish talk, Danny thought, but it was not his job to fix it. He reminded everyone of his commitment next door, wished Brad a happy birthday again, and took off. He definitely preferred casual Saturday night suppers, even though the food wasn't as good.

Some people were already giggling at the backdoor, including—
"Roe!"

"Shhh," she said, giving him a quick hug. "I was hoping to surprise you, too. We'll talk later."

Now, Danny almost wished he were going to the party. But Roe had a suitcase. She'd be staying over, and they'd find time to catch up.

Danny reminded everyone to hide and that he'd text Kylie when they were ready. He wasn't sure how Kylie planned to get Brad to the basement, but that was her problem.

Porter knocked on Hannah's front door, not entirely sure why he was there. Both Hannah and Danny needed help on their math? Porter doubted that, although that was Danny's reason to leave his house. Did he really need an excuse? Porter shrugged. Oh, well, it didn't matter. The only thing weird about seeing his friends on a Saturday night was the pretense of math.

Hannah's dad answered. "Oh, hi, Porter, come on in. Hannah is next door, helping Danny escort the guests to the basement. But they'll be here soon."

"Uh, thanks." This was Porter's chance. Should he take it? Mr. Rendina had always been kind and understanding to all of them. And he might be able to answer Porter's questions, once he could figure out what those questions were. "Mr. Rendina, I was wondering if I could talk to you about something — something personal."

"Of course, Porter. Do you want to do it now?"

"Well, no. It's kind of private, and you said Hannah and Danny would be here soon."

"Right. How about my office at Community after school someday this week?"

Porter spotted Danny and a giggling Hannah leaving the Kennedy's side door. "Would Wednesday be okay?"

Mr. Rendina nodded. "Wednesday after school, it is."

"Oh, you're here, Porter! You should have come over. It was so much fun!"

Porter blinked before grinning. No one was prettier than Hannah when she was in an exuberant mood. "I just got here. It's okay. Beth gave me all of the decorating details. More than I wanted, really. Is everyone there?"

Danny nodded. "A huge crowd, but Dad is going to keep an eye on things. And, guess what, Porter? Roe came, too!"

"Wow! They are having a reunion!"

Suddenly from next door came an enormous cry of "Surprise!" followed by a deafening cheer.

Mr. Rendina laughed. "And you three are planning to work on math? Doesn't seem fair."

"Don't worry about us, Dad," Hannah said. "With Porter helping, it won't take long. Then, if it's okay with you, maybe we could go see a movie?"

"Get the math done, and then we'll talk about it," Hannah's dad said, before heading to his office to grade art portfolios.

Silence. What was wrong with them? "Okay," Porter said, "what's going on?"

Hannah squirmed. "Well, actually, we don't have any math. Danny just used that as an excuse to leave his dinner early in order to help Kylie."

"But I've got a pie for all of us," Danny said.

"And you needed me, why?" Porter persisted.

"Well, we didn't need you, exactly. I wanted to justify my lie."

Porter shook his head. "That's ridiculous. You didn't lie to your family. That was part of your cover to help with Brad's party. The only ones who didn't know it was a lie were Brad, Hannah's father . . . and me."

"Okay," Hannah said. "I guess we just wanted you to come."

"So why didn't you ask me? It's Saturday night. What would be so weird in asking me to hang out? It's not like you ever do homework on Saturday, anyway."

Silence while Danny and Hannah looked at each other.

"What's going on, guys?"

Danny tried. "We were afraid you wouldn't come."

"You've changed so much lately," Hannah said. "You're so quiet, and you act as if you're keeping something from us."

"Oh," Porter said quietly. He couldn't deny what they were saying, but he needed to come up with something. "It's just that you and I, Hannah—"

Hannah gave him a dirty look. "Oh, that. Look, Porter, I get that you don't want to be my boyfriend. I don't mind, really. But do I have to lose one of my best friends? I don't need a boyfriend, but I do need a friend who happens to be a boy."

"Right," Danny said. "We're the SSC! Best friends forever! Now, what are we going to do? The movies?"

"I didn't bring any money," Porter said. "Can't we just hang out? I got the feeling Mr. Rendina doesn't want to drive us into town."

"He doesn't," Hannah said. "He's got a lot of schoolwork, even if we don't."

Video games were Danny's suggestion, even though Hannah didn't have many good ones.

Porter shook his head, suddenly feeling better about everything. These were his friends, no matter what. "How about we work on Hannah's basement? Make it a creepy meeting place for SSC meetings only."

"Yes!" Hannah shrieked. "We've got all those cool screens down there. We can post pictures on them from magazines or our own drawings. It won't take up the whole basement, so Dad and Uncle Martin won't mind."

"And let's not talk about anything serious for the rest of the night," Danny said.

Breakfast at noon. A rare occasion. Hannah finished her bagel and orange juice and quickly rinsed out the glass and tossed the paper plate. Caring for Betsy had come first, of course, but the little dog had settled in for a nap in her playroom. Perhaps Bingo and Boots would come over later. Hannah peeked out the window. No, still no signs of life next door. The Kennedys must be sleeping in, too. Missing church and dinner with the grandparents rarely happened.

Danny and Porter had stayed at her house until Porter's dad arrived at midnight, and Danny went home. Once the air with Porter had cleared, they'd had a terrific time. Their drawings and signs on the screens in the basement were juvenile—*SSC Headquarters. Keep Out!*—but that had made it more fun. The sillier the signs, the more they laughed.

Super cold today, Hannah thought. She kind of wished she could stay home and read. But, no, she'd promised Laurel a return to the Markey Home. She couldn't let her down on the very first Sunday of the plan. "The walk will do me good," she said. "I'll bundle up and walk fast." Dad and Uncle Martin wouldn't be home until dinnertime. Maybe she'd take a little money and get a snack somewhere on the way home. A bagel and juice weren't enough for both breakfast and lunch.

Hannah squeezed through the break in the fence. In time, she supposed, whoever was in charge of the property would notice the problem and fix it. The grove of evergreens hid the opening. So in the meantime— Hannah shivered. So cold! It felt as if it would snow any second. Hannah sat on the bench and waited. I'll stay for a half hour, she decided.

"Brrr!" What a difference a week made. Hannah wondered if she'd be able to keep her promise of coming every Sunday. There had to be a way she could see Laurel indoors, she thought. Laurel wasn't in danger, now that Avery was gone. And they were pretty sure she was. Last night, Porter said there was a For Sale sign in front of the Mullen house. She shrugged. The Markey Home was run by old people, probably used to rules older than they were. They were afraid to take chances.

Every ten minutes, Hannah stood and stamped her feet. The half hour was long over, and she needed to be home before Dad and Uncle Martin started to wonder where she was. Enough! She started walking toward the fence when she heard, "Wait!"

"Laurel?" No, it wasn't Laurel but that friend of hers. What was her name? Shaila. "Oh, hi, Shaila!"

Shaila rushed over to her. "I'm sorry I'm so late. I kept hoping Laurel would come out in time to catch you."

"Come out?"

"Can you stay a few more minutes? I know you must be freezing. Here!" Shaila handed her a cup of hot chocolate. "I stopped by the kitchen first."

"Thank you!" Hannah warmed her hands—she'd forgotten her gloves—and pressed the cup against her cheeks. The beverage was still too hot to drink. "This helps. But where is Laurel? Out from where?"

Shaila shook her head. "This whole day has been crazy. First, that theater teacher was here for most of the morning. That is, I saw him go into Mrs. Duncan's office about 10:30 and leave when I came downstairs for lunch at noon. I didn't see Laurel. She might have gone to church. Some of the kids are bussed to various ones. It's not required, so I don't go. After lunch, I saw Laurel's new social worker go into the office, and then maybe an hour later, Laurel was called to join them. She's still there! I'll bet she's upset. Fortunately, she told me you were coming. I kept waiting, but then I was afraid you'd be mad at her and leave. I guess I shouldn't have taken the time to get you the drink."

"No, I'm glad you did. I was turning into an icicle. I can't stay longer, though. I'm afraid my parents will worry."

"You're lucky to have parents who worry," Shaila said. She didn't sound bitter—just matter-of-fact. There was something hard and brittle about Shaila, Hannah thought, as if she'd become accustomed to disappointment.

"Well, tell Laurel I understand, and it's okay. I'll try to come back next Sunday, if the weather lets me. And thanks again, Shaila."

"Yeah, okay. I'd better get inside. I'm supposed to be doing homework, and the monitor is bound to check up on me. See ya, Hannah!"

And Shaila was gone. Hannah finished her hot chocolate and was wondering if she had time to go somewhere for a snack when her phone pinged. Dad? No, it was Danny. "Where r u? Bingo excited about snow. Come play with us!"

"Coming," Hannah texted back. I don't think I can run, she thought. But I'll walk really fast!

I hope Hannah isn't mad at me, Laurel thought. I hope she'll understand that I couldn't meet her. Of course she might not have come. It was snowing heavily now. The Castle Bluff kids were probably wondering if they'd have school tomorrow. Laurel sighed. That was a perk that would never happen here. School was downstairs, no matter the weather. Her Sunday afternoon had been spoiled. Such a long time with the new social worker, whom Laurel didn't really like. So many questions, often repeats of what must be in her file. Didn't people bother to read?

Time to grab Shaila and go to supper. Hopefully, Shaila had finished her homework and they could hang out this evening.

Scene Five – It's Okay to Coast

Before eighth period that Wednesday, Porter's only thoughts were about the upcoming conversation with Mr. Rendina at Community and the one-act plays Dr. D had mentioned yesterday. Then Porter discovered that he needed another book. Heading down the hall to his locker, he spotted a boy posting a sign on Hannah's. Then the boy dashed away, rounding a corner. Probably harmless, but Porter decided to check. He didn't recognize him.

Not harmless. The sign was dangerous, mean. Large black letters on white photocopy paper said, "Ask Hannah about her TWO DADS!"

Porter ripped it down, folded it, and put it into his pocket. Another nasty trick—one definitely meant to harm Hannah. At least Porter found it before anyone else could read it. But what should he do? Think about it later, he decided. For now, he needed to retrieve that book and hurry back to English class, where he doubted he'd be able to concentrate.

After school, Porter raced out of the building before Danny or Hannah could spot him. He'd told his mother he'd be late but, to his relief, she had her own concerns and didn't bother to question him. He'd lie if necessary, but he'd rather not. He shivered. Too cold. It might start snowing again before he made it home.

Now he regretted making the appointment with Mr. Rendina. It was too late to cancel. While he was not happy about the sign on Hannah's locker, at least he had an excuse to talk about something else. Normally, he'd bring up the matter with the SSC first, but this would give him an out with Mr. Rendina if he decided he needed one.

Porter had never been to Mr. Rendina's office, but he knew the location of the Arts building. The offices were on the third floor, according to the directory. Skipping the elevator to take longer, he started climbing, wondering with each step if he should turn around and flee. Oh, well, if Mr. Rendina didn't understand, who would?

"Porter, come in, sit down."

Mr. Rendina excused a woman, who seemed to be taking notes for him. A secretary? He must be pretty important to have a secretary. Porter looked around the office. It was larger than he'd expected. Many paintings hung on the walls. He recognized Mr. Rendina's work because of the framed paintings in Hannah's house.

"It's getting nasty out," Mr. Rendina said. "Can't offer more than a cup of tea and a leftover donut from this morning."

Porter shivered. "Thanks. I need warming up."

"Now what made you brave the weather on a day like this?"

Porter pulled the sign from his backpack. So, maybe he was stalling or maybe he wouldn't say what else was bothering him, but this was a good way to start. "This," he said. "It was taped onto Hannah's locker. I don't think anyone but me saw it."

Mr. Rendina whistled. "Well, whoever did this certainly meant to be cruel. Can you think of anyone who has it in for Hannah?"

Porter shook his head. "Other than Drama Club members, I don't think that many kids even know her. She's pretty quiet in most places. She gets good grades, but she never flaunts them. And she doesn't participate in anything but theater."

"Right." Mr. Rendina nodded., still studying the sign. "Different, of course, but it almost goes along with what happened to Danny. In other words, Porter—"

"I should watch my back."

"Exactly. If it were possible, I would think Avery was responsible. Well, I'll hang on to this and talk to Hannah about it tonight."

"Uh, I'd rather give it to her, if you don't mind. You see . . ."

"Got it. You don't want her to know you came here."

"Yeah," Porter said, "and I think I should probably go now."

"Okay—but first a question. When did you discover this sign?"

"During 8th period today." As he said it, Porter realized he'd fallen into the trap. Too late! "I mean . . ."

"But you asked last Saturday for this meeting. What's going on, Porter?"

He wasn't going to fool this man. Oh, why had he come? Probably Mr. Rendina had even guessed what he was going to say. "I—uh—just wondered how you knew you were gay?"

"How I?" Hannah's dad roared with laughter. "Oh, my—thanks, Porter, I needed a good laugh."

Porter turned red and headed for the door.

"Stop, Porter. I'm sorry. I did not mean to hurt your feelings. Sit down, and I'll answer sensibly as soon as I recover."

Porter obeyed but sat at the edge of his chair—just in case.

Mr. Rendina wiped his eyes, and then blew his nose. "I am so sorry. It took courage for you to come here, and then I reacted like an idiot."

"That's okay," Porter said softly, although it really wasn't.

"I gather that you've had some experiences that have made you wonder. For many people, that's normal. It just didn't happen that way for me. If you ask ten gay men the question, you'll probably get ten different answers. People are different you know, even gay ones."

"Okay," Porter said again. He wanted to leave—now!

"Martin would say that he figured it out when he was about your age. And he was fortunate to have a supportive family."

"But—" That didn't make sense. Hannah told him that both sides of her family had, basically, divorced the two men.

Mr. Rendina sighed. "I know what you're thinking. All would have been fine if Martin had chosen a different man to love. But I was married to Hannah's mother, Martin's sister. It was a big mess."

Porter nodded, not certain what to say.

"We hurt a lot of people. I did love Hannah's mother when I first married her. She was beautiful and fun, and I thought I was happy. True, I'd experienced some incidents that made me question myself, but I put them aside. My parents, especially my father, were very narrow in their views. He said art was for 'pansies.' My father was all about sports. He overlooked my interest in art as long as I played football in high school and watched the 'big game' on TV. I still watch because of him. After Hannah was born, though, my wife changed. She wasn't interested in the baby or me. And, well, she cheated. That's when Martin entered the picture."

"And you fell in love?"

"Eventually. I held out for a long time because of Hannah. Have I answered your question, Porter?"

Porter shook his head. "Not really."

"Did something happen?"

How much did he want to tell? Not much, but at least Mr. Rendina seemed sympathetic. "It happened in Colorado over the summer. This actor who was in the show I was in became my friend, sort of. He was a lot older than me. But he was fun, and we started hanging out together. Then, backstage, the night before I came home, he kissed me. I pulled away and left, but I kind of liked it. That's when I got confused. I wanted it to happen again."

"And how old was this actor?" Mr. Rendina frowned.

"Nineteen. I know he shouldn't have done it. But my reaction scared me."

Mr. Rendina nodded. "I understand. Did you see him when you visited your grandmother recently?"

"No, but I wanted to and didn't, at the same time. Does that make sense? Do you think I'm gay? I don't like sports, and I want to do theater and things like that."

"Porter, I have no way of knowing. My suggestion is that you wait and not worry about it. Just coast. Things will become clearer to you in time. There's a group at your church you could join."

Right. It was called Questioning Youth. His parents were supportive of it, but what if their own son became a member? He shook his head. "Not yet," he said. "Maybe someday."

"Take your time," Mr. Rendina said. He looked out the window. "Getting nasty out there. I'll give you a lift home. And if you return to Colorado next summer, stay away from that young man."

"I will. Thanks." Porter didn't want to talk anymore. What stuck in his head the most was Mr. Rendina saying he'd hurt a lot of people. Porter wanted to be true to himself without hurting anyone he loved. He resolved not to have any boyfriend or girlfriend for a long while.

"Come in," Danny called out. He grinned. It must be Roe. She was still the only one who bothered to knock.

"Hey, Danny. What are you up to? Schoolwork on a Friday night?" It was almost a week since Roe had made a surprise appearance. She sat on his bed while he gathered up papers and put them to one side of his desk.

"Auditions tomorrow at the castle, and I'm trying to make up my mind what to go for — if anything."

Roe reached for the scripts. "PDFs? Never heard of these plays — *The Valiant* and *Sorry Wrong Number*. They must be really old."

Danny laughed. "So is Dr. D. He calls them potboilers. I think that means they used to be done a lot. But they're great plays and won't cost a fortune to produce."

"He's doing two?"

"Yeah, at the castle; they're one-acts."

"What about sports?"

Danny had spent hours asking himself the same question. "I only have swimming this winter. I could take on a small part — either a policeman in *The Valiant* or a telephone operator in *Sorry Wrong Number*, although I'd rather be the murderer."

"The murderer? Wow!"

"Yeah, both plays are pretty intense." Danny's main reasons for auditioning were Porter and Hannah. Soon, they would go to high school, and he would be alone in middle school, except for his Drama Club friends. Somehow it was easier for him to make friends there. Everything was so competitive in middle school sports.

"Sounds exciting. I'm looking forward to seeing them." Roe winked.

"What? You're staying here?"

Roe nodded. "Here, but not here. In Castle Bluff anyway. My dad is going to rent an apartment near the high school while he and Mateo return to Mexico, to see if they can find Mateo's real father. Dad will still be Mateo's legal guardian, of course.

Danny shook his head. "Okay, but you're too young to live in an apartment alone. Just stay here." Danny liked Mr. Santos all right—he gave great gifts—but he wasn't always a very good parent.

"Well, I will stay with you and Kylie for a while. The plan is for my cousin Lucia to come from Spain and share the apartment with me. She's twenty-two and wants to go to Lakes Harbor College. It will all work out. You'll see."

His sister's old gang, back together again! "Roe, that's terrific," he said.

Hannah had stopped worrying about the poster Porter had found taped on her locker. She'd been scared at first, but nothing had happened in school yesterday or today. Perhaps the prankster had given up when there was no reaction. Prankster? That word was too tame, too jovial. But nothing more had happened to Danny, either. Porter, Danny, and Hannah would keep their eyes open, but it was time for them to move on.

This Friday night, Hannah, too, was examining the scripts and trying to make up her mind which part she'd like. Both had strong female leads. The tricky thing was that Dr. D had announced that the big spring play would be *Tom Sawyer*, and she could totally see herself as Becky Thatcher. The female lead in *The Valiant* was Josephine, a girl who visits a prisoner, but she was sweet and innocent, like Becky. The part in the other play was Mrs. Livingston, a bedridden old crab, much more fun to play. With her hair pulled back in a bun, perhaps Dr. D would consider her. "Mrs. Livingston," Hannah wrote on her audition sheet. She'd read the part one more time. Then she'd experiment with her hair.

The decision had been reached. The students at Markey Home would not be allowed to attend Drama Club meetings at the castle or middle school. Their board would not take a chance. "Too many of our children are being protected from adults who might hurt them," Mrs. Duncan told Laurel. "Some actually love them, but it's a destructive kind of love."

That doesn't apply to me, Laurel had wanted to say. No one loved her enough to risk anything. Laurel knew Mrs. Duncan was right, though. Shaila had told her enough for Laurel to realize she was one of those kids. Her parents were dangerous. Shaila was not allowed off campus, even to go to church. Fortunately, she had no interest in going, even though she pretended it was her choice.

"Maybe Drama Club could come back here someday," she said.

"Maybe," Mrs. Duncan said, in an unpromising way.

Oh, well. In the meantime, Laurel would look forward to Hannah's visits—until Hannah grew tired of coming. She could hardly wait for Sunday afternoon.

Scene Six — Audition time again

PORTER COVERED HIS HEAD WITH a black ski cap. Even Dr. D would have trouble imagining Porter as a dangerous prisoner facing execution if he had bright red hair. James Dyke in *The Valiant* was definitely the part Porter wanted. What an opportunity! Not a play most directors would even consider for middle school. Porter liked Miss Armstrong fine, but she would have picked something cutesy and silly — probably a fairy tale.

"I can do this," he told himself, "and I know I'm a better actor than Seth." He wondered if Hannah wanted Josephine. How would he feel about that? Porter shrugged. Fortunately, not his call.

Hannah shivered. Nothing about the ballroom felt the same. It looked as it usually did, but with no chance of Mr. Markey visiting, there was a sense of loss in the air. The room felt empty. But downstairs would seem even worse, she thought.

"Hannah, may I see you for a minute?" Dr. D beckoned her from the kitchen.

"Sure, Dr. D." Did he want her help with snacks? Snacks weren't exactly Dr. D's thing. No, the kitchen was bare of all food but somehow seemed more comfortable than the ballroom. All that was needed here were Gee's donut holes.

"I thought you'd want to know what the Markey Home board has decided," Dr. D began.

"Yes!" Hannah said eagerly. Please let it be good news!

Dr. D shook his head. "Sorry. They said no to anyone coming here or to the school."

Hannah had not expected a blank refusal. "That is so unfair. Why?"

"Mrs. Duncan didn't say, exactly. She just inferred that some of the students were at risk, that they needed to be protected."

"Avery is gone. She was Laurel's only risk."

"I don't know. Mrs. Duncan seemed to be saying that quite a few of the children were in possible danger. There's really nothing we can do about it, Hannah." He looked at his watch. "Nine o'clock on the nose. Time for auditions."

Hannah followed Dr. D back to the ballroom. She hadn't responded, but she was fuming inside. Well, she would not give up. Maybe Dr. D hadn't tried hard enough.

Surprisingly, very few students had arrived for auditions. Dr. D addressed the group. "We'll wait a few more minutes. I thought that having rehearsals over winter break might be a problem. I heard that you had that situation before, but it turned out fine."

Danny nodded. "That was two years ago when my sister ended up directing *Cinderella, Cinderella.*" He didn't mention it was because the director disappeared. "It was a very small cast. This time, we don't have enough kids for both *The Valiant* and *Sorry Wrong Number.*" He counted. Only ten students had arrived.

"I think there will be a few more," Dr. D said. "Let's get started. First thing to know is that I'm not going to pay much attention to gender. Father Daly could be Pastor Daly. It really doesn't matter. Telephone operators can be boys as well as girls. Doubling is possible. So is being in both plays."

Porter raised his hand. "You asked us to name the part we wanted. I never had that happen before. Does that mean you'll only consider us for the part we listed."

Dr. D shook his head. "No, casting will still be my decision. I had you choose a character because I wanted to be certain you read the plays. It's not often we can all get copies ahead of time. Thank goodness for computers, the Internet, and PDFs.

That made sense, Danny thought. The plays were advanced for middle school. He was a little surprised the school was allowing them. Cold auditions would be awful. The kids auditioning needed to know what they were doing.

A few more girls arrived, ones Hannah knew from the last play—all sixth or seventh graders. One girl was brand new and looked older. Competition or, perhaps, a new friend? Dr. D asked for their audition forms and then introduced the new girl. "This is Blair Cummings," he said. "She'll start eighth grade at CBMS right after winter vacation. Her parents got in touch with me about joining our group in some way, so she'll know some of you when school starts again."

"Welcome, Blair," Hannah blurted out. Well, as a Drama Club officer, she should be friendly. "I'll tell you about Drama Club once we have a break."

"Which won't happen unless we get started," Dr. D said. "You've read the scripts, so it won't be necessary to talk about the shows. With so few people here today, it's possible that I'll be able to cast all of you. You've seen the rehearsal schedule and have signed off on your availability. Any changes, let me know immediately."

Hannah thought she read well as Mrs. Livingston, the cranky, anxious invalid. Dr. D also had her read Josephine, a part she did not want. She thought the new girl, Blair, did best at that role, although Carol Tennant, the girl who played Ninetta in the last play, was also very good. Hannah liked the two plays a lot but was surprised Dr. D had chosen such boy-heavy ones when more girls were interested. The only boys here were not new. They had been in *Love for Three Oranges.*

Wow! Hannah thought, as she listened to Porter's audition for Dyke, the prisoner about to be put to death in *The Valiant*. No way, she'd decided when he was asked to read. Then he covered his head with a black wool cap and looked the part as well as sounding perfect. Seth had also tried for Dyke and seemed, Hannah thought, both unhappy and admiring as he listened to Porter. Soon everyone had had a chance to read.

"We'll take a break now while I pick the cast," Dr. D said. "Then I'll make the announcement and all of you can go home and" — he grinned — "learn your lines. Off book by next Saturday."

Everyone groaned. That was pure Dr. D, insisting on lines before blocking. Hannah didn't like this method, but she understood now that all directors were different and that there wasn't much she could do about it. Maybe he'd be a little understanding of those with huge parts, such as the one she hoped she'd get. And they'd find out their parts today. That was something else that was different about Dr. D. Usually, directors wanted to be as far away as possible when the actors learned their roles.

Hannah was hoping for a chance to talk with Blair, but Seth seemed to be demanding her attention. She thought about joining them when Danny stopped her. "What was Dr. D saying about Markey Home," he said. "I couldn't really hear."

"Their kids can't come here or school," she said. "They don't think it's safe. It's over, Danny — unless we can think of something."

Porter joined them. "Doesn't make sense," he said. "It's not like coming here would be advertised. Something else is going on."

Hannah nodded. "Yeah, I think so, too."

"SSC meeting? Your basement, Hannah?"

Porter and Hannah gave a thumbs up. Porter was spending the night at Danny's, so their meeting would be nice and long. With the SSC on the case, it would all work out.

Without their noticing, Dr. D had returned from the kitchen. He cleared his throat, causing the entire group to dash back to their seats.

Porter crossed his fingers. "This is it," he breathed. The only parts he would consider were Dyke, the Chaplain, or the Warden, but Dyke was definitely his number one choice.

"First, *Sorry Wrong Number*. I don't know if you realize this show began as a radio play for an accomplished actress named Agnes Moorehead, whom you would know as the Wicked Witch of the West in *The Wizard of Oz*." Most of the students looked bewildered. The Wicked Witch played Mrs. Stevenson? Porter vowed to Google the actress.

Dr. D resumed. "Now, the only difficult part in *Sorry Wrong Number* is Mrs. Stevenson. That will be played by Hannah Rendina." Hannah gasped, and a few of her friends applauded. "Now, Hannah, do your best to memorize as much as possible by Saturday, but I will give you some leeway. At least your blocking is easy. You stay in bed. The line load for the rest of you is not bad, and I do expect you to be off book next week." He consulted his list. "The first man will be played by Perry Hill, and the second man, George, by Danny Kennedy."

"Yes!" Danny blurted. Everyone laughed, including Dr. D.

"Fancy yourself a killer, do you, Danny? Beware, Hannah! Joe Pappas is Sergeant Duffy, Carol Tennant is the Hospital Receptionist—" Porter thought Carol looked crushed. After all, she'd been the main princess in the last show—"Kendra Yu is the Chief Operator, Sarah Barkley is the Lunch Room lady. Telephone operators are Julia Bennet and Maggie Jo Morgan."

Porter squirmed a little. It didn't seem quite fair. Everyone but Hannah had a bit part in that play. No matter what might be said about small parts, most of the actors must be disappointed, especially all of the girls but Hannah and one other. That other would be the new girl, Blair, who would probably get Josephine in *The Valiant*. Yes, she was good, but better than Carol? Porter was grateful not to be the one casting.

Perhaps Dr. D had an inkling of Porter's thoughts. "Just wait until we start rehearsing," he said. "All of you will love your parts. And if you think your part is too small, you will be relieved once the holidays are upon us and there are other things you want to do."

A few kids nodded, but most would need time to agree.

He would know all of his lines by Monday, Danny thought. An absolute first for him! And he knew his best line already—"Sorry, wrong number"—the last line of the play. They'd have to learn to use old-fashioned telephones. That would be hysterical. There must be plenty in Mr. Markey's storage room. Mr. Markey. Would they still be allowed to use his props? Danny would check with Kylie.

The biggest surprise in casting wasn't Hannah. Out of character, but he'd known how much she wanted the part and how hard she'd worked to get it. No, the shocker was Carol getting a bit part. That meant she would not get the lead she wanted in *The Valiant*, and that Dr. D was going to cast the new girl. Dr. D might be making a mistake. He might not have done Blair a favor if the other girls decided to take it out on her. She was cute enough to be accepted by the other kids at school, but maybe not with Drama Club members.

But how about the other show? Danny could tell the kids were becoming impatient.

Finally, Dr. D held up another sheet of paper. "Now for *The Valiant*," he said. It was pretty much what Danny predicted. Porter would be the prisoner, James Dyke. Once he pulled on the black cap, it was all but certain. Stephen Boulder, who was the wizard in the last show, would play Warden Holt and Seth, the prison chaplain. Seth had wanted Dyke, but the chaplain was a great part, and Porter and Seth got along fine. Kevin McCloud would have two parts, jailer and attendant.

"I was impressed by Blair's audition," Dr. D concluded. "I've decided to give her a chance with the part of Josephine Paris."

The room went silent, and most of the girls stared daggers at Blair. Only Hannah spoke up. "Congrats, Blair. We're glad you've joined us."

Hannah had changed so much since he'd first met her, Danny thought. She knew what it was like to be the new girl. He looked out the window. It had started to snow furiously. Looked as if they were in for a major storm.

Dr. D noticed, too. "Uh-oh. We'd better call it quits. Read-through of *Sorry, Wrong Number* in the Green Room on Tuesday, and *Valiant* on Thursday. I'll block both plays right here next Saturday, the first day of Winter Break.

Coming up—his birthday and Christmas, Danny thought. The year was going by so fast.

A S SOON AS SUNDAY DINNER was over, Shaila grabbed Laurel's arm. "Let's escape to our room," she said, "before anyone can organize us into something. Wait until I tell you what I heard!"

Laurel had no objection, although a big part of her wished she still had her single room. Shaila's roommate had just been fostered, and Shaila had pushed hard for Laurel to move in with her. Mrs. Duncan had thought it a fine idea. It was working out okay, but Laurel wasn't used to talking quite so much. At least she didn't have time to brood about herself, and she'd insisted that Shaila understand that study time meant exactly that.

"Well, okay, at least until I have to go meet Hannah."

"Are you kidding? Have you looked out the window lately?" Shaila shook her head. "You wouldn't even make it to the grove, and Hannah definitely isn't coming here. Barbara said she heard that Castle Bluff schools are closed tomorrow. It's really bad out!"

"Oh, well." Laurel sighed. Two weeks since she'd seen Hannah. Soon she'd be forgotten, even though she was certain Hannah meant well. But snow, plays, and schoolwork would give Hannah other things to think about.

Laurel stretched out on her bed. "One hour," she said. "Then both of us better write our book reports." No snow day for them! "So what did you hear?"

Shaila bounced on the end of Laurel's bed. "I found out why we can't go to the Drama Club meetings at the castle."

"So did I," Laurel said. "Mrs. Duncan told me. It's because some of our kids could be in danger if their relatives found them." Such as you, she decided not to add.

"Unh-uh, nope. Well, maybe that's true, but it's not the whole story. I heard Mrs. Duncan talking to her sister. They didn't know I could hear. Mrs. Duncan is worried about that teacher coming so often. Her nephew at the castle says he's okay, but she has a bad feeling about it. It seems he's been asking a lot of questions about you—personal ones."

"Oh, Dr. D is all right. He just wants to make sure I'm okay." In truth, Laurel did think Dr. D seemed too interested in her. Maybe it was because he knew about the awful mess with Avery and her family.

"Anyway, Mrs. Duncan told her sister not to let him in if he comes again, and if it keeps on happening, she'll see about getting a restraining order."

"Oh, wow! Too much!"

Then Shaila started to giggle. "I'm starting to wonder if I'm rooming with a celebrity—a very important person."

Laurel tossed her pillow at her. "That must be it. I'll give you my autograph after we write our book reports. First one done gets to eat the other's dessert at supper!" That threat insured that Shaila would get going. Laurel didn't much like dessert anyway.

Danny shivered. Mentally, he had planned on school being cancelled again today. No such luck! On days like this, he sometimes wished he hadn't joined swim team. Why would anyone swim when the temperature outside barely recorded zero? Oh, well, once he jumped into the water he'd change his mind. First making sure that a dripping coat wouldn't destroy his books and papers, he hung it in his locker. Today is Tuesday, he told himself firmly. It just feels like Monday.

But what a weekend! Porter was finally able to go home yesterday afternoon. Worst storm in decades, people said, although Danny remembered some just as bad. They'd had their SSC meeting but didn't accomplish anything. Yes, the sign on Hannah's locker was menacing and serious, but what could they do at this point? And other than Hannah trying to visit Markey Home on Sundays, there wasn't a thing they could do to help Laurel. Their SSC meeting was the shortest on record. Decorating Hannah's basement was fun, though.

Danny stopped suddenly. It wasn't over. There, on Hannah's locker, was another sign. "Two Dad's wears Mom?" He folded it into his gym bag. So he knew two things about the culprit: he or she was a swimmer and a terrible student—at least in English!

There was a Drama Club officers' meeting after read-through today. He'd stick around and talk to Porter and Hannah then.

But the officers' meeting never happened. Read-through went fine, Hannah thought. Because of yesterday's snow day, everyone but her knew their lines. She did fine with the first five pages, though, and her personal goal for completion was next Saturday. Dr. D was pleased with her. "You won't have trouble learning your part," he said. "The trick will be the character. Yes, you need to age yourself, but try to get in touch with Mrs. Stevenson. Although she is unlikable, you must like her. Try to find some empathy. Picture someone you really don't like but understand what made them that way. You may not like them but do understand their circumstances."

Avery's mother, Hannah thought. That's who will be my model. Not a pleasant person at all, but you can't help feeling sorry for her when you learn her circumstances. Mrs. Stevenson may or may not be an invalid, but she certainly thinks she is. And she's stuck in bed and can't get help. She's terrified. The poor woman! Hannah began to figure out how to play the role. She would be whiny, but not so much that the audience would be pleased when she was killed.

"We'll block on Saturday," Dr. D said. "The telephone operators will use music stands and stools, and the rest of you will simply stand in a spotlight. Hannah, of course, will be in a bed Leland says we can use. *The Valiant* won't be much more difficult. Two simple adjacent offices, that's all we need."

Although the read-through had not taken long, Hannah could see it was growing dark outside. More snow? It had better be a short meeting, she thought.

Then Porter joined them and said all after-school activities were cancelled because of the new storm coming in. "School will probably be called off again tomorrow. My dad is coming to pick up Hannah, Danny, and me right now."

Dr. D shrugged. "At least we finished the read-through."

Porter, Danny, and Hannah exchanged looks. Porter's dad wasn't normally what you would call jovial, but now he was beyond solemn, even for him. His hands gripped the stirring wheel, and he stared straight ahead. Maybe the roads were icy, Porter thought.

Dad said nothing when he dropped off Hannah and Danny. "Call me," Danny mouthed as he left the car. Porter nodded.

"Dad, is something wrong?"

Dad paused, and then pulled over. "It's my father in Colorado. He died this morning."

"Oh, I'm sorry, Dad. And poor Grams!" The news was not unexpected. Gramps had been in and out of the hospital for almost a year. Porter sort of wished he could feel some sorrow, but he didn't really like him much, and it seemed to him that Grams was happier when he wasn't around. "What will Grams do?"

"Too soon to say. I'm in the middle of a big case, and I can't possibly go out there. I'm afraid we're in for a big discussion at home."

"I guess." If there was one thing Porter was not in the mood for, it was a big discussion.

The whole family, with the exception of baby Zoe—mercifully asleep—had gathered in the kitchen. Also present was Aunt Jane,

Danny's mother. Mom's best friend—that made sense. Mom was definitely flustered.

"Oh, good, you're home, Porter. You've heard the news then. Now, how would you feel about spending Christmas with Grams? She's going to need your help again."

"What?" he blurted. "But I was just there!"

"Yes, I know," Mom said, "but you get along so well with her." In other words, Mom did not. Grams had wanted Dad to marry someone else that he'd dated before he even met Mom.

Both parents were smiling at him, expecting that he'd bail them out again. Porter, the good child, the one who always helped and made peace. This, at last, was too much!

"No," he said, quietly but firmly. "I love Grams, but I was there last Christmas, most of the summer, and just a few weeks ago at Thanksgiving." He looked at his sister for help.

Beth understood immediately. "He has the lead in a play, and the performance is right after winter break. He wouldn't be able to keep the part."

"Then you go, Beth," Mom said.

Slowly, Beth shook her head. "We should all go to the memorial service, I think, but that's it. I want to spend Christmas at home this year. Besides, there's a dance at Crofts, and . . ."

"And everything," Kelly said. She'd refused to leave the room. "I'm old enough to have an opinion. I think Grams should come here, where all her friends are."

"And the service could be held in her old church," Porter agreed.

"But she needs help out there right now," Dad said. "And I can't possibly go. That leaves you, Sue."

"Your sister is there."

Porter bit his tongue. Aunt Sandy was a total flake, and everyone knew it.

"But Zoe!"

Porter was about to rush in with an offer to take care of Zoe but stopped himself just in time. Was taking care of Zoe how he planned to spend winter break. No! And he could see the same reaction on Beth's face.

"I'm sure your mother would be glad to come over and help," Dad said, and then seemed to wait for the next objection. But it was Aunt Jane's turn.

"You don't want to go alone," she said. "I understand. I've always wanted to see Colorado. I'll go with you."

And one, two, three, the problem was solved, without Porter being part of the solution—for once. Aunt Jane would be the mediator between Mom and Grams. It was about time for them to come to terms.

"I'll call my mother and tell her you and Jane will be there as soon as you can get a flight out of here."

It was over, Porter decided, heading for his bedroom. There was still tension between his parents, but it didn't have to be his problem. Beth had followed him, but he wasn't in the mood to talk it over again. Evidently, she wasn't either. She patted him on the shoulder before retreating into her own room. "You stood up for yourself, Porter," she said. "I'm proud of you."

"So what was that about?"

Danny shrugged. "No idea, but I don't think I'd like to be Porter right now. Look, Hannah, I need to talk to you and your dad about something that happened. Could I go over to your house after supper?"

"Sure, but can't you tell me now?"

"Better to talk later. I've got to let Bingo out before the snow gets any worse." Danny hurried inside, knowing he was leaving Hannah in the lurch and that he was not being fair. But he needed a few minutes away from disturbing thoughts. He needed his well-adjusted family. Mostly he needed Mom.

But Mom was not to be. Instead, Danny found Dad rummaging through the refrigerator. "She's with your Aunt Sue," Dad said. Quickly, he let Danny know what was going on at Porter's house. "I don't think she'll be home anytime soon. Trying to figure out what we might have for supper."

"I'll help," Danny said. Hot dogs and baked beans would be a good option, something Mom thought more suitable for a summer picnic.

Dad fell in with the plan immediately, adding a bag of potato chips to the suggested menu. "Let's eat early," he said, and told Danny to fetch Kylie and Roe.

At the table Danny considered bringing up the subject of the new poster on Hannah's locker, but then decided he didn't want to. This was nice, just the four of them. He told them about the read-through at the castle, learned about Kylie's upcoming audition, and shared Roe's pleasure that Eric, her old boyfriend, had finally asked her on a date.

He offered to do the dishes—just stalling—but Kylie and Roe insisted he'd done his share. No putting it off any longer. It was time to go to Hannah's.

Scene Eight — Is it possible?

Mr. Rendina studied the sign "I wonder —" He shook his head. "You wonder what?" Hannah was shaken. She'd really thought it wouldn't happen again.

Uncle Martin answered. "He wonders if the writer is that poor in English or is being ignorant intentionally."

Danny nodded. "That's what I was thinking. At first I thought I'd take it to an English teacher to see if they recognized the person. Then I thought that might not be the best idea."

"At least not yet," Hannah's dad agreed. "You found it early this morning. So do you think that person may be on a swim team?"

"I did at first, but it might have been left Friday after school. No school yesterday."

"My problem is the only person I can think of doing such a thing to any of you is Avery. Could that be possible? What about the group of girls who were her friends?"

Hannah shrugged. "I don't think so. They pretty much ditched her even before Betsy was kidnapped." The little dog yipped at the sound of her name. Hannah picked her up and held her close.

"I agree," Danny said. "I don't think they're even friends with each other now. And Porter saw a boy racing around the corner when the first sign was hung."

"And a girl would be noticed in the boys' locker room. The person who's being mean to us is a boy," Hannah concluded. "I don't know what we should do next."

They sat waiting, thinking. Finally, Uncle Martin made a point. "Nothing more happened to Danny because the boy —and I agree about that—succeeded. A second attempt was made on Hannah because the first didn't. What if you allow it to happen? In other words, if he posts something again on your locker, leave it there."

"Could you handle that, Hannah?" her dad asked.

Hannah shook her head. "I don't know. What if someone does ask me about my two dads? What do I say?"

"The truth," Danny said. "We talk about your two dads, but we're just being friendly. No one has more than one biological dad. Say you live with your dad and your uncle. Most people will think your Uncle Martin is your dad's brother. That's what I thought for a long time."

"Maybe. I don't know."

Dad and Uncle Martin shook their heads. They didn't know either.

Hannah spent the entire day learning her lines. For the first time, she could see the wisdom of doing it that way. While she preferred learning lines and blocking together, for this particular part, Dr. D was right. She would have no blocking because she would remain in bed the entire time. Even though there were a lot of lines, learning them was the easy part. Character was what mattered. How could she portray an unhappy, unpleasant woman, whose husband probably wanted her dead?

"I need to do something else. Any ideas, Betsy?"

Betsy yawned and gave a half-hearted stretch before curling up again into a tiny ball.

Hannah laughed. "No, I don't want to take a nap, and you're obviously not up for a walk." She looked out the window. "Still snowing, but it should stop fairly soon." Maybe she could talk Danny into coming over — to work a puzzle or play a video game, or something. "I'm bored," she told Betsy. "That doesn't happen to me often." She picked up her phone. "Danny, I'm bored. Can you come over, or could I go there? Okay, I'll see you tomorrow."

Hannah stretched out next to Betsy. "Danny can't," she said. "They're driving Mrs. Kennedy and Porter's mom to Union Station. All the planes have been grounded, so they're taking a train to Colorado. In this weather? Crazy!" Betsy gave a slight sympathetic whimper. That is, Hannah decided it was sympathetic. More likely, Betsy was telling her to go away.

But darn, she did not need to nap. And she didn't feel like reading. "I know! I'll work on *Stage Directions*!" She hadn't done one in ages, and if she worked hard, maybe she could distribute copies during the Drama Club meeting tomorrow. If not then, there wouldn't be another until after winter break.

She grabbed her theater bag and headed downstairs to the kitchen. A change of scenery and a snack might help. Coke, a bowl of pretzels, paper and pen—she was all set. She started with the descriptions of the plays that Dr. D had included, followed by the cast list and theater schedule. True, practically everyone already had the information, but this was for the record, the club's history. Then she turned to the computer and looked up Agnes Moorehead. Everyone knew *The Wizard of Oz* and some might be interested that she'd once played Hannah's part. Possibly include the last poem from Laurel, and maybe a George Spelvin letter. Hannah reached into her George envelope. "Whatever it says, I'll answer it," she whispered. She read it over. "Typical," she said. "People keep talking about the same darned thing. They're jealous because someone else got the part they wanted. Ho-hum. Oh, well, this feels a little different."

Dear George Spelvin,

I feel kind of spoiled talking about this. I was cast recently in a play and got a lead. It's a fine part, and I should be grateful. The thing is, it's not the part I wanted. That went to one of my best friends. I know they'll be great, but I think I'd be better. Also, I look the part, and they don't. Do you have any advice on how to get over these feelings?

Signed: Spoiled and Jealous

Hannah wished she knew how long this had been in the George envelope. She thought the writer must be talking about the one-acts. Clever of "S and J" to say they. It was impossible to tell whether the writer was a boy or a girl. If it were a girl with a lead, the writer would have to be the new kid, Blair. Each play had only one female lead; the rest were bit parts. Did Blair even know about George Spelvin? Hannah didn't think so.

There were three male leads in *The Valiant*. She knew the writer wasn't Porter, who definitely got the part he wanted. So it must be Seth or Stephen Boulder. No way would roly-poly Stephen think he looked like murderer, James Dyke. Until Porter put on the black cap, Hannah considered Seth a shoe-in. Yes, Porter and Seth were friends, but Hannah had always noticed some tension between the two boys. Just as well she didn't want either for a boyfriend anymore. She needed to write humorously, but, at the same time, seriously. This was important to Seth.

Dear S and J,

You are making me, George Spelvin, the anonymous actor, grateful. I never have anything but small parts and am never given proper credit for the parts I do play. Thank you for making me happy to be me.

You got a lead! Congratulations! I'll bet most of the people who auditioned got bit parts or nothing. You must be a very good actor. You say you would have been better than the person who got the part you wanted. Maybe you would. George has no way of knowing. Sometimes you just have to trust the director. Surely you can't blame your friend for wanting the same thing.

Your job now is to do the best you can for the good of the play. As far as your feelings go, they belong to you. Go ahead and feel them, without acting upon them. Maybe you should examine your friendship. Why are you friends? What do you like about your friend? If it helps,

George wants you to know that being jealous of a friend's success is perfectly normal.

Your friend, who is jealous of you,
George Spelvin

"That's rather good, Hannah," she congratulated herself. And special thanks to the advice columnist in the Trib, who gave her clues as to what to say about feelings. Now, what else might she put in the newsletter? The last meeting before Christmas, even though there would be rehearsals all during break, they needed a special activity. Food, of course, and gifts!

"Got it!" But was there enough time, and did she need permission? The rest of the officers would go along with it, but what about Dr. D?

Her cell phone rang. Danny maybe? No! "Dr. D! You must be psychic!"

Dr. D laughed. "I've never been accused of that before."

"No, really, I was just wishing I could talk to you. I've got an idea for tomorrow's meeting, but there's so little time to make it happen." Quickly, she told Dr. D her plan. "And I could bring lots of extra stuff for people who don't look at their emails in time."

"As long as you take that into consideration, I'm fine with it," Dr. D said. "We don't really have much of anything on the agenda tomorrow — assuming we have school."

"I'll have a new *Stage Directions*," Hannah promised. Then she remembered. "But you called me. I'm sorry. I should have let you talk first."

"Not a problem. I wanted to talk about tomorrow, too. Hannah, I was wondering if you'd be my assistant director for *The Valiant*?"

"Wow! I'd love to!"

"And you didn't even stop to think it over. Most of the rehearsals will be for both plays, so you'll be there anyway, but most of *The Valiant* cast will leave when their rehearsal is over."

Hannah agreed. "Or not come until it's time for them. Any particular reason you chose me?"

"Several, although I think you'll be good is the main reason. But also because there's only one girl in the play, and I think that it would be wise to have another girl present."

That made sense—for Blair's sake, as well as Dr. D's. "It wouldn't hurt to have an adult woman there, too," she said.

"Any ideas? I don't know people as well as you do."

"Yes," Hannah said. "I could call Gee. I'll bet she misses us as much as we miss her—and her donuts."

"Good thought. Oh, one more thing. After rehearsal tomorrow, I'd like to discuss something with you, Danny, and Porter. Would you ask them to stay behind?"

Odd, but Hannah agreed. Dr. D thanked her profusely, and the call ended.

Danny and Porter's text responses were pretty much the same. Danny was sorry, but he had to get right home after Drama Club. He had to take the activity bus because Dad was working. He liked the gift exchange idea. "Sorry, Hannah.," Porter wrote. "I have to go home to help Grandma with Zoe, who is not happy Mom is gone. I can stay after rehearsals Saturday."

Hannah decided to assume Danny could stay Saturday too, and she texted Dr. D about the change of plans. A thumbs-up reply followed immediately.

Goodbye boredom, Hannah thought, as she opened the file of Drama Club members. "Thanks, Grandma, for always accusing me of being inappropriate. Well, Grandma, I'm about to be extremely inappropriate!" Quickly, she wrote and sent the evite.

> *How Frightfully Inappropriate!*
>
> *And terribly last minute, but your editor just got the idea. Tomorrow at the Drama Club meeting, we will hold our first Inappropriate Gift Exchange. Please bring a badly wrapped gift that no one could possibly want.*

Open those dresser drawers! Rummage through your closets. Clean out your school locker. Don't go out shopping in the snow. If you pay money for it, it cost too much! Bring a gift — get a gift! That's how it works!

Now to clean her room for extra presents. And then maybe she'd bake some cookies. This was going to be so much fun.

"You seem a bit down," Laurel's music teacher said. "I thought voice lessons were the highlight of your week."

Laurel smiled, and then sighed. "They are, Mrs. Hill, thanks to you. I guess I'm just wishing we could have snow days, too, like the other schools in town. Not that I had much to do when we did have them."

"I know exactly what you mean," Mrs. Hill said. Even when I was way past school age, I always found snow days exciting. They always took me right back to childhood. I always seemed to forget how annoyed I was when we had to stay later in springtime to make up for it."

Laurel giggled, feeling much better. "The snow doesn't keep us from walking downstairs at this school."

"And we'll get out on time in May when your town friends are wishing their schools had air-conditioning. Now you'd better warm up that voice, and then we'll find the perfect song for your solo at the holiday assembly."

Her town friends — that's what Hannah, Danny, and Porter were now. It didn't seem right or make sense that she wasn't able to see them, except in secret. Other kids at the home had visitors, at least some of them did.

IF IT WEREN'T FOR HANNAH, today's Drama Club would have been a big fat bomb. At least, that was Danny's opinion. He thought most people would have skipped the meeting if it hadn't been for Hannah's email. The Inappropriate Gift Exchange was a brilliant idea, so much better than just calling it a grab bag. And Hannah put a theater spin on things by insisting that everyone pretend to be delighted by the gift and explain what they would do with it. The chocolate cookies and latest issue of *Stage Directions* added to the fun.

Danny opened his gift, wrapped in old newspapers that were turning yellow. He checked the dates first in case they were the real gift. "A tutu!" he exclaimed finally. "Excellent! Just what I wanted!" When Hannah and others stared, daring him to continue, he thought fast. "You see, since Dr. D loves old-fashioned plays, he's bound to put on *The Nutcracker* next year. If I start practicing right away, he might decide I'd make a perfect Sugar Plum Fairy." Danny pulled on the tutu and pranced around, accompanied by roars of laughter.

Blair's gift was courtesy of Hannah's extras, since her email address was not yet available. A bag of pencil stubs inspired Blair to rave about all the wonderful stories and poems that had come from these tired remains. "I'm inspired," she said. "I will start my own writers' museum with these. People shall come from miles and miles to visit. I will make tons of money, but I won't charge my Drama Club friends." She grinned.

Not bad for someone brand new, Danny thought. It couldn't be easy to move in December in your eighth-grade year.

Hopefully, the smiley faces at the end of the meeting taught Dr. D something. Drama Club needed to be fun, as well as worthwhile, or they would lose members. Dr. D was great, but he still didn't quite get it. Not everyone wanted to act or help put on a play.

Whatever Dr. D wanted to talk to them about had to do with Laurel, Porter decided, munching on a leftover cookie before the read-through began. He'd noticed Dr. D listening in when Hannah said she was hoping to see Laurel on Sunday. When was that, exactly? Maybe last Saturday, and then Hannah couldn't go to the home the next day because of weather. Why in the world was Dr. D so interested in Laurel? True, having Hannah be assistant director so that Blair wouldn't be the only girl was a good idea—Hannah would be a big help—but Porter would bet money that another reason was for Dr. D to learn more about Laurel.

The read-through was late in starting because of lingering members, chatting about possible activities after the plays were over. Danny was telling people about a possible trip to the high school to see the play his sister was in—*Gaslight*, a scary thriller. Porter's own sister, Beth, was thrilled at the chance to design the lights, but he'd share that another time.

While waiting, Porter read a copy of *Stage Directions*. He'd forgotten to pick up one on Thursday. Could the George Spelvin letter be about *The Valiant*? Did an unknown boy want his part, or was a girl unhappy not to have Hannah's? The writer did get a lead, though, and there were no male leads in Hannah's play. Seth could have written the letter, although Porter hoped not. It was also possible that Hannah didn't have a letter, and wrote a mock one, herself.

Oh, good, a poem! Porter wondered if Dr. D knew that Laurel was the prolific poet. He didn't think so.

<u>*The Twelve Days of WB*</u>
by a prolific, poetic prodigy

On the first day of Winter Break
Great Thespis gave to me
A voice so the crowd could hear me.

On the second day of Winter Break
Great Thespis gave to me
Two shiny spotlights
and a voice so the crowd could hear me.

(Continue in this fashion)

Three acts of script
Four stage directions
Five vital props
Six sides of blocking
Seven costume changes
Eight crowded exits
Nine tricky sound cues
Ten dress rehearsals
Eleven directors crying
Twelve in the audience

And a voice so the crowd could hear me.

Porter just managed not to laugh out loud. Most people—especially English teachers—had no idea Laurel was so talented!

"Okay, cast," Dr. D cried out. "Please arrange your chairs in a circle."

The best thing about being assistant director, Hannah thought, was that she and Blair had become instant friends. Maybe because during *Valiant* rehearsals they were the only girls present, but Hannah thought there was more to it than that. They both loved animals and books and trees and probably had lots more in common. Now that they had each other's contact info, the texts flew back and forth.

Gee had joined them this Saturday, and the welcome aroma of donut holes wafted in from the kitchen. "Don't get used to it," Gee warned. "This is just a welcome." But Hannah thought something yummy would be a common occurrence. Gee had been thrilled to be invited back.

Blair had asked her over to her house after rehearsal. Darn! Hannah would have loved to go. But today, she, Porter, and Danny had to stay to find out whatever Dr. D had in mind. The date had been fixed when they couldn't on Thursday, so that was that. "Sorry," she said, "but my dad has plans. I can another time."

"Deal," Blair said. "Sometime over break would be great. Uh, almost forgot. I saw a weird sign on your locker about two dads. What was that about?"

Hannah shrugged. She'd seen it yesterday morning and had let it hang until after school. No one else had asked her, although she'd received a few strange looks. "I'm not sure," she said. "I don't have two dads. My parents are divorced. I live with my dad and uncle."

Blair nodded. "Someone is trying to be mean, to hurt you."

"Well, that someone won't succeed." Hannah hoped that was the end of it, but she'd stay alert.

Blair had been complementary about Hannah's acting. It was going well, Hannah thought. *Sorry, Wrong Number* was completely blocked, and a double bed had been brought into the ballroom from one of the castle's many bedrooms. Hannah had been completely wrong about the part being easier because she was in bed all the time. It was hard to show expression without the use of her legs. She'd never realized how much of her acting came from bodily movement. Dr. D had been right about that. The whole body acts; not just a person's voice and face. At least she'd learned her lines. Now she must concentrate on the rest.

Scene Ten – Dr. D's Story

THE GROUP GATHERED AROUND ONE of the tables in the kitchen. All seemed nervous. No one spoke. After all, Dr. D had called for this meeting. It was up to him to begin. Porter nibbled on another half sandwich Dr. D had provided — and waited.

Danny was on his third half sandwich and about to grab the remaining donut holes when the others stared at him. Shrugging, he took one and then glanced out the window. Cold, of course, but the sun was shining. They'd skip calling a parent today, he decided, and walk home along the cliffs. They'd talk over whatever Dr. D said — if he ever got around to saying it. It wasn't like him to be so hesitant.

Hannah was positive Dr. D wanted to talk about Laurel. Nothing else made sense. Porter and Danny weren't involved in both plays, only Hannah. This was not about assisting. She was happy to help, of course, and being at rehearsals was good for Blair. But that wasn't the real reason Dr. D had requested this meeting. He knew she tried to go to the Markey Home every Sunday. That's what he wanted to talk about.

Dr. D held up a small bag that looked as if it contained a box. He started to open it but put it down again and shook his head before speaking. "I hardly know where to begin."

"Begin with Laurel," Porter said. "That's why we're here." Hannah and Danny nodded.

Dr. D stared at them, and then sighed. "My story starts much earlier, but you're right. It ends, or it might end, with Laurel." He took a long sip of water. "For many years, I lived in Des Moines, Iowa, with my wife and daughter, Melissa, whom we called Missy. Missy was always a troubled child. I'm not sure why. As a teen, she fell in with the wrong crowd. At least that's what we thought, but it is possible she influenced her friends as much as they did her. That took a long time for her mother and me to accept."

Hannah exchanged glances with the boys. Why had Dr. D chosen them for such an adult conversation?

"Then when Missy was a junior and struggling badly in school, my wife was diagnosed with cancer, and my attention was on her—when I wasn't directing a show for our community theater and teaching English. Soon, I gave up both."

"And Missy got worse?" Danny wondered, thinking about Roe's brother. In some ways, the stories seemed similar.

Dr. D nodded. "Margaret died, and Missy dropped out of school and—disappeared."

"And you never saw her again?" Hannah guessed.

"Well, not for a long time. I got occasional postcards and requests for money, which I honored occasionally by sending checks to a P.O. address. Finally, when I never heard back, I stopped sending them. She'd made her point. The only thing that interested her was my money, and I barely had enough for myself anymore. I returned to teaching."

Porter squirmed. When would he get around to Laurel? Dr. D confiding in them was—he grasped for the word—*inappropriate*. "We need to start home soon," he said.

"And I'm making you uncomfortable. I understand. I'll try to get to the point. Six years later, Missy knocked on my door. With her was a young child, a girl, maybe around three. Both were unkempt and, I thought, hungry. Had Missy been at all contrite, I might have reacted differently. But she was arrogant and demanding, and I'll admit I saw red. I told her if she was going to act that way, she could just leave. And she did. She grabbed the child's hand and pulled her down the stairs. Several years later, I received word that Missy had died, but there was no word about the child. My granddaughter."

Hannah gasped. "You think Laurel is your granddaughter?"

Dr. D smiled. "I think there's a very good chance. I've been searching since I learned Missy died. I hired a detective for as long as I could afford to. He tracked her down to a church in Des Moines, where she had been abandoned as a young child. We were lucky in finding a few possible placements, but then the path stopped."

"Laurel told me you asked if she ever lived in Des Moines," Hannah said, "but she didn't remember. She said she'd lived in lots of places."

"She told me she hadn't," Dr. D said. "Well, in early spring last year, another detective I'd hired said she might have been placed somewhere in northern Illinois, perhaps Gurnee. I was unfamiliar with the area. While staying in a motel in Waukegan, I happened to see an ad for your school's *Secret Garden*. I guess I was feeling nostalgic and homesick, for it was my wife's favorite book, and we both loved children's theater, so I came down here, and —"

"And saw Laurel Mullen," Danny finished.

"That's what happened. And she looked almost identical to Missy as a young teen, and her voice . . . Well, I determined to learn more about the girl, and early last summer, I applied for a teaching position. Normally, I might have been considered too old, but the principal was very interested in my theater background."

"We're glad about that," Porter said. "We might not have had any plays or Drama Club this year if you hadn't come. I hope you decide to stay."

"I have decided to — whether or not I find my granddaughter. I'm convinced she's Laurel, but I have no proof, and Mrs. Duncan isn't about to help me."

Hannah nodded. "And you want us to. How?"

Finally, Dr. D took a small box from a paper bag. "By giving Laurel this," he said.

Porter whistled. "I know what that is. My grandmother in Colorado is into that stuff. It's an Ancestor DNA kit. Grams just discovered that some of our ancestors were Seneca Indians."

"Fascinating," Dr. D said. "Yes, you can find out a lot from your own spit sample. Many people use it to find their relatives, to learn who they are. I am hoping, Hannah, that you'll tell Laurel my story and give her this kit."

Hannah reached over to take the box but noticed Porter staring at her — a warning stare, she thought. Porter didn't think she should. She grappled for an excuse. "Dr. D, I might not see her tomorrow. The weather forecast isn't great, and my parents were talking about doing something. The next time I see her, I will tell her your story. Perhaps she'll remember more."

"And the kit?"

"Hannah should think it over first," Porter said, "and maybe you could talk with Leland about it. After all, Mrs. Duncan is his aunt."

Dr. D did not look happy, but how could he object? "I understand. I'll hang on to the kit for now and will think about telling Leland. He's not the easiest person in the world to talk to."

"I think he's just shy," Danny said. "Try Janet, his wife. We'd better get going. My dad is going to wonder where I am."

Quickly, they gathered their belongings and escaped — that's what it felt like — down the back stairway.

"Wow!" Hannah said, once they were outside. "I didn't expect that. I don't know what to do."

"We do what we decided when we knew Laurel needed help. We'll talk to our parents, starting with Danny's dad and your uncle."

"Agreed," Danny said. "Now let's clear our heads by taking the long way home."

I WAS THINKING," PORTER SAID, as they neared the cliffs, "that we should talk to my dad, too—maybe after Zoe goes to sleep tonight."

"Why?" Hannah asked. After all, Mr. Walters hadn't been involved so far.

"Because he's a lawyer," Danny said. "Good idea, Porter. Dr. D needs a lawyer. Maybe if your dad is the wrong kind, he can recommend someone."

Hannah walked a few steps ahead. Talking to a lawyer was probably a good idea, she thought. The situation seemed too grownup for the SSC. Would she have taken the kit if Porter hadn't stopped her? Maybe. And then she would have regretted it once she got home. She didn't know much about DNA kits, and she thought Porter was right. The kits probably weren't meant for kids. Somehow, she felt used, and she didn't like it one bit.

"Hannah, stop! Get away from the cliff!" Hannah looked down, and then retreated quickly. The cliff had eroded massively since her last walk here. One more step, and down she'd go. Not into Lake Michigan, fortunately, but it would have been a long slide down to the beach.

"Oh, gosh! Thanks, Porter!" She was cold and scared now, and she wanted to go home. "Let's walk faster," she said, "away from the cliffs."

"Too much rain and melting snow," Danny said. "Leland will be lucky if he doesn't lose his castle."

Porter shook his head. "Not for many years, but someday."

There wasn't much more to say. None of them wanted to talk about Dr. D's story or why he had reached out to them. They were lost in their private thoughts until—

"Help! Oh, please, help!"

They rushed forward and saw a complete breakaway of the cliff, directly over Lake Michigan. Below, in the water, someone was struggling to stay afloat. Danny gave orders as he found a safer place to descend.

"Quick, Hannah, give me your jacket. Now, call 9-1-1. We need an ambulance fast. Porter, follow me. I'm a better swimmer than you, but I'll need your help—and your jacket!"

The SSC was used to acting quickly in an emergency. Hannah called for an ambulance, and then to her father and Danny's. She gave clear directions to the sudden ending of Cabot Drive, where the only way forward was directly into the mighty lake that was acting like a fierce ocean today.

Danny could tell it was a boy, and he kept calling out encouragement. "I'm coming. Help is on the way. Try to stay calm." What a stupid thing to say, he told himself. He'd taken off his jacket, shoes, and blue jeans that would have weighed him down. He plunged into the ice-cold water, as he heard a siren in the distance.

Porter stood watching, prepared to follow Danny into the water. He couldn't help hoping it wouldn't be necessary. He wasn't a strong swimmer or strong anything, he decided. He'd always thought being smart was enough. It wasn't, but he should use that brain to figure out what they should do next, once the boy was out of the water. Porter recognized him now. He was the one who'd put the note on Hannah's locker. Maybe they'd finally get some answers.

Just as Danny was certain he'd failed and both he and the boy would drown, he reached shore, and Porter helped drag both of them onto the cold sand. The boy was unconscious. Porter threw the largest jacket, Danny's, plus Hannah's over him, and handed Danny his own. Porter wished he could help Danny, who was white and shivering all over, instead of this stranger enemy, but the boy would certainly die without aid. He started CPR, although he'd only watched videos of how to do it.

Then the ambulance arrived, along with Hannah's and Danny's fathers, and Kylie and Brad, who'd been at Danny's house when Hannah's call had come through. Porter and Hannah dropped back. They watched helplessly as the ambulance carried Danny and the boy away. Danny's father was about to follow when Brad yelled out, "I'm going, too. That's Nick, my brother!"

Shaila had been in Mrs. Duncan's office all Saturday afternoon. Earlier, Laurel had seen people going in and out, including a couple with a small child. What was going on? The Markey Home was either a total bore or too stressful. At the moment, it was both. Laurel stretched out in bed to read and wait — until . . .

"Finally! You've been gone for hours. What happened?" Laurel simply couldn't read Shaila's expression. It was happy and sad at the same time. She guessed that was possible. "Please, Shaila, I've been going nuts here!"

Shaila sat on the opposite bed. "The craziest thing." She sighed. "Let me catch my breath."

Laurel put down her book. More waiting seemed intolerable.

"Okay, I'll tell you, and then let's go for a walk. It's cold, but I've got to get out of this building. I found out this afternoon that my parents have dumped me."

"Oh, no! That's terrible!" Laurel didn't know what else to say.

Shaila shook her head. "No, that's the good part. If they had claimed me again, I would have run away. But they've totally relinquished me. That was the actual word on the paper. My father is in jail, and my mother is in some combined rehab-mental institution. It's over. I don't have to be scared anymore."

Laurel would have loved to have real parents, but maybe having no parents was better than what Shaila had. "So, what's the bad part?"

Shaila stood and wandered around the room. She didn't seem to want to meet Laurel's eyes.

"Shaila?"

"I'm going to be fostered out."

"What?" Was she going to lose another friend?

"It's a young couple with a little girl. They can't have more children. If it works out, they may adopt me."

"And that's bad?"

Shaila's eyes welled with tears. "No, that's good, too. They're really nice, and the little girl is darling. They live in a beautiful home in Winnetka."

"How do you know they're not just looking for a live-in babysitter?"

"I don't, but Mrs. Duncan asked them every question imaginable, and she believes them. I do, too, and I can come back if it doesn't work out." Shaila crossed to Laurel's bed and put an arm around her. Stiffly, Laurel shrugged her off.

"The bad part is leaving you, Laurel. I am sorry about that."

"I'm fine. Grab your jacket. Let's go for that walk now." She wasn't fine, and both girls knew it.

LATE THAT NIGHT, DANNY STOPPED shivering. He'd wanted to go home, but his doctor was probably right having him stay in the hospital overnight to make sure. The shivering was due to—well, the lake had been damned cold, and it had taken forever for him to be completely dry. It was also caused by fear. Fear of not being able to save Nick. Fear that both of them would drown. And finally, fear that the doctor would find something wrong with his legs, considering that the accident that had nearly cost him his ability to walk was only a year ago. But he was okay, and Nick would be, too. Now he could sleep.

And in the morning, Kylie and Brad were at his bedside, and he felt just fine. "Well, hi," he said.

"As soon as you have your breakfast and your doctor checks you over, we're going to spring you," Kylie said. "We need you home. Bingo and Boots are being absolute brats."

Danny smiled. "Animals always know when something is off. I can't wait." Then he looked at Brad, who looked way more serious than usual. "How is Nick doing?"

Brad wiped away tears that had formed suddenly. "His doctor wants him to stay here a few more days, but he'll be okay, thanks to you." Then Brad seemed lost for words. He looked down and shuffled his feet.

"Go ahead, Brad. Danny will understand. It will be all right."

"I'll try," Brad practically whispered. "Well, you know that Nick wasn't doing that great—"

"You said he was in trouble a lot," Danny said.

"Trouble is right—one thing after the next. I-uh-was alone with him for a few minutes last night. He's pretty shook and also ashamed. You saved his life, and he's the one trying to cause all the trouble for you, Hannah, and Porter."

"Oh, wow," breathed Danny. "Why?"

"I don't have all the details yet, and I know he's planning to talk with you, but it has something to do with Avery paying him and giving him ideas what to do."

Danny nodded. "We thought Avery might be involved, but we couldn't figure out how. We couldn't see how she could get into the boys' locker room without being seen, and we don't think her family is still in Castle Bluff."

An important mystery was about to be solved, Danny thought, wondering why he wasn't furious. Maybe that's what happened if you saved someone's life. You kinda wanted to continue to be there for them.

"Nick will talk to you as soon as he's allowed to," Brad said. "But—"

"But Brad has a favor to ask," Kylie said, "and it's totally up to you, Danny."

"Okay."

Brad started. "This is hard. The thing is, Danny, we—that is, Mom, Dad, and me—wonder if you could hold off telling your parents what Nick did. We're afraid Nick will be in a lot of trouble if the police find out. And your dad's best friend is Sergeant Lodge, and your mom—"

"Is a hot head," Danny finished. "Yeah, I get it. I think Hannah and Porter need to know, but I'll ask them not tell anyone, except Porter can tell Beth. And Kylie or I should tell Roe. Then I'll decide more after I talk to Nick. That's the best I can do for now, Brad."

"Thank you, Danny. That makes a lot of sense. It's time for Nick to grow up."

Other than wishing she'd worn a different winter jacket yesterday, Hannah was fine the following morning. She definitely planned to see Laurel. But Dad and Uncle Martin put an end to that. One, because they felt she needed to keep warm because of her chill yesterday, and two because she made the mistake of telling them about the DNA kit. Porter was right; they didn't approve at all.

Uncle Martin was particularly enraged. "The idea! Basically trying to talk a minor into participating in an illegal conspiracy!"

"Well, maybe not that bad," Dad said, "but certainly a foolish idea. I'm glad Porter stopped you. Yes, you are too young. Porter's suggestion that Dr. D talk to Leland was right on target. But I can't help hoping Laurel is Dr. D's granddaughter. He's a fine man, Martin, and it sounds as if his life has been extremely difficult. Keep it to yourself, Hannah, but he lives in a run-down motel in Waukegan. He doesn't even have a home for Hannah and himself."

Uncle Martin nodded. "Well, one step at a time, as long as Hannah stays out of it."

But Laurel is my friend, Hannah thought. It feels like ages since I've seen her. Maybe next weekend. But I won't say anything about Dr. D's suspicions. She couldn't shake the feeling, though, that Laurel needed her—now! Taking a big chance, Hannah texted Blair and filled her in as much as possible. "Could you take my place?" she pleaded. "I can give you directions. I know it's a little weird. I just think she needs me."

"An adventure," Blair texted back. "Thanks. My parents are decorating the synagogue for a party tonight. I need something to do. Wish you could come, too. I'll tell you how it goes."

Hannah sighed. She wished she could, too. This might be better, though. She might be too tempted to tell Laurel about Dr. D.

Porter slammed down his cereal bowl, causing the milk to splatter all over his school shirt and pants. "I have officially lost my temper!"

"Then I suggest you find it soon," Grandma said. "We don't have time for such shenanigans."

Kelly giggled. "Shenanigans! That's a great word, Grandma. And you don't even have to tell us what it means. We get it!"

"As long as it isn't directed at me," Beth said, rising from the kitchen table. "Gotta rush. Meeting Priyanka to work on props." Beth grabbed her coat and school bag before escaping. Her brother and his friends were okay, but she no longer wanted to be involved in middle school drama. Her high school theater director had advised them to keep the drama on the stage. An excellent goal!

It was good Grandma was here, Porter thought, but he missed Mom, who would be as angry as he—once she learned the truth of what happened. He really wanted some time alone with Beth.

"I'm sorry," he said. "I was wrong to dump on all of you. But when I think of what could have happened to Danny."

"But Danny was released from the hospital and is just fine. And now, all three of you are heroes. Go change your clothes, and Kelly and I will clean up. I'll fix a breakfast tart for you to eat on the way to school."

A sudden wail complicated that plan. Zoe was definitely awake.

"You go, Grandma. I'll clean up after my messy brother." Kelly grinned at Porter, letting him know she sympathized.

"Thanks, Kelly. I'm sorry, Grandma."

"You're forgiven, but do try to settle down."

Porter bolted. "Mom come home, Mom come home," he muttered as he climbed the stairs. Dad was involved in a difficult legal case, and Grandma was doing her best, but it wasn't the same. Sure, Mom helping Grams was important, but they needed her right now.

Of course Porter hadn't minded helping Danny rescue Nick, even though it had cost him a winter jacket, but to learn that Nick was the person who used Danny's phone and posted the mean notes on Hannah's locker . . . He guessed that whatever Nick was planning on Saturday involved an anti-Porter scheme. *Why* was his main question.

Why would Brad's brother want to hurt his girlfriend's brother and friends?

"Please be there, Hannah. Please be there," Laurel whispered as she made her way toward their private bench. Such a lonely weekend! Without Shaila, she had no one. She finished all of her homework last night and got a head start on upcoming assignments. She'd looked around the tables at lunchtime to see if there was anyone even close to her age she might befriend. She'd probably spend the evening reading. That would be fine—if she could have a good catch-up with Hannah first. "Please," she said again.

But no! A stranger was sitting on their hidden bench. Someone who clearly didn't belong! Fighting tears, Laurel turned to start back.

"Wait," the strange girl called out. "Hannah sent me!"

"Hannah did? I'm afraid I don't know you."

The girl laughed. "Not many people do. My name is Blair Cummings. My family just moved to Castle Bluff, and I joined the Drama Club. Hannah thought it important that you know she can't come today."

Well, Hannah got that right, Laurel thought. "Why can't she come? The weather's okay."

Blair patted the seat next to her. "Sit down. Wait until you hear! It's quite the story." She pulled two Snickers candy bars from her jacket pocket, one for each of them.

Laurel liked Blair immediately. There was something about her—friendly but in a natural kind of way. She wasn't making a big deal out of coming. She was just there.

"So what happened?"

Blair told as much as she knew, which wasn't a great deal. "All I know is that Hannah, Danny, and Porter were walking along the cliffs when they spotted someone drowning. Danny jumped in and saved the kid's life. Porter did CPR, Hannah made phone calls, and they all gave up their coats. They're okay, but Danny had to stay overnight at the hospital, just to be sure. He's probably going home today. Hannah's dad kinda freaked out and said she had to stay home. I don't know about Porter."

"Wow! But who is the kid?"

"I don't know him. His name is Nick Michaels, and he's a sixth grader."

"I don't know him either. Is he okay?"

"Probably. He has to stay in the hospital longer."

Thank goodness Blair came, Laurel thought. She needed to think about something other than herself. "I'm glad you're here," she said. "Tell Hannah, please."

"So her vibes were correct," Blair said. "I know you used to go to CBMS, and that they still consider you the vice president of Drama Club."

Laurel gave a brief summation of why she was back at the Markey Home. "I am safer here, but I get lonely. Tell Hannah that my friend Shaila was fostered."

"I'll tell her. Hope things get better for you, Laurel," Blair said, standing to leave. "Maybe I can come again?"

"I'd like that," Laurel said.

"It's too bad we can't see you inside, especially when the weather is bad. Aren't you allowed visitors?"

"I don't know. I never had any when I lived here before, so I didn't think about it. I guess I'm afraid to ask because I'm afraid Mrs. Duncan will say no."

"Well, think about asking," Blair said. "It would be too weird if you can't."

"I'll try," Laurel said. "Thanks, Blair. See ya."

Laurel headed back to the house. But she felt better now. She'd just made another friend.

SHE GOT ON THE BUS to a chorus of "Hi, Hannah!" She was enjoying her fifteen minutes of fame, as Dad called it. She thought that meant it wouldn't last long, so she smiled and waved at her busmates. Hopefully, they would move on soon. Other things, like the plays and Laurel, were more important.

No rehearsal on Wednesdays, which Hannah thought was a good thing. This evening, she and Porter were to go to Danny's house to meet up with a reporter and photographer from the Chicago Tribune. They would tell their story of Nick's rescue and have their picture taken for the Sunday paper. But they would not reveal what Hannah had learned from Danny only last night—that Nick was the enemy who had tried to hurt them through his phone call and signs. Of course, they were right to rescue him, but still . . .

It was not being able to tell an adult that was hard, but Danny wanted to wait until he had a chance to talk things over with Nick. "I'm afraid the grownups won't act, well, grownup," he said. His father would be certain to call the police. Hannah's dad and uncle would feel threatened, and Porter's family had enough on their plate with a death in the family. Danny's and Porter's moms weren't even home yet.

Hannah shrugged. She guessed it was enough for now that Kylie, Roe, and Beth knew and agreed they should wait. She felt a little guilty not confiding in the adults. But what did they know, for sure? Just that Nick was in sixth grade and Brad's little brother. What could he possibly have against them?

As the bus approached the parking circle, Hannah's thoughts returned to after school and tonight. Porter was going home with

Danny, and Blair would accompany her — for the first time. Blair was going to help her pick out something to wear and pretend to be a reporter asking questions so Hannah could practice telling her story. Danny was the hero, of course, with Porter second in line. All she really did was give up her jacket and make emergency phone calls. But each part was important, like in a play. Blair hadn't had much of a chance to talk about her visit with Laurel. That was also on the *agenda*, as Seth would say.

Danny and Porter walked home, although they could have taken the bus. The thing is they needed to talk. The bus wouldn't be private enough for a conversation. Sure, the crowd was noisy, but Danny and Porter were celebrities. Someone was bound to listen in. And Danny's home was probably crazy, with Mom arriving home and deciding the house was a mess and that she had to clean it up before the reporters arrived. The house was fine, but Mom wouldn't think so.

"So what's in the bag?" Danny asked. "Your fancy tux?"

Porter laughed. "The way Grandma was carrying on, you'd think I needed one. No, I just packed some clean school clothes, nicer shoes, and a comb. I had to pass inspection before she let me leave the house."

"Your mom coming home soon?"

"Maybe in a few days. We're still not certain what Grams is going to do. I think she should come here, but we don't have any room to spare."

Danny nodded. With Roe staying at the Kennedy's until her cousin arrived, they didn't have room, either. "Well, let's talk about Nick. I got to meet him, officially, last night. He's mighty scared."

"He should be. So what are you going to do?"

"Well, I don't know if I'm right or wrong, but I think we should give him another chance. Remember Marla speaking at Mr. Markey's memorial service at the castle? She did even worse things than Nick, but she changed because of Beth, mainly, and also Kylie and Roe. We were wondering if Avery could have been different if people had helped her. And Nick is Brad's brother and that family has had an awful time. Okay, Avery paid Nick to do bad things to us, and Nick was angry and jealous, and who knows what else?"

Porter shook his head. "But isn't that still the case?"

"I don't think so. Without us, he would have drowned, and he knows it. I've made a deal with him, as long as you and Hannah agree. No more chances. We'll be his friends as long as he changes. For starters, he's going to join Drama Club and offer to run lights and sound for the plays at the castle. I know Dr. D doesn't have anyone."

Porter shrugged. "I suppose it's worth a try. What if he doesn't come through?"

"Then I go directly to Sergeant Lodge. Remember, Nick's parents and brother, and Kylie, Beth, and Roe know about it and agree with the plan. We think he'll do better if no one else knows?"

"And Avery?"

"A big unknown. Nick said she gave him $50.00 before she left, and he never heard from her again."

"And I hope we never do. Okay, Danny. I have some doubts, but I'm behind you."

"All the way home. Let's go see if we can calm Mom down."

Porter grinned. He knew his Aunt Jane.

Dr. D and Leland were heading into Mrs. Duncan's office! What in the world was going on? Leland was Mrs. Duncan's nephew, so that made sense, but Dr. D back again? Shaking her head, totally puzzled, Laurel started up the main staircase toward her room.

"Laurel, wait up!"

She stopped. "Uh—Okay." She sort of knew the girl, who was a few years older than she. "I'm sorry. I don't remember your name."

"I'm Joanie. I suppose I have a last name. I just don't know what it is."

Laurel grinned. The girl was so casual about it. "I don't know mine either."

"Maybe they should assign us one when we come here. Duncan or Markey probably wouldn't work. What do you think?"

"Hmmm"—Hannah decided to play the game—"Maybe Home? We could be Joanie Home and Laurel Home."

"Cool. But what about when we're not here?"

Laurel laughed. "I choose Away. I'll be Laurel Away."

"That's actually kind of pretty. Uh, well, Mrs. Duncan asked me to talk to you about maybe hanging out sometime. She said you lost your friend Shaila and were feeling lonely. So, do you want to? Hang out, I mean? I'm older, but you're way smarter. I'm having trouble with English, and Mrs. Duncan said maybe you could help me because we're not in the same class."

"Sure," Laurel said. Inside, she shrugged. She didn't know if she wanted to or not, but it was something to do. Something to keep her mind off her pathetic life.

"Laurel, stop!" Another person calling her. It was Wendy, an older girl who often ran errands for Mrs. Duncan. "Come back down. Mrs. Duncan wants to see you."

Joanie smiled. "Looks like you're popular today."

"I have no idea why," Laurel said. "I'll come find you later, Joanie. We'll figure out your English."

Laurel followed Wendy into Mrs. Duncan's private apartment. "I don't think you're in trouble," Wendy said, before making a quick escape. Wendy sounded wary, as if she wasn't sure her words were true.

Laurel was grateful she'd seen Dr D and Leland before. At least she wasn't surprised to see them seated around Mrs. Duncan's coffee table. "Sit down, dear," Mrs. Duncan said. "You must be very puzzled."

"Maybe it's about another Drama Club party?" Laurel guessed, although she couldn't imagine why Mrs. Duncan would change her mind.

"I'll let Dr. Drake explain," the house mother said.

Both men seemed uncomfortable, Laurel thought. That was normal for Leland, but not Dr. D. He remained silent for a few minutes, and then seemed to gather his courage.

"Well, it would be wonderful if we could plan another party," he said, "but the reason I'm here is about you, Laurel."

"Okay . . ."

"You and your friends must think I've been paying too much attention to you." Silence, but Laurel nodded.

"And people have been asking you a lot of questions," Mrs. Duncan continued.

"Yes," Laurel agreed. "In all my other places, people wanted me to forget. They thought I should start over each time I went to a new home."

"As if you had no past at all," Dr. D said. "Well, those questions and the few answers you've had have caused the adults in your life to start digging. And we've started to get answers."

"You know who I am?"

"We're getting close," Dr. D said. "Laurel, do you remember when I asked you if you'd ever been to Des Moines?"

Laurel nodded. "I said no, but I wasn't really sure."

"The answer is yes, you were, but it's doubtful you'd remember. You were dropped off at a church there when you were only three years old."

"Who?"

"Who dropped you there? I believe it was your mother—my daughter."

"That would mean you—" Hannah couldn't finish. "Is my mother—? My father?"

Dr. D shook his head. "Your mother died some time ago." He opened a folder. "I've brought some photos to show you. I don't know anything about your father. I don't think he and your mother were married." He held out a photo. "This is Melissa when she was about your age. We called her Missy."

Laurel stared at someone who could have been her twin. Missy. That was Missy, her mother. Missy. Missy. It was coming together. And she screamed, "Don't leave your baggage here, Missy! I'm not baggage, Dr. D. I'm not baggage!" Laurel began to sob. She cried as she hadn't in years.

HANNAH REACHED OVER AND GRABBED her cell phone. Who in the world would call her so early on the first day of winter break? The last week had been so crazy with rehearsals and school papers, she'd hardly talked with anyone. She checked the ID. "Dr. D?"

An excited voice on the other end giggled. "No, it's Laurel!"

"Laurel? How?"

"Long story. No time now. Can you come to the castle for lunch? Danny, Porter, and Blair are coming. Danny's dad can give you a ride. It's snowing again."

It was way too much to take in all at once. "What time?" was the best Hannah could do.

"11: 30. I'll tell you everything then."

The call ended. "I guess I'd better get up," Hannah told Betsy. "No way can I sleep now!"

Danny knew the results of Laurel's DNA tests, but he promised to let her tell the rest of their group. Yes, she was Dr. D's granddaughter, and she felt good and bad at the same time. She was thrilled to have family, even though it was just one person, and that she'd return to CBMS after the holidays, but she still had a bad memory she couldn't quite shake.

She'd confided in Danny. "When my mother finally went home, he didn't welcome her. I guess she was kind of snooty, but still . . . And he called me baggage."

"I don't think he meant that," Danny said, although he had no way of knowing. Who knew what had been in Dr. D's mind eight years ago? He was probably thinking of all Missy had put him through. Suddenly, Danny thought of Roe and her father. Mr. Santos wasn't always the best of fathers, at least compared to Danny's, but Roe loved him. She was the right person to talk to Laurel. Roe would understand what Laurel was going through.

They met at the Markey Home—Danny, Laurel, and Roe—and Roe was as super as Danny knew she'd be. "Grownups are people," she told Laurel. "Somehow we forget that. I do sometimes about my father. He made a lot of mistakes, but he was in a tough place. I always knew he loved me."

"It's different for me," Laurel said. "We don't know each other. I guess he loves me, but it's hard to tell."

"Please try to remember what your grandfather was going through," Roe said. "His wife died, and he was hardly making any money because of taking care of her. The only time he heard from Missy for years was when she wanted money. Then she sashayed back and basically acted like a spoiled brat. I don't think he meant for a second that you were baggage."

"And he never stopped looking for you," Danny added. "He spent his money on detectives, and he lives in a shabby motel room in Waukegan."

"You're right," Laurel said. "The thing I should do, I guess, is start over. There's nothing I can do about the past."

Roe gave Laurel a hug. "That would be the mature thing to do. It won't be easy, but you can always talk to us."

Danny hadn't told anyone about this conversation. It was Laurel and Dr. D's story. He called Hannah. "Dad can drive us now," he said.

Porter would have preferred staying home. Mom and Grams would be home early evening, but Dad shoed him along. "Nothing to do here," Dad said. "Your Grandma, Beth, and Kelly are in charge, for now. And I like your idea, so you really need to talk with Leland."

"Okay, Dad. I guess you're right." It just felt weird to be leaving when so much was happening right here. He and Dad would be the least inconvenienced by Grams' arrival. Very little would change for them. Dad could always claim work and go to his office. Kelly had twin beds in her room, so Beth was going to bunk in with her. (Beth would not like that.) Grams would take Beth's room, until they figured out where she was going to live, and his other grandmother was anxious to go home. He crossed his fingers. "Here's hoping Mom and Grams are getting along better."

Dad nodded. "You said it!"

A honking outside announced that Mr. Kennedy had arrived. "See ya, Dad," Porter said.

Dad held up crossed fingers. "May we all break legs!"

Laurel met her friends in the downstairs parlor. "Sit down, everyone," she said. "I have so much to tell you and need to do it quickly. Janet expects everyone at the table two seconds after the bell rings."

Hannah nodded. "I remember." She was the only one who had eaten a meal at the castle.

Laurel continued. "Danny knows some of what's going on, but not everything."

"We're assuming that the DNA tests have proven that Dr. D is your grandfather," Porter said.

"Right, although so far I'm still calling him Dr. D."

"But you're here at the castle," Hannah said. "How does that make sense?"

"Long story, but I'll try to shorten it. As you know, Dr. D has been living in a motel room in Waukegan. It isn't very nice, and I can't go there. Even if I could, it would mean I couldn't go to school here."

"Whoa!" Danny said. "You're coming back?"

Hannah gave him a nudge. "Don't interrupt!"

Laurel smiled. "Yes, at least once the holidays are over. And I'll help out with rehearsals here. Leland is renting us two rooms on the second floor for what Dr. D's motel room cost. You see, practically all of Dr. D's money went toward finding me. We're also paying extra for food and will help Leland and Janet in whatever way we can."

"I'm too new to know much," Blair chimed in. "But in a way, it will be just like the Markey Home. When the weather is bad, you won't even have to wear a coat to go to rehearsal."

Laurel laughed. "On Saturdays, at least. I'll go up instead of down. I never thought of that before."

It wasn't always going to be easy, Laurel thought, but for now, her life was certainly improving.

Then they heard the bell.

"To the dining room," Danny ordered. "And, Laurel, I don't know when the next dance is, but you are definitely my date!"

Before leaving a few hours later, Porter managed to grab Leland and tell him his idea.

"Sounds as if it might work," Leland said. "I'll talk to my aunt and see about setting up an appointment."

Fingers crossed again, Porter thought.

Late that night, Laurel thought over this wonderful day. Her friends were terrific, she lived in the most special house in the world, and she was starting to love her grandfather. She even felt warmly toward Mrs. Duncan and the Markey Home. She wondered if someday she might continue voice lessons with Mrs. Hill, even if they couldn't afford to pay her now. Maybe she could by helping students like Joanie. And she'd ask Mrs. Duncan for Shaila's address. She'd like her only real friend at the home to know what happened to her. Winnetka wasn't far away; maybe she could visit Shaila sometimes. Or maybe Shaila could come here for a party, or even a dance.

A party or a dance! What if . . .? What an incredible idea! She wanted to wake up everyone and ask. Danny wanted a dance and a date, and his birthday was almost here. She'd ask Janet tomorrow, and if Janet said yes, she'd call Kylie. After all, Danny's sister was in charge of the ballroom. What if they had a surprise birthday dance for Danny right there? It could be another square dance, this time without any interference from Avery.

Laurel was so excited she thought she'd never get to sleep, but eventually, of course, she did.

Scene Fifteen – Happy Birthday and Happy Holidays

As usual, Winter Break began with Danny's birthday. Danny was worried. No one had said anything about it.

"Has everyone forgotten?" he asked Boots and Bingo. Two giant yawns were his only reply. They didn't care either.

But someone did — big time!

Laurel, with Hannah's and Porter's help, had distributed invitations to everyone they knew would be home winter break. This would not be Danny's first surprise birthday party, but it definitely would be the most amazing.

The party would be a square dance in the castle ballroom. Gee was arranging it with the Senior group that had led the middle school dance. Gee, Hannah, and Mrs. Kennedy were sewing skirts for girls who didn't have them. (Laurel's would be a yellow print.) They were also hemming bandanas for the boys to wear around their necks. The boys were asked to wear blue jeans and plain tee shirts. Dr. D found plenty of straw hats in the CBT costume cage.

True, they wouldn't have the middle school band, but Gee had plenty of old square dance music CDs and records. "I collect them," she said.

Best of all, Shaila was coming from Winnetka, as well as Joanie and a few others from the Markey Home. Porter's Grams would chaperone them. In time, Laurel thought Drama Club and the Markey Home would join together often.

Danny scowled, although he vowed not to let anyone know how he felt. "It's different for you, Boots," he said to the fully grown black and white cat. "We don't even know when your birthday is. But I'll be thirteen tomorrow, officially a teenager. And no one cares!"

True, he'd had a surprise party two years ago, but that was only because the weather was so awful his regular party was postponed at practically the last moment. The only reason for the surprise party then was because his sister's friends had been snowed in here for two nights! But he smiled, remembering. No one had ever had such a terrific party. The best part was camping outside in the snow and "getting you, Bingo." Getting Boots from Hannah on his next birthday was great, too, even though he'd felt awful because of his accident.

Stop feeling sorry for yourself, he scolded. At least you can walk and do just about everything you used to. Maybe he'd consider running again in the spring. I'm sure no one forgot your birthday. They're just being sneakier than usual. That was for sure. He'd gone searching, but he hadn't found one single present!

"Danny, are you ready?"

"Coming!" He, Mom, and Dad had been invited to dinner at the castle. It didn't have anything to do with his birthday; Kylie even had a date. No, Leland and Dr. D wanted to thank them for all they'd done for Laurel. Oh, well, at least Janet was a great cook!

Danny was about to use the castle's famous troll door knocker when the door burst open. Foolishly, he was displeased. When would it be his turn to knock? But he got over it fast at the sight of Laurel's happy face. She was a whole new girl, and she definitely considered Danny her boyfriend.

"Come on in," she said. "Let me take your coats, Mr. and Mrs. Kennedy. Dinner isn't quite ready, but Dr. D wants you to come up to the ballroom, Danny, and see the set for *Sorry, Wrong Number*. It's amazing!"

Mom and Dad declined, saying they'd join Leland and Janet in the kitchen.

Weird, Danny thought. Dr. D must have changed his mind. All that play needed was a bed with a side table for a phone, and music stands and stools. The whole point of both plays was to keep them simple. But he followed Laurel up the stairs. He shrugged. Why didn't they take the elevator?

Laurel turned on the lights of the ballroom. Where Danny expected to see a set was, well, nothing. Just a bare platform stage! What was going on? Maybe . . . Perhaps . . .

"Surprise!" Just about everyone he knew dashed into the room — from the kitchen, backstage, hall, elevator, and behind chairs in the ballroom. Then everyone yelled, "Happy Birthday, Danny!"

"Wow! This is great! Thank you!" Then Danny noticed that all the girls were dressed in square dancing skirts, and the boys all had bandanas around their necks. He, of course, was wearing his "Sunday Best."

Kylie, who could practically read his mind, gave him a bag. "Now go into the bathroom and change, little brother."

Danny glanced into the bag. There were his jeans, a plaid shirt, gym shoes, and a red checked bandana. "I'll be right back," he said.

"Take your time," Porter whispered in his ear.

And when Danny returned, he understood Porter's advice. Like magic, the ballroom was decorated with balloons, streamers, and a few bales of hay — nothing that couldn't be removed quickly. A large table housed sandwiches, chips, pickles, glasses of lemonade, and Gee's homemade donut holes. In the center of the table was a huge cake with chocolate frosting. Another table was loaded with gag gifts — just for him.

As soon as they'd eaten supper, lit thirteen candles, sang and consumed the cake, Danny opened his presents — rubber chicken, whoopie cushion, slinky — and the square dance began. It was almost as good as the one at school. Better, if you considered that Laurel was his partner and Sergeant Lodge, simply one of the guests.

Winter break flew, of course, as it always does. Rehearsals at the castle were practically every day. The gang, Hannah, Laurel, Danny, and Porter, were invited to Blair's house to celebrate Hanukkah. The holiday was new to all but Danny, who had inherited Roe's dreidel from her *Diary of Anne Frank* days. Blair had become a firm member of the SSC, as had Laurel. Members were without mysteries at the moment, but they all agreed it was just a matter of time.

The older gang—Kylie, Roe, Beth, Imani, Brad, Kurt, and Eric—attended Priyanka's Diwali party, another festival of lights. Joe, still dating Imani, attended that one. They learned that many Hindus celebrated Christmas as well, believing that Jesus was an avatar.

Totally cool, Danny decided.

Christmas was extra special this year. Roe's cousin came from Spain, and the two were finally settled into their new apartment in town. Roe's dad and brother were staying at the Kennedy's for a short period of time. They still hadn't been able to locate Mateo's real father, but they hadn't quit searching. Danny sighed. If the SSC could only go to Mexico, they'd be sure to find him.

Thanks to Porter and Leland, Grams was hired by Mrs. Duncan at the Markey Home. She wasn't paid much, but she had her own suite and was able to return to her long-ago job as school counselor. And because she was Grams, she helped in every way possible. She and Porter remained especially close, and he confided to her things he would never tell anyone else. Mainly, she just listened.

Everything was going fine, Danny thought. Rehearsals were fun and smooth; everyone knew their lines.

Scene Sixteen – Showtime Again

DANNY AND BETH RAN LIGHT CUES with Nick. Danny didn't know much about the lightboard. All along, Beth had been the real teacher, but Nick seemed more comfortable with Danny there. Danny was growing fond of the kid. Maybe it was true about saving a life—that life would end up mattering for the rest of yours. Next year, Nick would be in seventh grade, and Danny eighth. The two boys might end up being close friends. Kind of like in that movie Dad made them watch over break—like Bing Crosby and Danny Kay, the two soldiers in *White Christmas*.

"You're going to do fine, Nick," Beth said. "This lightboard is easier to manage than the one at school. I hope you'll learn that one for the spring play."

Nick smiled. "I will, that is, if Danny is going to be around."

"Count on it," Danny said. "I don't know if I'll act or be on a crew, but I'll definitely do something."

Sorry, Wrong Number and *The Valiant* would have two performances each. *Sorry* was tonight—Friday—and there'd be a matinee tomorrow. *The Valiant* would be tomorrow night and Sunday matinee. At first, they were going to present both plays each time because the plays were so short, but this was better. Because so few kids were involved, each cast would crew for the other.

"I should get into costume," Danny said.

"And go over your lines," Nick said.

Danny grinned. "You mean my line. *Sorry, wrong number!*" Actually, he had a few growly lines with the man who'd ordered the hit on Mrs. Stevenson, but whether or not the audience heard his words didn't matter. He could be reciting favorite ice cream flavors, and they wouldn't know. Maybe he'd like more lines in the next play. Maybe.

Hannah had worked herself into a panic. That is, her character, Mrs. Stevenson had. She no longer felt superior. She was alone, scared and about to die. Perhaps the telephone operator would call the police. Surely, the police would stop the murderer in time.

You've got to hear me. Oh, please you've got to help me. There's someone in this house. Someone who's going to murder me. And you've got to get in touch with the . . . Oh, there it is . . . he's put it down . . . he's coming . . . Hannah started to scream and cry at the same time. *Operator, give me the Police Department.* She thrashed in bed, desperately trying to get up. The bedside lamp crashed and the stage was in darkness.

Police Department, Precinct 43, Sergeant Duffy speaking, said the actor playing the part.

But it was too late. George, played by Danny, stabbed Mrs. Livingston, and then noticed the phone. "Sorry, wrong number," he said into the receiver and hung up.

The play was over. When the lights came up again, The actors, including Hannah, were standing in a line downstage, with Hannah in the middle.

The show was terrific, Hannah thought, and I get to do it one more time!

And now it's our turn, Porter thought. If *The Valiant* was as good as *Wrong Number,* he'd be more than pleased. Dr. D was right in not presenting the plays back-to-back. Too much emotion, especially for an audience used to folk and fairy tales. He was also correct in not including children. Kelly was over the moon to be in the audience. She'd started counting the months until she could be in Drama Club. Once summer came, she'd be counting the days.

Porter's family was finally in a good place. Beth and Kelly were among his best friends, as well as sisters, and Zoe had begun to realize that the word "no" applied to her. Dad was Dad, always calm and steady, no matter what faced him in court. Mom seemed at peace and was getting along with her mother-in-law. Grams having plenty of her own activities helped. In many ways, Grams was his best friend — other than Danny, of course. Porter didn't think there was anything he couldn't discuss with Grams. She'd advised him to tell his parents about wanting to attend Questioning Youth at church. Mom and Dad swallowed hard, but then seemed to be okay. He'd start as soon as the play was over. He needed to be around other people who had questions and doubts about who they were.

Laurel, who was stage manager for both plays, gave Porter a hand signal. It was time for him to get into character, to have thought lines before going on stage. Like Miss Armstrong, Dr. D was a strong believer in doing this — especially before a dramatic performance.

The play begins with the Warden and Father Daly, played by Sean, discussing Porter's character, Dyke, who is about to be executed for murder. Again, Porter wondered how the audience was going to react to such an intense, unhappy story.

The Warden: *You've got to hand it to him, Father, I never saw such nerve in my life. It isn't bluff, and it isn't a trance, either, like some of 'em have. It's just plain nerve. You've certainly got to hand it to him.*

Father Daly: *That's the pity of it — that a man with all his courage hasn't a better use for it. Even now, it's difficult for me to reconcile his character, as I see it, with what he's done.*

In spite of Dyke being a convicted murderer, Porter realized the two men actually liked him and didn't want him to die.

Porter couldn't decide with whom he enjoyed playing opposite the most—the Warden, Father Daly, or Josie, played by Blair. All scenes were terrific. Ah, there was his cue. He gave Laurel a thumbs up and a smile before taking the stage.

Thanks, he said to the Warden before sitting down.

Warden: *Dyke, you've been here under my charge for nearly four months, and I want to tell you that from first to last you've behaved yourself like a gentleman.*

Dyke: *Why should I make you any trouble?*

Everyone at the prison—the Warden, Jailor, and especially Father Daly—wants Dyke to identify himself before he is put to death, guilty of murder without a doubt. Surely, he must have family worried about him. But Dyke insists there is no family. Father Daly believes he was trying to protect someone. Many letters have come to the jail from people who think Dyke might be their missing son or brother or fiancé. One of those people will talk with Dyke. Josie, played by Blair, believes he might be her brother, Joe.

Dyke: *A year ago, nobody'd have crossed the street to look at me, and now they come a thousand miles!*

Josie: *What's your real name?*

Dyke: *Dyke. James Dyke. You don't think I'd tell a lie at this stage of the game, do you?*

Josie was only three when her brother Joe disappeared. She has no way of telling if Dyke is Joe.

He is her brother, of course, but does not want her or her ailing mother to know. Dyke gives her an envelope to give to her mother and says it's from Joe, whom he met at Vimy Ridge, the site of a terrible battle in World War I.

Josie does remember that Joe used to quote Shakespeare when he said goodnight. After she leaves, Dyke finishes the line of poetry she had begun. And then he quotes another.

> *Of all the wonders that I yet have heard,*
> *It seems to me most strange that man should fear;*
> *Seeing that death, a necessary end,*
> *Will come when it will come.*

Father Daly and the Warden try to interpret what Dyke is saying. Will Dyke finally tell them who he is?

Dyke struggles to remember the rest of the quotation. Ah, yes, that was it!

> *Cowards die many times before their death;*
> *The Valiant never taste of death but once.*

A door opens and the Jailor beckons.

Dyke: *All right. Let's go.* (He starts toward the door.)
Father Daly: *I will lift up mine eyes unto the hills.*
Dyke: *The Valiant never taste of death but once.*
Father Daly: *From whence cometh my help.*
Dyke: *The valiant never taste of death but once.*
Father Daly: *My help cometh from the lord which made Heaven and Earth.*
Dyke: *The valiant never taste of death — but once.*

(He goes through the doorway, and the Jailor closes the door.)

The Warden and Father Daly stare at the door, and then — Blackout!

There was no applause—only silence. And then clapping began, and then cheering. There was no curtain call. That's the way Dr. D wanted it, and it made sense. To have the executed Dyke come out, smile cheerily, and bow would look silly. This seemed real.

Backstage, Porter was frozen. What had just happened to him? He wasn't Dyke, but he wasn't Porter either. Who was he?

Dr. D rushed up to him. "Porter, that was absolutely amazing. Well done!"

Porter tried to smile, but a few tears rolled down his cheeks instead. "Please, oh, please," he said. "Please may I play another part like that again someday?"

INTERMISSION – THE REAL THING

ETH, IN TEARS, TURNED TO Kurt, seated next to her holding her hand. "Kurt, I can't believe that was my brother. I don't know how we can afford it, but shouldn't he go to Crofts next year?"

Kurt shook his head. "No, Beth, he's too good for Crofts. He'll only be starting high school, but he's better right now than anyone else at Crofts, including me. We don't have anything to teach him. If I weren't so proud, I'd be jealous. Don't you get it? He's the real thing!"

Porter's mom was also crying. "I knew he was good, of course, but this . . ."

"It's hard to know what would be best for him," said Porter's dad. "Maybe Dr. D will have some ideas."

Porter, minus his black wool hat, came from backstage, not realizing his bright red hair stuck straight out and that he didn't, under any stretch of the imagination, resemble a murderer. He hugged his mom and two sisters.

"I'll be here next year," Kelly said, obviously thrilled to be old enough to attend.

"That's right, you will," Porter said, suddenly not sure about himself. Where would he be? Nowhere seemed like a good fit.

Roe, Dr. D, and two men came toward him. One, he sort of recognized, but the other was a stranger.

"This is Mr. Warner, who directed me when I played Anne at Crofts," Roe said.

Mr. Warner shook Porter's hand. "That was a fine performance, Porter. I'd love to see you at Crofts next year, but these two men might have a better idea."

Dr. D then introduced the stranger. "Mr. and Mrs. Walters and Porter, I'd like you to meet Dr. Robert Landis. He and I have been friends for years. Robert is the principal of The Chicago Academy for the Arts."

Dr. Landis shook everyone's hand, and then laughed. "I never expected Dyke to be a young boy with bright red hair and freckles," he said. "You totally fooled me." He handed Mr. Walters a card. "This isn't the time or the place for a discussion, but I'd like to offer Porter a full scholarship to attend the Academy next year. Could we talk about it sometime next week?"

Porter's dad shook a little as he took the card. "That would interest us very much," he said.

"A fine job. By you, too, Don." He addressed Dr. D. "It takes courage to direct meaningful shows in middle school."

Hannah, too, was in for her share of compliments. Hugs from Dad, Uncle Martin, Laurel, and just everyone. Someone said she, too, should consider Crofts next year. She shook her head. No, she had lots of interests, not just acting. She'd go to Castle Bluff High School with most of her friends. "I think I might run a training school for dogs someday," she said. "I think I'd be good at that. Or maybe I'll teach German or work for a newspaper." There was plenty of time to figure it out.

Both plays were great, Danny thought, but he was glad they were almost over. In his opinion it was past time for cookies and ice cream.

ACT THREE

Life is a fairly well-written play, except for the third act.
–Tennessee Williams

Life is like theatre.
Each new day is a new scene with new acts and roles to portray.
The sets always change.
— Melody Joy

L AUREL HELPED HER GRANDFATHER PASS out the scripts. She'd decided it would be better for everyone if she didn't audition for *Tom Sawyer*. If she got a good part, the other kids might think it was because Dr. D was her grandfather. Also, she was behind in school and needed to work hard to catch up. Instead of acting, she'd help Gee with costumes. It would be handy to learn to sew, and she could use Janet's sewing machine. Because of Janet and Leland, she was starting to understand how kids with real parents felt.

Maybe next year she'd audition again, at least for the musical that Dr. D would not direct. For now, she was allowed to continue voice lessons with Mrs. Hill here and at the Markey Home. Dr. D said the lessons were her birthday present. One of their goals this summer was to locate her birth certificate and finally learn for sure when her birthday was. Of course, she'd be in the advanced choir at the middle school. Life wasn't perfect, but it was certainly a lot better. And, finally and officially, Danny Kennedy was her boyfriend.

All scripts and pencils distributed, it was Dr. D's turn to take over. "First," he said, "I knew *The Adventures of Tom Sawyer* was the right story to present this spring, but I had a hard time finding a script that made me happy. I needed Miss Armstrong's input badly. Finally, I decided on this one. I see a lot of you looking for your parts. Please hold off on that for a few minutes." He waited until everyone put down their highlighters.

"This is a good adaptation of *Tom Sawyer*, despite it being something I dislike," Dr. D continued.

At that, everyone looked alert.

Dr. D smiled. "I hate three-act plays. Too much to decide. Should you have intermission between the first and second act, or second and third? Or maybe you should have two intermissions and a very short curtain call. We'll decide that together. Three-act plays are too much like life. Exciting, fulfilling, and then a downward spiral and a final thud. Cumbersome. Act three, if there must be one, should be a blip. Finish and leave before the audience gets sick of you."

Laurel touched his hand briefly. They were getting good at non-verbal communication. Her grandfather was saying too much. She sort of understood what he meant, but the kids didn't care. They wanted to see their parts and didn't want to hear his theories of acts, scenes, and life.

Dr. D nodded. "I'm talking too much, a fault of both teachers and directors. Take a quick peek at your scripts while I take a short break."

Laurel noticed that a few people with terrific parts looked glum, especially Danny, who would play Tom Sawyer and have the most lines. He would be wonderful, Laurel thought, as soon as he got over his fear. As soon as the read-through was over, she'd offer to help him with his lines.

Porter, cast as Tom's buddy, Huck Finn, also looked disappointed, although Laurel thought him perfect for the part. It seemed that Porter wanted to play Injun Joe or Muff Potter. Seth would play Joe, and it was a much smaller part than Huck. Laurel shrugged. Porter would see that as soon as he read the script.

But what in the world was wrong with Hannah? She'd wanted Becky Thatcher and had succeeded. Why wasn't she thrilled? Then Laurel saw Carol glaring at Hannah. Oh, right. Carol wanted Becky, too. Carol would have been good, and she'd still be in middle school next year. Why hadn't her grandfather picked Carol? Laurel wondered if Dr. D knew that people always blamed the person who got the part, instead of the director.

Dr. D returned. "Just a quick comment before we start read-through. I know some of you are disappointed. I'm sorry about that, but I trust you to put the play first and to act your part the very best you can. Please keep that in mind when we read. Also try to look at the play as a whole, without thinking about your lines and how you fit in. Try to pretend you're a member of the audience because the production is about pleasing them."

Laurel knew it would take a long time before disappointed cast members understood his point of view.

Danny

WELL, IT CERTAINLY WAS THE best part he'd ever had or likely to have again. Danny had been hoping for a bit part, like maybe Joe Harper, with only two lines, or Tom's brother, Sid. Nick would play that part. At least Danny could keep an eye on him.

Maybe Nick could help Danny by holding the script while Danny recited lines.

Suddenly, Danny puffed up in pride. He was Tom Sawyer. He had the lead in the year's main play. No, he wasn't as good an actor as Porter or Seth, but he must be pretty good for Dr. D to give him so much responsibility. He would not let anyone down, he vowed.

What an amazing year it had been! Last year at this time, he was just deciding to take the part of Colin in *The Secret Garden*, not so much because he wanted it, but because it would be the best trick in the world to play on Mom and Dad — to surprise them by finally walking again.

He supposed sports and his pets still mattered most to him, but theater mattered, too. Acting, lights, sound, props, all of it — especially friendship!

Porter

PORTER GUESSED THE DIRECTOR WAS right after all. Huck Finn was the correct casting for him. In fact, he'd been pretty arrogant thinking he knew more than Dr. D. The part was terrific — not as huge as Tom Sawyer but more challenging. Injun Joe, in this script anyway, was a small part, but Seth would be great, and he finally got the part he wanted. If Porter played another villain, he would be setting himself up for type casting. If, that is, he were staying in Castle Bluff.

It appeared now that he wouldn't be. He'd received the scholarship to the Chicago School of Performing Arts, and the adults in his life were figuring out the details. Grams would pay for his room and board in the school's dorm, and he would take the train home on weekends or get a ride from Hannah's Uncle Martin.

It would all work out, somehow. No, it didn't seem real, but neither did being a freshman at CBHS or Crofts. He'd never had lots of friends, so that didn't matter. He'd make a few in the city and be back with the SSC on weekends. Most likely, there's be new mysteries to solve.

Hannah

HANNAH STAYED AFTER READ-THROUGH to talk with Dr. D.
"What is it, Hannah?" he asked. "I can tell you're not happy. Becky Thatcher is what you listed as first choice."

Hannah nodded. "I know, but now I'm wondering if you've made a mistake casting me."

Dr. D did not look pleased. As director, he did not like his decisions questioned. "Why in the world would you think that?"

"It's Carol. She's really disappointed, and she'd be just as good as Becky — maybe better than me."

"Her turn for a larger role may come next year," Dr. D said, "if she improves at learning lines. That was the main reason I didn't consider her. Don't you remember how she never made a deadline in *Three Oranges*?"

"Oh," Hannah said. "I guess I forgot. She's really mad at me for getting the part. I would have been happy with anything, really."

Dr. D smiled. "Somehow, I doubt that. Just relax, Hannah, and enjoy your part. You earned it. I've never understood why actors blame other actors when they don't get what they want."

"Yeah, that's what happens. I don't get it either. Thanks, Dr. D. I'll do my very best."

Hannah practically skipped home. Her last part at CBMS was going to be such fun. She and Danny would start working on lines immediately!

Curtain Call

GRADUATION WAS OVER. NOT THE two big ones ahead, of course. A middle school graduation was important, but not in the same way a high school or college one was. As Porter said as he spoke to his classmates and the entire audience, graduation implied an ending. "For us, it means we are no longer children. We are saying goodbye to childhood days. Our friendships now have more to do with helping each other than enjoying the same games. We are trying more and more to be true to ourselves and others. We will try to confine our acting to the stage."

Those who knew Porter laughed at that.

"Curiously," he continued, "the ceremony we'll attend at the end of high school is also called graduation. Another ending of childhood. Finally, many of us will complete at least four years of college. Then, instead of graduation, the ceremony will be called commencement, which means beginning. We will be beginning adults with bottom of the ladder jobs."

Porter's speech continued. He started talking about going in different directions but still remembering what they'd learned at CBMS. It was deadly boring and pretentious, Hannah thought. It didn't sound like Porter at all.

She shrugged. Dad and Uncle Martin had warned her about graduation speeches. "No one likes to listen to them," Dad said. "It might be an honor to be chosen, but soon the speaker wishes someone else had been picked."

That was true enough, Hannah thought. Porter had been complaining about his speech for weeks. "I used to think I knew how to write," he'd said. "Good thing I won't get a grade for it."

It was finally over. She stood in a long line with all of her classmates whose last names started with R.

"Rendina, Hannah," read the president of the Board of Education. Each name so far had been pronounced clearly and correctly. Some of the kids in her class had really weird last names that were totally lacking in vowels. Hannah wanted to congratulate the president for getting them right, but that might seem too weird. Instead, she gave him a huge smile as well as a thank you.

Porter Walter came after her of course, and she waited for him.

"Good job, Porter," she said. "I liked what you said about directions. I think that applies to you and me."

Porter gave her a hug. Well, that was a first—and a surprise!

"The best part of the speech is that it's over," Porter said. "I think I sounded way too old. But I meant what I said about directions. I think we'll always go in different ones, but we'll always stay friends."

Hannah smiled. It was the perfect thing to say.

Danny forced his way through the crowds. Having graduation outside was better than being stuck in the auditorium or gym, but he could tell already he was headed for a nasty sunburn. He needed to find Laurel and Porter, in that order, if possible. He'd see them later at his graduation party. That's where he and his whole family would be, but he wouldn't really have much chance to talk with Laurel. Tonight, she'd have a sleepover with her girlfriends, and then tomorrow she and her grandfather were taking a long vacation together. They'd start in Des Moines, where Laurel was born. In a way, they were going on a mystery hunt to locate all the places in Laurel's past.

"The SSC spreads its wings," Danny told Laurel, once he found her. "If you need our help, call or text."

Laurel had smiled. "I'll do that, Danny. I don't really feel like I need answers anymore, but my grandfather does."

Danny nodded. It was going to be strange not having her around this summer. He hoped that when she returned, he'd still have a girlfriend. As for him, Dad promised a vacation this summer.

Somewhere far away—just the two of them. Probably a camping trip. Well, as long as he could take Bingo.

Oh, there was Porter. "Porter!" he called.

Porter struggled through the crowd. "Phew! I'm glad this is over. Let's find our parents and get out of here."

"Your speech was —"

Porter laughed. "Pompous and ponderous? That's okay, Danny. I didn't much like it either. But that's what the principal wanted."

Danny shrugged. "At least I could hear you. I couldn't say the same for anyone else."

"Hooray for Drama Club, where one learns to project!" Then Porter said what was on both of their minds. "Danny, don't worry about next year. We've got all summer to hang out and find a new case for SSC. And next year, it will be kind of like before middle school. We'll still see each other practically every weekend."

"I know," Danny said. "We'll be fine." Inside, though, Danny knew they weren't telling the truth. Yes, they'd always be friends, but they'd grow at different rates and have different interests. It was time for him to start making new friends.

Old best friends, Kylie, Roe, and Beth sat on the Kennedy's front steps, watching Laurel, Blair, and Hannah come out of Hannah's house. Hannah was lugging an oversized bag.

"Why in the world is Hannah taking so much on a one-night sleepover?" Kylie wondered.

"No idea," Roe said. "But she looks as happy and nervous as if she were going on a hot date. They're just going to Blair's house, aren't they?"

Beth smiled. She knew Hannah better than the other girls did. "It's Hannah's dream come true. She finally has girlfriends who are going to stick around. Forget about the suitcase. Look at the three of them. Really look!"

Hannah had put down her bag and had her arms around Laurel and Blair. All three beamed with happiness.

Roe gasped suddenly. "Oh, I know them!"

Beth laughed. "Of course you do. They're us three years ago. Three best friends about to have an overnight."

"The first of many," Kylie said. "Do you remember our pledge?"

Together they stood, arms around each other, and chanted. "We promise that we will always share our problems and help each other the best we can."

Beth nodded. "And we've always kept that vow."

"I'll bet they make the same one this very night," Kylie said.

About the Author

STAGE DIRECTIONS ENDS MARILYN LUDWIG'S theater trilogy that began with *NO SMALL PARTS* and was followed by *JUST A STAGE*. Many of the characters have been with her for years, and she will miss them as they leave middle school, and she leaves the fictional town of Castle Bluff, Illinois.

STAGE DIRECTIONS is Marilyn's thirteenth novel, ninth for middle grade/young adults. She is the director of her own children's theater and a proud member of the Society of Children's Writers and Illustrators.

www.ingramcontent.com/pod-product-compliance
Lightning Source LLC
Chambersburg PA
CBHW032027310726
48972CB00002B/564